Terri Paddock is a freela... reviewer and writes regularly for the *Evening Standard*, the *Mirror*, the *Express*, *What's On Stage*, *Playbill* and various women's magazines. *Beware the Dwarfs* is her first novel. She is married and lives in London.

BEWARE THE DWARFS

Terri Paddock

An *Abacus* Book

First published in Great Britain in 1999 by Abacus
This edition published in 2000

Copyright © Terri Paddock, 1999

The moral right of the author has been asserted.

*All characters in this publication are fictitious and any resemblance to real
persons, living or dead, is purely coincidental.*

The author gratefully acknowledges permission to quote from the following:
Résumé by Dorothy Parker. Copyright © 1944, Dorothy Parker.
Copyright renewed 1972 by Lillian Hellman.
Reprinted by permission of Gerald Duckworth & Co Ltd.
An Inspector Calls by J.B. Priestley. Copyright © J.B. Priestley.
Reprinted by permission of The Peters Fraser and Dunlop Group.
'Circle' by Edie Brickell. Copyright © 1998 Edie Brickell.
Reprinted by permission of MCA Music.
'I Feel So Good' by Richard Thompson. Copyright © 1991 Beeswing Music.
Reprinted by permission of Bug Music. All rights reserved.
Every effort has been made to trace the copyright holders and to
clear reprint permissions for the following:
The Book of Laughter and Forgetting by Milan Kundera
The Sea by Edward Bond
Fragments of Lear by Bill Goodman
If notified, the publisher will be pleased to rectify any omission in
future editions.

A CIP catalogue record for this book is available from the British Library.

ISBN 0 349 11116 2

Typeset in Berkeley by M Rules
Printed and bound in Great Britain by
Clays Ltd, St Ives plc

Abacus
A Division of
Little, Brown and Company (UK)
Brettenham House
Lancaster Place
London WC2E 7EN

For David and Mamaw,
my role models

CHAPTER ONE

THE WHEAT TEST

'Scars are blessings in disguise,' Rebecca has told Charlotte time and again. 'At least mine is,' she would add with one of her dazzling smiles. A blessing dressed up as a molten strip of devastated flesh? A funny disguise, Charlotte thought, but Rebecca was adamant. If Charlotte thinks about it now, she can hear Rebecca recounting the story, the one Rebecca's mother told her about the accident that happened when she was only three. Gorgeous Rebecca – the lilt in her voice, the tilt of her head – sad story.

Charlotte herself has always believed that life is a series of precise moments, definitive moments that shape the future. There's a hierarchy to these moments: some are watersheds, real turning points which divide stages of life; others are just vivid snapshots of emotions, flashes of happiness or grief or frustration; or coins of memory of a period that felt important at the time. Sometimes Charlotte can recognise these moments when and as they occur, but usually they only become clear afterwards, when she's had time to reflect on them and can tease out the precision of the outline and the significance in the details. As she looks around her now at the piles of clothes scattered across her unmade bed, clothes in the process of being folded, separated by season and packed away, at the blank spaces on the walls where she has removed posters and her framed photomontages, at her tapes stacked neatly by the hi-fi, Charlotte wonders if tonight will qualify for the abridged annals of her personal history.

In any case, Charlotte is certain that Rebecca's accident qualifies, an early but crucial determinant for who her friend would become. Whenever Charlotte explained this, Rebecca would shrug and pull her lower lip down in a who-knows expression; Rebecca didn't remember the accident, or how much it hurt, how much she cried when it happened.

But Charlotte can remember or thinks she can, as if it were one of her own precise moments. It is early one dull, winter, weekday morning and toddling Rebecca is in the kitchen. She isn't dressed yet but she doesn't feel cold in her cotton knickers and pink ankle socks because she's running madly around the room helping Mummy get breakfast ready for Daddy who needs to go to work. From the gas stove-top, she can hear the eggs and bacon sizzling and popping and the smell of the cooking meat is all mixed up with the warm toasty aroma coming from the grill. Daddy likes his cooked breakfasts. Mummy must go upstairs for just a second to make sure Daddy is out of bed and hurrying along because he mustn't be late. Before she leaves, she tells Rebecca to sit still and be good, she'll be right back. Mummy clump, clump, clumps up the stairs to the first-floor bedroom, but she seems to be gone a long time. Way up there, she won't be able to hear that the kettle is nearly ready, that it is starting to dance around on the stove-top, jostling the neighbouring frying pan. Not to worry, Mummy, Rebecca can cook too, she knows what to do. She pushes a chair from the table over to the cooker and climbs up to move the kettle so that it will stop whistling. Ouch! But the handle is hot, it stings her palm as she tries to lift it and it is too heavy for her. She drops the kettle which clatters into the frying pan and they both tumble towards her and then there is boiling water and grease pouring all down Rebecca's bare side and she is screaming and screaming and there is a stampede of footfalls on the steps. And she is screaming and screaming and, oh Mummy, it hurts.

Rebecca doesn't remember any of this, but she knows the scar well enough, she says. As far as she's concerned it has always been there – the long strip of scorched skin that stretches from her right armpit, to half-way down her right thigh. She's learned to live with it. And, as she has always told Charlotte, it's a blessing in disguise because it helps her to separate the wheat from the chaff. That's how she puts it. Men who could love her as she was are the wheat, the others aren't worth knowing.

Charlotte had admired her for that. She admired how easily Rebecca could pretend that the scar wasn't there and how she expected others to do the same. One summer they'd gone to Ibiza on a package holiday with the rest of the girls – old school chums Liz and Joyce and Liz's flatmate Harriet. Charlotte thought Rebecca would refuse to go to the beach, but in fact, it was Rebecca's idea to organise the outing. Instead of hiding behind a stripy windbreaker or under her towel, Rebecca presented herself for all the world to see in a minuscule red bikini. And in profile, from the left, she looked just like the choicest beach babe – hard little body, long blond hair swept up with a twirl, evenly cocoa-tanned skin that glistened with baby oil and sweat – an almost perfect silhouette. Sometimes lads would approach greedily from this side with their tongues wagging, but then when faced with her head on, they would see that the tan was not quite so even, they would see the blob-like scar, the stretched and distorted melaninless skin that rejected the sun's rays. Then they would gulp their tongues back into their mouths and move on, announcing their disappointment loudly, knocking over castles and kicking up sandstorms.

Little kids and stupid Spanish goons would turn and gawk when Rebecca stood up from her towel and strode to the water's edge. Some even pointed or tossed their Frisbees in the girls' direction so they could move in for a closer inspection. They stared at Rebecca even more than they stared at Joyce who had her own problems what with so little hair and all. The girls, Charlotte included, urged Joyce to wear a hat in the sun but she refused, said she despised hats. So she'd try to discreetly rub SPF 15 into her scalp when no one was looking or sit with a bag or a book tepeed over her head. Though she hated to admit it, Charlotte almost enjoyed being on the beach with Rebecca and Joyce, she felt almost normal, even desirable compared to them. Her body wasn't so bad really, was it? Of course, there was nothing wrong with Liz and Harriet, no physical deformities or anything. They looked pretty good in their cossies if truth be told, certainly better and fitter than Charlotte, or so she thought. But then they had boyfriends and weren't on the pull even if they were in Ibiza. Still, attached or not, Charlotte avoided sunning next to them on the beach. She preferred to position her towel between Rebecca and Joyce – a real battle as Joyce always tried to claim the nearest patch of sand to Rebecca.

For all her own insecurities, Charlotte felt sorry for her friends, terribly sorry, for Rebecca especially. At least in the harsh light of day. Rebecca, on the other hand, didn't seem to care at all. And it was hard to feel sorry for her all the time, because then, in the evenings, Rebecca would pull her bright-white mini and skin-tight T-shirt over her scar and go out and make heads turn again.

Often for Charlotte, sitting next to Rebecca was like not being there at all, or at best, just existing as an unnecessary appendage. In pubs, when Charlotte would leave their table to go to the loo, men would stop her and ask to be introduced to her friend or she would return to the table to find her seat usurped by several young hopefuls. Other times, she felt too obvious sitting next to Rebecca, as if Rebecca's petite frame and figure-flattering clothes accentuated her own bigger body, her flabby backside and her thickening waist. It was safer to be beside Joyce, who couldn't cover her problem up with a miniskirt and a flirtatious laugh, or Liz, who did her best to take Charlotte's mind off her worries. Sometimes, when Charlotte would confess her feelings to Rebecca, her friend would laugh, though not unkindly. Rebecca told her it was all about attitude and how you carried yourself – who you were not how you looked. But it seemed easier for Rebecca somehow and Charlotte wondered if this had something to do with her scar. Rebecca seemed so cosy and comfortable in her body. Like it was the favourite outfit in her wardrobe, she wore her skin with a smile, zipped up by the scar into a perfect fit, snug and confident.

Charlotte examines herself in the full-length mirror which, not quite long enough to live up to its name, is nailed into a position on the wall so that it cuts off her ankles and feet and shaves an inch from the top of her head. Why couldn't it subtract a bit from the middle? Not a chance. Hello, Mrs Blobby, in the track-suit bottoms, baggy pullover and pale, pale skin. She frowns. She might not have any noticeable gashes or burns or slice marks, but nor has she Rebecca's angelic face (make-up or none) or her Cindy Crawford body which clothes and men cling to with pleasure. Charlotte's lumbering mass fills all the edges of the mirror's frame. Everywhere she looks, from every angle, there it is – fat, fat,

fat. Pinching more than an inch is a laughable understatement. She can grab whole yards of the stuff. Charlotte tilts
her head back until her double chin is stretched taut.
Through slitted eyes, she views this more flattering reflection. If only she could walk around like this without
tripping. Why was she cursed with this body? It wasn't fair.

In the beginning with Peter, Charlotte insisted that he
turn the lights out when they went to bed. She couldn't bear
for him to see her cellulite or her ample bum. Even in the
dark, it embarrassed her to have his hands moving over her,
over the folds of her belly, back over the bumpy, rough hills
of cellulite and the stretch marks which cut like tributaries
through them. He traced the bumps and grooves curiously
as she tried to restructure their landscape in her mind. She
held her breath and sucked in her stomach, moulding it to
him as he held her.

Pathetic! She sticks her tongue out at her reflection. 'I
hate you,' she says to the mirror. She imagines another more
perfect face staring back at her and jabs at the image with
her thumb which leaves its smudgy print on the glass. 'I
hate you, Rebecca.'

No, no, none of that, Charlotte scolds herself. She drops to
the floor and rips into a rep of sit-ups. Crunch that tummy,
crunch, crunch. In her head, she recites another refrain of
her mantra. Get rid of it. Get rid of all her feelings for him,
get rid of all the pain. Squeeze it out. No place for that on her
new lean body. With each droplet of sweat, each time she
pees or takes a shit, she'll be squeezing out a little more.
Purification of body and mind. The food and what it does to
her body, that is the pain, same as Peter, same as Rebecca. No
place for it. Get rid of it. She won't even feel hunger any
more because she doesn't want it, has no need for it. She'll be
fine, better without it, better without them. Get rid of it all,
Charlotte! No more food, no more fat, no more dumb

dreams, no more lies, no more doubts, no more self-pity, no more pain, no more Peter, no more Rebecca, no more!

Charlotte has been doing this every night for two weeks now. Every night which Charlotte spends alone in the flat while Rebecca is out with *him*. By next summer, she tells herself, she will be a sleek new Charlotte, capable of wooing men far superior to Peter, capable of leaping over competition like Rebecca in a single bound. It's only September remember, she's got plenty of time, especially at this pace. She is up to 500 sit-ups and 500 leg-lifts a session. Crunch, crunch, crunch. Lift, lift, lift. Then she runs in place for about 20 minutes, sometimes she jogs around the flat or jumps on Rebecca's bed, chanting her mantra at the top of her voice. She collapses now, on her stomach on the floor, panting hard. She doesn't exactly feel good about the situation, but she's beginning to feel better. Or in any case, the pain is starting to recede. Slightly. It seems more muted, removed, remote. There is still sadness, and that ache in her gut, but it feels elsewhere, buried. Like someone else is experiencing it, experiencing all these humiliatingly precise moments of agony over her friend and her boyfriend, ex-boyfriend, ex-friend. Someone very close, someone Charlotte can relate to intensely and feel sorry for, but still, it is someone else, someone else's moments, and she is just observing, safely from a distance. It's strange, this remoteness, but more comfortable than the other.

Thinking of her imminent move helps, too. She pictures the flat in West Hampstead. Her own room – small but private. And Liz, her best friend, her real and true friend, just on the other side of the wall. And Harriet too, of course. All together, a whole new flat, a long way from here. Emotionally distant, now physically distant. Distant in every way. Whenever she hears the phone ring, and knows it's him for Rebecca, whenever she imagines them walking hand in hand, both of them radiating their beauty and health shamelessly and making heads turn in envy, she thinks of her new home, of her new flatmates standing at the door, waiting to welcome her with open arms. A refuge, escape. The upside of this whole terrible débâcle.

Charlotte waited up for Rebecca one night last week to tell her. She wasn't sure how Rebecca would act but figured Peter had already warned her. Charlotte was in bed when her flatmate tiptoed into their room. Rebecca tried for quiet as she fumbled in the dark but the detritus Charlotte had strewn in the path from the door didn't help her progress. Evidence of Charlotte's fitness programme littered the floor – piles of exercise books, trainers, sweat-dried T-shirts and more. Charlotte gagged the giggle in her throat when Rebecca stubbed her toe on a tin of baked beans which she'd earlier been using as a makeshift weight.

'Shit!' Rebecca gasped as Charlotte switched on her bed-side lamp to find her friend teetering on one foot.

'Oh hi,' said Rebecca, hopping the remaining few feet to sit down on the edge of her bed. 'I didn't mean to wake you.'

'You didn't. I've been awake for hours.'

'Oh?' Rebecca focused on her raincoat, still dotted with the evening's shower, as she unbuttoned it.

The summer was over but giving in reluctantly with still warm temperatures punctuated by flash downpours. Often the sun shone through the rain and you didn't know whether to reach first for your sunglasses or your umbrella. You never knew on any given day what you'd need. At least Charlotte didn't. Each morning was a tussle to decide what to wear, what to pack – why were umbrellas so bulky? – and, it seemed, she always chose wrong. Not Rebecca, though. She knew how to dress properly for every occasion and keep dry too. Her raincoat splayed open now to reveal her toned legs and the hem of another pristine minidress.

'I've got something to tell you,' Charlotte told her.

'Oh,' sighed Rebecca. Her fingers fell from her coat, mid-button-hole.

'I'm sure it won't come as any surprise, maybe you'll even be relieved. Anyway, I'm moving out. Harriet and Liz have got a room spare now and I'm going there.'

'Charlotte, you don't have to do this.'

'Yes, I do.'

'Come on. Let's not be silly. I can't believe you're letting a guy come between us. No guy is worth ruining a friendship over.'

Deep breath, count to ten. '*I* didn't let him come between us, Rebecca.'

'But Charlotte, isn't there another way? There must be another way.'

'Hmmm.' Charlotte plucked at the fold of skin beneath her chin. 'Well, you could give him up.'

'No!' Rebecca flinched, excess raindrops spattering her duvet. 'I mean, I don't know. Would it really help if I said I'd never see him again?'

'Who knows? Say it and let's see.'

'Okay, I'll never see him again.'

Charlotte leaned back against the headboard and closed her eyes. She tried to imagine life before either of them had met Peter. If only she hadn't let her workmate Wendy drag her to that god-awful night-club. She hated night-clubs; she was a terrible dancer, three left feet and a Zimmer frame kind of co-ordination. She should have known it would all end in tears. And so predictable, so bloody typical. That she would have to endure the humiliating, deafening, sexually tawdry, meat-market experience to find Peter only to deliver him on a platter straight into Rebecca's arms. Charlotte wished she could believe Rebecca now; she almost could. But there had been too many lies, too many broken promises. Even if Rebecca meant it this time, it wouldn't stop Charlotte from wondering, worrying, continually wanting to know everywhere her friend had been and with whom, always assuming Peter was there somewhere, hidden from view. Charlotte felt like the jealous husband in an American made-for-TV film that Channel Four showed late on week-nights during insomniac hours. 'It almost doesn't matter any more,' she said. 'Besides, you don't really mean it. You couldn't really just give him up – for me – could you?'

Rebecca shook her head, refocusing on her remaining buttons. 'No, I guess I couldn't.' Her coat turned inside out as she wrestled free of it and dumped it on the floor. 'But you probably already know that.'

'Yeah, I know. So, you can't give him up and I can't stick around and watch you two, right in my face. I mean, shit, Rebecca, right in front of my face!' Charlotte felt the tear ducts kicking into action. She dug her fingernails hard into the palm of her hand to make them stop.

Rebecca's arm twitched as if to reach out to her friend, but her hands remained clasped and locked between her thighs. Instead she shook her head again. 'Well, I know you won't believe it, Charlotte, but I really am sorry. If it were any other guy . . . I mean, it's not just any guy, you know. I really think Peter might be the one for me.'

'Funny. I thought exactly the same thing once.' Charlotte yanked the cord on the bedside lamp and rolled over, leaving Rebecca once again in the dark.

Whenever Charlotte tries to explain to herself why it mattered so much, she sifts through the various scenes and precise moments of her relationship with Peter. Again and again, the same one keeps popping up. They are in Peter's bed. His room is library quiet, black around them, and close

10

with a welcome summer claustrophobia. The night is too warm for a duvet, but Charlotte can't bear to lie next to him completely naked, in the open. She stretches for the discarded pile at the foot of the bed and pulls Peter's duvet up and over their bodies, enjoying the coolness of its cotton cover against her skin and the weight of it pinning them down to this mattress, this moment, each other. It will become too heavy in a moment but, for now, Peter doesn't seem to mind. He lies on his back staring at the ceiling; she lies on her side, her elbow tucked up under her head, gazing at him. Her heart is still beating a bit fast, slowing, slowing slowly, and she leaves her hand resting on his wrist. His pulse throbs warmly beneath her fingertips. He pushes the duvet down to his waist as he leans over to the bedside table. Propping the ashtray on his bare stomach, he pulls a fag from the pack with his lips. He points the pack in her direction but she shakes her head.

She just wants to watch. For a second, the flame of the lighter shoots through the darkness and then is gone, leaving a little spot of orange ember at the end of Peter's cigarette. She follows its trail from the ashtray to his mouth, flitting back and forth like a firefly. And when he takes a puff, the ashes burn faster and brighter, illuminating his face. Ledge-like cheekbones, ruler-straight nose, darkened brows and a firm, stubbled jaw. In the glow of the cigarette, he's almost too beautiful to bear. He exhales and she can feel and smell the smoke mixed with his breath circling in the air above them. She breathes in deeply, holds it there, and then releases it with a sigh which makes him turn to regard her.

'Happy?'

She smiles. 'Mmmm.' As if she is still savouring the moment and it is too delicious for comment. He nods and sucks on his cigarette again and the silent, mesmerising fireworks continue.

Charlotte recounted the scene for Rebecca later. Detail for detail, smoke-ring for smoke-ring. The two girls sprawled on the sagging sofa in their lounge, their heels kicked up against the yellowed, floral wallpaper. They were eating Twiglets which Charlotte pretended were cigarettes as she demonstrated Peter's seductive smoking. Marmite-flavoured memories. 'I'm so happy for you, Charlotte,' Rebecca squealed, upending the Twiglets as she turned to hug her friend. 'You really deserve it.'

Now sitting surrounded by her packing, Charlotte can still see and feel the scene with Peter vividly, can almost detect the cigarette smoke in the air, and she thinks that perhaps she was never happier. She remembers afterwards, when he put the cigarettes and the ashtray away and turned to hold her. 'I'm no good for you,' he said. 'You do know that, don't you?' And she laughed it off because she had never felt so good in all her life and didn't know what he could mean.

In later days, when she was depressed and dubious, Charlotte would think of that moment and it would all seem okay and worth enduring. She had her suspicions – like when Peter would show up early for their dates even though he knew she wouldn't be home yet, like when he invited Rebecca to join them because 'the more the merrier', like when Rebecca answered the phone first and then talked for 15 minutes before handing the receiver over to Charlotte, like when she was home alone and wasn't exactly sure where Rebecca was and when she called Peter's flat, his flatmate Martin just said he was 'out'. She would call Liz and blubber and Liz would comfort her, as usual, and say things like 'that doesn't sound like Rebecca' and 'friends don't do things like that, Charlotte'. Well, exactly. Liz assured Charlotte that she must just be imagining it, why didn't she just ask Rebecca? And so she did ask Rebecca, all the time, about every little thing in a parental paranoia fashion – where had she been? who was she with? why was she so late? Just out at the pub, just with Anita from the office, just lost track of the time. It was getting Charlotte nowhere. On Harriet's more forthright advice, Charlotte then started to confront Rebecca directly, demanding to know if she was seeing Peter, if she would ever do that. And Rebecca would deny it up and down, and tell Charlotte to stop being so schizo and that of course she would never do that to her best friend. And Charlotte would believe it. She would think of those moments with Peter and she would need to believe it.

Peter didn't come round to the flat any more; he and Rebecca met elsewhere. Charlotte told Rebecca that it must be that way, and besides, she knew that Peter wouldn't want to risk seeing her. Was he afraid of her? Or perhaps not afraid, perhaps just disgusted. The last time they'd seen each other was the worst. Whenever she visited that searing memory, it was like returning to the scene of a crime.

He had picked her up in his car and taken her to dinner. It was raining again and the windscreen began to fog. As usual, she didn't know where they were going: 'The best Indian in all of London,' he said. She never paid attention to the roads when he was driving; she trusted his taste in restaurants, as with everything. At the pink- and white-clothed table, after placing orders with the bow-tied waiter, the conversation seemed stilted. They ping-ponged comments on the weather for at least five long minutes before the waiter came to the rescue with a plate of poppadums and a wheel of sauces which Peter made a big show of tucking into. Charlotte dabbed some mint sauce and chutney on her own plate, stared at the series of Taj Mahal-in-all-seasons watercolours on the wall and racked her brain for something to say. As innocently as she could manage, she asked what he'd been up to that weekend.

'Oh, you know, this and that. Actually, you'd be proud of me, I went to see a play the other night. That new Andrew Lloyd Webber.'

She felt hurt but was determined not to show it. She loved musicals and had been wanting to see that one for months. She'd even read a review last week which she showed to Rebecca and they thought they might save up to see it together, splurge on the top price tickets. 'Really?' she said. 'I thought you hated the theatre.'

He karate-chopped a whole poppadum and dipped one of the shards into the chutney. 'Yeah, well, it wasn't so bad.' He stuffed dripping poppadum into his mouth and crunched loudly. 'And a friend went with me, she recommended it.'

A friend? *She?* 'Oh, great.'

He hesitated then said, rather too loudly, 'A mutual friend, in fact.'

She was inspecting the pool of chutney on her plate, swirling it round and round. No, no, no. She didn't want to look up.

'Actually, that's not quite right. She's rather more than a friend. To me, that is.'

Then the sickness began. Charlotte never knew that a few words, just hearing a few words – that she didn't want to hear, that she wasn't prepared for – that a few words could cause such pain. Not a vague kind of fuzzy 'emotional' pain, but real, intense, physical pain. He went on – he thought they should get it all out in the open. Charlotte and he, well they were really just mates, he said; but he and Rebecca, that was something different. The chutney after-taste was now sickeningly sweet on her tongue. She was going to vomit, she was certain of it. She had to excuse herself.

The ladies' room was just a single broom-cupboard-sized

cubicle. She rushed in and bolted the door. Sitting on the toilet, she could lean forward and rest her forehead on the icy lip of the sink. Her hands were trembling and the tremors spread quickly and more violently to the rest of her body. Was she shaking or nodding her head? Everything – the black, broken tiles on the floor, the rusted water pipes sticking out of the wall, the bin and its contents of wadded bog roll and cigarette butts – everything seemed to be leaping around in front of her eyes. Then it was sliding down and to the left, slick on the tears that were beginning to dot her eyelashes. She retched a few times into the basin but nothing would come. When she tried to stand up, she had to immediately hunch over again because there was an explosion in her gut that surged up through her chest flamelike, clutching and ripping at internal organs. Is this what a heart attack feels like, she thought; was she going into cardiac arrest? She held her breath. After a few minutes curled around the toilet bowl, the fire seemed to abate and the pain nested, hard and knotty at the base of her throat. The path the blast had taken through her body felt parched and hollow. She flushed the toilet, splashed handfuls of cold water on to her face, then dried off and returned to the table.

The main courses had arrived. The waiter, head bowed, hovered round the table politely to guide Charlotte back into her chair. She raised her eyes to thank him and noticed the razor's width scar from a cleft lip, glowing white against his dark skin. When the waiter smiled, as he did next, the scar stretched taut; it looked like the skin might just rip open again. Maybe his whole face would split right down the middle, starting from the top lip, splintering his nose, peeling away from his skull. Charlotte shuddered and the waiter resealed his lips and backed off. But the macabre vision remained; her appetite would not be reappearing tonight. Which might have offered her one small glimmer of satisfaction at the calorific savings if she hadn't been so certain she'd over-compensate the next day.

As normal, Peter had chosen the spiciest thing on the menu and now ordered a second Kingfisher to slake his thirst. He asked her if she was okay and, without waiting for a reply, continued talking as he served himself generous helpings of pillau rice and lopped spoonfuls of Chicken Vindaloo on top. He needed to get it all out, he said. They never meant to hurt Charlotte, of course. It was just that the attraction was undeniable, they couldn't fight it. After all, Rebecca was so beautiful, probably the most beautiful woman in the world, probably the one who would change his life. Certainly, even she could understand that.

Beautiful, beautiful, beautiful! 'No,' Charlotte said. 'I don't understand. What do you mean, beautiful?'

'Well, you know, gorgeous.' He chewed fast.

'You told me I was gorgeous when we first met.'

His chomping slowed as he swallowed and reached for more sauce from the hotplate. 'Yes, yes, I did. And you are gorgeous, too, of course. But, well, Rebecca's different. It's hard for me to admit, it's hard for her, too. But I feel differently about her; I just can't help it.'

She pierced a chicken chunk and raised a small forkful to her mouth, then lowered it again. 'Tell me, Peter, have you . . . have you two . . .' She gulped. 'Well, have you slept together yet?'

'Come on, Charlotte. It's not like that. Rebecca's different, she's special.'

Different, special! He and Charlotte had hit the sack after their second date. She was embarrassed and shy. She held her stomach in and made him turn the lights out, but they had done it and she hadn't regretted it. But now Rebecca was *different*. Did he know just how different? Had Rebecca told him about her scar yet? 'She's not as beautiful as you think.'

'I know you're hurt, but you don't have to be petty.'

'I'm not being petty, I'm being serious. She's . . .' Charlotte so wanted to tell him, just to see how he would react. Was he the wheat or the chaff? 'You don't know as much about her as you think,' she said.

He tore off a hunk of naan bread and dipped it into her Tikka Masala. 'No, maybe not, but I'm looking forward to knowing more.'

Charlotte pushed her food around on her plate, mashing the chunks of chicken into the rice. The smell of the curry was pungent. She couldn't eat another bite. Her breathing was shallow, and swallowing, even so much as her own saliva, was impossible – the knot in her throat had swelled. She started to consider some options, reeling them off in her head. 'I don't suppose Rebecca and I can live together any more, I don't think I could handle it.'

He laughed at that. 'Maybe you have a point there.'

Why the hell was he laughing? 'Do you think that's funny?'

He shrugged non-committally but couldn't manage to erase the grin from his face.

'Does that make you happy that I don't want to live with one of my best friends any more because of you? You are sick, Peter, seriously sick.' The parched path inside her was starting to sizzle again. Please let this be anger, better angry than hurt.

He nodded. 'I suppose maybe I am. But I did warn you, Charlotte. You knew what I was like from the beginning.'

No, she thought, not the same person who breathed life into the firefly, not the same person at all, it wasn't possible. Charlotte couldn't talk any more, she couldn't listen, she couldn't look at him. She just wanted to go home. But she didn't know where they were or where the nearest Tube was and she didn't have money for a taxi. So she waited. And he sat there eating and eating – finished his own food, picked through the remnants of hers and even ordered dessert and coffee.

Finally back in the car, the silence grew. There had frequently been silences in their relationship, Charlotte realised. Peter did the majority of the talking; if he didn't have anything to say, they struggled. But words weren't always necessary. In the past, like that night in his room, the silence was shared, comforting like the duvet thrown over both of them, a silence they could snuggle up in together. Or so she had thought. This silence in the car was different, it was malevolent. And the longer it lasted, the harder it was to break.

Peter flicked the radio on for a minute, then turned it off. Get rid of it, get rid of it, get rid of it, Charlotte told herself. She stared out at the wet streets and the burn of the yellow streetlamps, bobbing her head as if to punctuate her chant. I don't want to be jealous, I don't want to be hurt, I don't want to be angry, she thought. It's not their fault, they can't help it, it's not his fault; get rid of it, get rid of it, get rid of it. But then he started to whistle. It was a tune she vaguely recognised from one of those battered cassettes without cases that sat jumbled in his glove compartment. He was actually whistling!

Suddenly, the fire in her gut was licking and spitting again – and it felt like rage. Before she could stop herself, her right arm lashed out, and all this rage came shooting through her shoulder and her arm and the back of her hand where it whacked itself into his chiselled face, her silver ring chiming coldly against his teeth. She hadn't intended to hit him that hard, certainly not in the face. It was just meant to be a backslap on his chest. But then he had lowered his head and there was his face and then there was her hand and her rage. His body jerked back from the force of the blow and the car swerved into oncoming traffic. Horns blared and another driver roared at Peter as he pulled over to the side of the road.

Yanking up the handbrake, Peter launched into a torrent of abuse – what was the big fucking deal, when the fuck was she going to grow up, it had been going on for weeks with Rebecca and she should have realised, why was she so fucking stupid, she knew the score, she knew what he was like. No, Charlotte told him, she thought he was different. He snatched open the glove compartment and, tapes and windshield flyers spilling out, rummaged around for some tissues. His nose was weeping small teardrops of blood. Had she really hit him that hard? She wondered if it would swell or bruise at all. Would his perfect profile be damaged, if only temporarily? She hoped so. Tilting the rear-view mirror to a better angle, he examined his nose and dabbed the tissue beneath his nostrils. He raised his upper lip and scowled at his reflection, running his tongue speculatively over his teeth and gums.

'Dammit, Charlotte, are you really thick enough to think you meant anything to me?' He spat into the now crimson-spattered tissue, crumpled it up and tossed it on the floor with the rest of the rubble at her feet. 'You can't really be that stupid. Rebecca means something, Rebecca is special. You mean *nothing*.'

She whispered that it didn't have to be her friend, her flatmate. 'As if that makes a difference,' Peter snarled.

He wiped a hole in the gathering steam on the windscreen and peered out. A few yards ahead, at the end of his gaze, were some shopfronts and a blinking red neon sign – mini-cabs, minicabs. Fishing his wallet from his jacket pocket, he handed her a twenty-pound note and told her what to do with it. She didn't want to accept his money, she didn't want anything of his, but she had no other way home.

'Now just go,' he said. 'Just get the hell out.'

She was of course umbrella-less – it had looked so promising this morning – as she stepped out into the rain. She felt as if she should slam the door, but all her strength had gone. So she didn't slam it, she didn't even close it, she left it hanging wide open, scraping against the pavement with the rain pouring in on to his nice leather interior. As Peter reached over for the handle, he screamed out at her – 'You are *fucking* crazy!' Then he slammed the door shut and screeched off.

Get rid of it, get rid of it, get rid of it. Sometime during the long minicab ride home, Charlotte recognised that another precise moment had passed between herself and Peter. At the precise moment when her hand smashed into his face, something died, Peter died, shrank right back out of her life. He never wanted to see her again. The twenty pounds could just as well have been a farewell note. She might have framed it if she hadn't had to pay the cabby. So all she had left of Peter was a few pound coins and some spare change. The finality of it made her feel rather desperate. She could hardly believe it – but that's what had happened. She wasn't drunk, she wasn't hysterical, she wasn't overreacting. She felt it, she watched something die in that car, she knew that was the end. No going back, no attempts to revive the corpse. Now she just wanted to forget it, if she could.

When she got home, she heard Rebecca in the lounge watching television. She couldn't face her yet. Instead, Charlotte searched in the kitchen for an empty jam jar which she found under the sink. She put the leftover change in there, shook it up like a maraca and listened to the jangling of the coins. An urn for the ashes. Next, she marched to her bedroom, the bedroom that she'd shared for all this time with her friend and enemy. She grabbed some tapes from the table by the hi-fi – tapes he'd bought her, some mixes he'd made – and a Martin Amis novel he'd lent her, tore down the birthday card he'd given her just two short months earlier, and the photos of them she had taped to the mirror, where they'd been waiting to go into a new photomontage dedicated to their relationship. There weren't many photos, only a handful, but they stopped her in her tracks. There he is in one, his arm draped casually over her shoulders as he plants a kiss on her cheek; she is beaming. Those people are dead, Charlotte told herself. Time to dispose of the remains.

In her top dresser drawer, she found one of Peter's Bic lighters. She sat down on her bed with these things in a heap in front of her. What a pathetically small pile of rubbish, she thought. Then she began to destroy them. She pulled all of the tape out of each cassette until she had a mountain of shimmering brown ribbon. She ripped the photos and the card to pieces. She burned the book, ignited it with his lighter.

Just as Charlotte was stuffing the debris into her jammy urn, Rebecca ventured into the room. Charlotte had been rehearsing in her mind the many things she wanted to say to her friend, but right then she just wanted to crawl into bed.

'Don't talk to me about it,' she warned Rebecca. 'As far as I'm concerned, Peter doesn't exist any more. I don't want to talk about him, hear about him, see him, or even have his name mentioned around me. Ever. If you see him, don't tell me. I don't ever want to know.'

Rebecca's face crinkled up as if to protest or apologise, but she did neither. She didn't say a word before returning to the safety of the lounge and the telly. Charlotte closed the door behind her.

For weeks now, Charlotte and Rebecca have led separate lives. Rebecca is out late each night; Charlotte assumes she is with Peter while she, Charlotte, is home alone, crying on the phone to Liz, an ear whose sympathy seems to know no limit. Charlotte makes sure she is tucked up in bed asleep, or pretending to be asleep, by the time Rebecca comes home. In the mornings, she wakes first; her internal alarm clock set to pre-dawn early. As she gets up, she checks the bed opposite. Rebecca is there, asleep or pretending to be asleep, twisted up in her sheets, her night-shirt riding high, her knickers hiked up into a wedgie, her scar sticking out like a petulant tongue. If only Peter could see her from this perspective. Charlotte wonders when the night will come when Rebecca won't make it home. But she doesn't ask. She doesn't speak to Rebecca at all. If she times it right and is quick with her shower and her cup of tea, she can be out of the flat before Rebecca stops snoring long enough to tumble out of bed. She can go days without having to interact with her flatmate.

And so tonight has finally arrived and Charlotte is home alone again. Liz and Harriet have just phoned in their encouragement, talked up what a great time she'll have in her new home. They're taking her out tomorrow night for a welcome gathering at their local, drinks on their dutiful boyfriends ('Ha, ha!' cackles Harriet), Alex and Edward. For now, Charlotte is still packing to move out. In the morning, Liz and Alex will arrive with a hire car to help her with the transport – the earlier the better.

'You'll hardly have to lift a finger,' Liz promised her when they last met for Sunday lunch. 'Alex'll do everything,' she said, gesturing towards her boyfriend whose wallpaper smile had worn thin. 'Isn't that right, Alex?' Liz pressed until he replied in the affirmative. 'The easiest move you'll ever make,' Alex said. 'The girls – I mean, we all – are really look-ing forward to having you around.' To which Liz had smiled her approval and rewarded Alex with a kiss on the cheek. And though Charlotte knew he didn't really mean that, she knew Liz did. It was like Liz was a puppeteer, speaking through him. Charlotte was wanted – by someone – and that felt good. Escape was almost here.

Charlotte told them not to ring the bell when they arrived, just to beep the car horn and she'd come down. Hopefully, she can avoid dealing with an awake Rebecca tomorrow as well. She doesn't own any suitcases so she's packing her clothes into big, black plastic bin-liners and a few old gym bags. All her tapes go into her backpack. The hi-fi is Rebecca's so it, sadly, must stay. Posters are rolled up and fastened into scrolls with dusty rubber bands. There are a couple of boxes of books, papers, photos and the urn, of course; her toiletries; and some carrier bags of groceries in the kitchen – the tail end of a pack of Digestives, some potatoes, half-empty bottles of tomato sauce and chutney, a bag of pasta, some crisps. Not much really. She carries everything out into the hall and stacks it beside the door. She'll strip her bed, bag her mountain of colourful pillows and fold up her duvet in the morning.

What now? Charlotte returns to Rebecca's hi-fi and punches the button for the radio – all her tapes are packed away and she's always hated Rebecca's taste in music. She twiddles with the dial. London's Love Songs on Capital? No thank you. Boring talk show on Radio Four? Unh-unh. She settles on GLR which is playing an upbeat Eurhythmics number. Twirling the volume knob all the way to the right, the music becomes almost deafening – the windows are rattling and she can feel the floorboards vibrating through her slippers. She climbs on to Rebecca's bed and starts to jump and shout, trying to make herself heard over Annie Lennox. The downstairs neighbours will hate her, but what does Charlotte care. Only Rebecca will be around tomorrow to deal with their complaints. One last parting gift. Get rid of it, get rid of it, get rid of it, *GET RID OF IT!*

By the time Rebecca comes in hours later, Charlotte has turned the sound down a decibel or two and is back on the floor doing more sit-ups. Crunch, crunch, crunch. Her shoulders tighten as the key clicks in the lock and the front door opens then shuts. There are no further steps. It's only when she hears a sob muffled into a cuff that she swivels her head round for a look. From her stomach-crunching position on the carpet, Charlotte has a clear view through the open bedroom door to the front hall where Rebecca hesitates over Charlotte's moleish mountain of worldly possessions. Surely, her flatmate hasn't forgotten that tomorrow is moving day?

Rebecca stoops down to peer into one of the cardboard boxes. Lifting the flap, she picks up the urn which had been tossed in on top. She lets out another sob, less muffled. 'Oh, Charlotte, you're not really moving out, are you?'

"Fraid so.' Charlotte sits up, throws her legs out spread-eagle and begins to stretch her arms in a bouncing motion towards her toes. She keeps her head up, eyes locked on Rebecca.

'You don't have to. Honest, you don't.'

'I do.'

'No really, I swear I'll never see Peter again. I mean it this time.'

'What happened?'

'Nothing really. I mean, nothing. There's no reason to go into it. I just realised that he isn't worth ruining our friendship over.'

'What happened?'

Rebecca is struggling to control the sobs, but tears are forming runways down her cheeks. 'Oh God, Charlotte, it was just terrible. I mean, he really is a god-awful prick, isn't he?'

Charlotte refuses to ask the question again. She folds her

legs up, crossing them Indian-style, and waits. Carelessly, Rebecca drops the urn back into the box and trips over the open flap as she shuffles into the bedroom and collapses on her bed.

'I thought he was different – you know, all the talks we had, he's such a great talker – I thought maybe he was the one. But he's the worst ever.' Her sobs quicken, turning to loud barks as she gulps for air. Charlotte is afraid her friend – ex-friend – may hyperventilate and pass out. But after a short pause, Rebecca continues. 'You know, it's been several weeks now and he's been so wonderful and generous, and I was sure this was becoming something very serious indeed and I figured it was time. And so tonight, after dinner, we went back to his flat for coffee and we were in his bedroom and were kissing, and I thought, well now I want something more, I feel like I want to go further and of course, I knew he'd felt like that for a while already. And so I said I had something to tell him. I said that if he was serious about us then he needed to know everything about me. And he seemed very enthusiastic and said, yes, yes, he was looking forward to knowing everything. So then I told him the story about Mum and breakfast and the kettle. And he held my hand and made all these sympathetic noises and said how horrible it must have been for me. I said, well, you know, I didn't really remember it, it was no great hardship, but that there was this scar . . .'

In a flash, Charlotte is there, crouching on top of Peter's creaky wardrobe, spying down at the room and them in it. It's very bright, both bedside reading lamps and the overhead light are on – Peter had always preferred it with the lights on – and the white walls and the glass from the framed National Gallery prints zap all the rays back like stagelights on to the couple lying on the bed in the middle of the room. They're stretched out on top of the down duvet with the blue and yellow chequered cover; they're still fully clothed but have discarded their shoes and are playing footsie. Propped up on their sides, facing each other; Rebecca is telling him the story – that tilt of her head, that lilt in her voice – just the way her mother told it to her, she says, how hot and heavy the kettle was, and Peter is sympathising and thinking to himself what a good sign this is that Rebecca is really opening up to him, baring her soul and making it his for the taking. Some soft, jazzy music is playing on his CD-player in the corner, sounds like Louis Armstrong. Perfect, he's in. And then she mentions that there is a scar. His finger stops drawing little circles on the back of her hand. Scar? Yes, she's telling him, a scar from the accident. A big scar? Well, yes, suppose it is rather big. He had better see it. She simultaneously lifts her T-shirt with one hand and inches her leggings down with the other.

There it is, exposed and uncensored. It's awfully bright in the room now and there are no shadows to soften it. Ghastly. What a blessing. And he recoils, jolts back with nearly the same force as he did in the car when Charlotte hit him. It's just a scar, Rebecca tells him. No big deal, right? He can touch it if he wants to. His right hand makes a move to do so. His fingers flutter over her puckered, purplish skin. His eyes shine, wet and slippery. Then he pulls away again as if he himself has been burned.

'Can you believe it?' Rebecca is saying. 'He had tears in his eyes. And I was silly enough to think for half a second he was crying because he was thinking of my pain or the accident or something. But it wasn't that at all. He didn't want to *touch* me.' Rebecca pulls a tissue from her pocket and wipes at her own eyes.

'After that, he got me out of there quick, saying all this shit about how tired he was and how he needed an early night. In the car home, he waffled on and on – how he'd

26

been worrying about it and how he didn't want to split you and me up and how maybe we should all just rethink the situation a bit, take a step back. I couldn't think of a single thing to say, not a single thing. And then when he dropped me off, he just said he'd see me around. He couldn't even bear to kiss me goodbye.'

Charlotte flies back from her spectator's seat on the wardrobe. Blinking, she tries to refocus on Rebecca's tear-stained face in front of her. That was a precise moment if she had ever seen one. 'You ruined his plans,' she says.

'Yeah, I ruined his damn plans. My God, he's nothing but the fucking chaff.' Her tears are beginning to dry in salty, mascara-tainted streaks on her cheeks. She sniffs and blows her nose. 'What a waste of space he is, what a waste of time.'

'Definitely.'

Rebecca smiles feebly. 'But the good news, of course, is that you don't have to move out any more. Not now that I've given Peter up.'

'It sounds more to me like Peter gave you up.'

'Not exactly. After all, I would never go out with anyone who didn't pass the wheat test. That's the whole point of it. That's the only good thing about having this scar.'

Charlotte locks her arms across her chest. 'Did you ever think, Rebecca, that someone who didn't pass your precious wheat test, someone like Peter for instance, would never go out with *you*?'

'Well, I prefer to think of it the other way around, thanks very much. Besides you don't have to rub it in, you know.' The sniffling is starting again and her eyes are juicing up. 'I mean, really, Charlotte, you just can't imagine how terrible it is to have to live with something like this. Sometimes I feel like I'm cursed.'

Under her pullover, Charlotte flexes and releases her

stomach muscles repeatedly. Maybe it is possible to restructure your body. Shapeless becomes shapely? 'But, Rebecca, you always said your scar was a blessing. You should be thankful.'

'Yes, you're right, Charlotte. We *should* be thankful, because now you don't have to move out. This changes everything.'

Charlotte spins herself around, away from Rebecca, to look in the wall mirror again. Captured on the glass, there she is sitting Indian-style in her track-suit bottoms and pullover, and there's Rebecca's face and creased-up body, broken but still beautiful, on the bed behind her. 'Not really, not as far as I'm concerned. I mean, I may not *have* to move but I *want* to and I'm going to. Tomorrow morning, as planned.'

Rebecca is bawling good and proper now. 'Charlotte, how can you say that?'

'Easy. That's nothing anyway. I can say a lot more than that.' She spews out words that have been ripening for a fortnight. Hate, despise, loathe. They gurgle up from the pit in her stomach like a geyser, cooling her still charred insides, sweeping some of the knotted pain out with them. Detest, disgust, can't stand the sight of. Rebecca races out of the flat before Charlotte can finish. As she passes, the gale she and the door stir up topples a bag of groceries that was perched atop the pile of packing in the hall.

'And another thing,' Charlotte calls after her. 'You have shit taste in music!' She turns back to the stereo, increasing the volume again. The Rolling Stones – Mick rasps into the room.

As she reclines on the carpet and closes her eyes, the music subsides and Charlotte is back in Rebecca's childhood kitchen. She pops out from behind the refrigerator where she's been hiding. Rebecca's mother has already clumped her way upstairs and if Charlotte listens carefully, she can just hear, over the sizzling of the bacon, the sounds of a couple having one last tumble before work – the scrape of the bed-posts, the ping of the mattress coils, the rustle and squelch of the soiled sheets. But little three-year-old Rebecca doesn't hear it, or even notice this stranger in the room with her. She is too busy reaching stupidly for the whistling kettle and then there is that hot, hot water and grease raining down on her. Charlotte can hear the toddler crying, she can see it all, she can see that it is her own hand gripping the handle, pouring this vitriol down on to Rebecca whose eyes stare up at her, too big for her sweet, angelic face. So vivid, so precise. And she is screaming and screaming and screaming.

CHAPTER TWO

FEELS SO GOOD

You recycle your little sister for Emmy. Emmy is the conquest of the moment for whom your sister has died. Last night with Melissa, who was having a fight with her buxom twin (little did she know you were the cause of it), sis was alive and well, a horrible twelve-year-old brat with an acne problem, greasy hair and a training bra. Last night her name was Helen and she was healthy. Tonight her name is Viola and she is dead. You have recycled your childhood and your little sister, you have killed her for Emmy whose father died in a car accident when she was thirteen.

'How'd it happen?' Emmy shouts, trying to be heard over the DJ's music.

'Drunk driver,' you shout back. 'She was riding her bicycle down our street. Just about dusk on a summer evening. It wasn't dark yet, not even close, and besides she had reflectors laced in the spokes of her wheels. She was easy to see, she was safe. She should have been safe, that is.' You choke back a whimper. Cue the dampness at the corners of your eyes.

'Oh, Pete, I'm . . . I'm real sorry.'

You wave her off heroically. 'Please don't, you have nothing to be sorry about. It's not your fault.'

Emmy reaches out for your hand. 'I mean I'm sorry it had to happen. It's really terrible.'

'No, the really terrible thing is that it *didn't* have to happen. If only I'd ever got my hands on that driver . . .' You grip her fingers and stare up into her eyes to make sure she gets a full-frontal view of your pain-ridden face.

'Yes, I know, I know exactly how you feel,' she says as she strokes your arm. Tears are starting to well in her eyes, too. God, you must really be on target tonight. What a performance, what conviction.

Better drag this out a little more. 'I can still see little Vi's face and I ask myself what she would look like today if she was alive. She would be about eighteen now.' You pound your free hand into your thigh. 'God, she was such a cute kid!'

Emmy leans forward to comfort you with a hug. Medium-sized, firm tits press against your chest. Her shirt, a horrible shade of subtropical fuchsia but conveniently scoop-topped, allows you to dip your head into her bare neck where it curves into her shoulder, press your icy nose against her warm skin, sniff two brimming nostrils full of Eternity. Not your favourite scent but still pleasant. Her loose hair falls around you, tickling your eyelashes. Not bad. Not bad, will certainly suffice. For later. But the night is still young and you have invested the last 45 minutes in wringing the story of Emmy's father's death out of her, feigning interest in her bubble-gum pop philosophies, and then matching her whimper for whimper, stoicism for stoicism with the tale of poor Viola, cut down in the prime of childhood. You deserve a break now. Scanning the tiers of writhing bodies, your eyes settle on the lads still camped out in the balcony seats where you left them. Thankfully, Martin is already looking in your direction so, behind Emmy's back, you give him the thumbs up and a beckoning finger to set him in motion.

You clear your throat. All this shouting has left you a little hoarse. No time for that now. You pull away from Emmy, just as Martin slides into the seat across the table from the two of you.

'Pete, old man, where have you been? We thought you might have deserted us,' he says to you while keeping his eyes appraisingly on Emmy. 'Giles keeps asking about you and is most distraught that you aren't there to join in the toasts to his future.'

You launch into a blusteringly long-winded apology which hinges on being distracted for so long by Emmy's charming company. You introduce her to your flatmate with further effusiveness, taking special care to stretch-rack your vowels in a Sloane Ranger kind of way that the Yanks cream themselves for. Martin takes your cue. 'Yaaaahhhh, hullo,' he says as he dribbles kisses on to the back of her hand. 'How do you do? So nice to make your acquaintance.'

Suitably flattered by the aristocratic attention from you both, Emmy's cheeks seem to redden although it is difficult to see in the dim, flashing, coloured strobe lighting of the club. After a few minutes of chit-chat, Martin stands and loiters genteelly, his arms clutched behind his back, waiting for you.

You turn to Emmy and grin further apologies. 'Thank you, Emmy, thank you for being so understanding. You can't imagine how much I appreciate it. I wish we could just sit here and talk all night. But I'm afraid you'll have to excuse me now. I must get back to my friends. It's Giles's bachelor party after all and I don't want to upset him. Quite a chore really, at the moment – I'm in no mood for a party, as I'm sure you realise.'

Emmy nods her understanding and you promise to find her later in the evening once you've put in an appearance of polite length with your friends. As you move off through the crowd with Martin, he asks you her name again.

'Is that as in the American music awards?'

'Telly.'

'Her name's Telly? You're kidding.'

'No, her name's Emmy as in the American telly awards.'

'Really. God, that's so septic. Still, not bad looking for a dyed-in-the-wool Yank. So how many phone numbers does that make tonight?'

Five, you tell him as you touch your breast pocket. Martin clucks admiringly and you both proceed to rate Emmy against the others. A definite nine – she compares quite favourably to the competition. If she'd been English, she'd have just scraped by with an eight but foreigners get extra points. When you reach the balcony headquarters, the rest of the assembled lads want a full run-down. You are sure to turn your back in the direction you've just come from in case Emmy or any of her gaggle are still watching. The lads laugh at your report from the field and reward you with a round of applause.

You sidle up next to Giles. 'Change your mind yet?'

'Not in the least. Lily is a wonderful woman.'

'So's Emmy. So were the last four before her.'

'Yes, but Lily is *the* wonderful woman with whom I want to spend the rest of my life.'

You groan. What on earth has happened to Giles? He's the first of the lads to get married and you feel as though he has betrayed the whole group. You all know what will happen next – Giles and Lily will move out and buy a nice commuter cottage in the Home Counties. Every evening after work, Giles will be in a rush to catch his train back and will only have time for one measly pint, if that. Then, the inevitable, Lily will go and get herself pregnant and Giles will become truly, unbearably boring. He may eventually leave London for good and you'll only see him a few times a year at school reunions, christenings, or oh God, worse yet, more weddings. You look around at the rest of the lads – Martin, Simon, Gregory, John. They have all sworn they're not considering it but everyone is looking more and more susceptible. Simon and John have both had the same girl-friends for well over a year now, for fuck's sake, and Gregory has also just started seeing someone. Even Martin, your very own flatmate, seems a likely target – he doesn't want to go out on the pull nearly as much as he used to. No, it's obvi-ous, Giles's wedding is the death-knell for the lads. You're dreading having to attend it. Perhaps you should wear all black to signify the passing of an era.

'It's the end of an era,' you announce to the lads. They all nod wistfully and Giles laughs in a way that you imagine to be twinged with remorse.

'It was good while it lasted,' Giles says. In front of your very eyes, he begins to age and you realise that, once he is gone from the group, you will all slowly but surely start to talk about him in the past tense, as if he were dead. But not yet. For now, you decide, he's still with you and he's not pissed enough, none of you are quite pissed enough. You declare that it's time for some slammers and the others agree; Giles and Simon none too enthusiastically you think. Fuck them, they're going to enjoy this night whether they want to or not. You flag down a cute young cocktail waitress and place your order of tequila slammers and pints of lager for chasers, also remembering to order another round to be sent over to Emmy and her friends. That'll impress her.

When the drinks arrive, Martin raises his shot glass and toasts, 'To the end of a great era.' And you add, 'And to the hope that Lily has invited lots of attractive, single women to the wedding.' You all clink your glasses loudly and belt your shots. Giles sips at his and you elbow him.

'Down in one,' you tell him and the others start to sing. 'Down in one, down in one, down in one . . .' until he obliges.

Siphoning the lager, you turn to survey the dance floor and lower tiers. You've always loved this night-club. An old converted theatre, it is still velvety plush and lavish. There are bars on three levels – the ground floor, mezzanine and upper circle. The pit where the stalls once were is now a heaving dance floor with the DJ camped out on the stage before it. Pulsating strobes and mirror balls twirl from the ceilings, their reflections cutting kaleidoscopically through the darkened haze and loud, ravy music. Away from the dancing mob, the theatre layout means that there are plenty of seats, corners and recesses to take a break, have a snog, jot down a phone number or engage in meaningful conversation. Your favourite bit by far is the box-seats. From these balconied viewing platforms, the whole club sprawls out beneath you; creating the perfect vantage point for analysing, strategising, seeing and, most importantly, being seen by all the eager young women in your audience.

Your gaze moves over the mezzanine. There is Emmy sitting with her transatlantic peers just nipping into their rum-and-Diet-Cokes (so American), compliments of you. She sees you, mouths a gee-thanks-a-lot and you wink at her. Down on the dance floor, you can just make out the bobbing brown heads of Louise and Hillary. You can't find the first two conquests of the night and assume they've already left. Not to worry, their telephone numbers are safe in your pocket. Besides, their departure means you can strike them off the drinks list which is getting a little long. You must remember to send Louise and Hillary their drinks when they take a break from jumping around. They'll be thirsty then and will certainly appreciate it. Like Emmy, they're still students and can't afford the cocktail prices in this place. If you didn't buy them drinks, they'd have to slurp from the tap in the loo just to wet their tongues.

You've never minded spending money on women, especially once you started earning so much of it. Your belief is that the expenditure is an equitable exchange – you get what you pay for. The more the woman's worth, the more you'll spend. You find it enhances the image to spend quickly and extravagantly in front of witnesses. This trick works especially well with students because they're still young and poor enough to be in awe of money. Financial pygmies, you've dubbed them. At the moment, it's even better with American exchange students like Emmy. Even though Daddy – or in Emmy's case Mummy, sorry Mommy – is bankrolling their year abroad, they're shocked at how little their almighty dollar is worth here. Parental allowances only go so far. Thank goodness, sweet old you is here to supplement them. Twenty quid spent with that lot always buys you infinitely more. Real VFM, which appeals to your consumer sensitivities.

For the most part, you prefer your conquests to be five to ten years younger than you. It's more than just their lack of hard cash and the increased chance of finding a virgin (always good for a laugh and a few white-knuckled bruises). It's the ideals and silly dreams that these students or recent graduates carry around in their pockets, like a currency substitute, that gets you going. Some of them, usually the ones who studied business or marketing, look up to you, they want to be like you, or at least to earn as much as you do. You sometimes hint to these ones that there just might be a vacancy coming up at your firm, and their eyes and legs open wide to be interviewed.

Some, usually the less business-minded ones who are still

glistening with their liberal-arts degree hopes, are the opposite – they're afraid of becoming you. To them, you sob a story about how you, too, once had ideals and how they'd been beaten out of you, how you hate your meaningless job and can't imagine doing it for the next thirty-odd years, how you feel your youth running away from you as you slide towards the big three-oh. You lay it on thick with these judgmental bitches. Sometimes, you tell them, you find yourself entering a kind of self-destruct mode where you drink to excess every night and sleep with every tart who comes by in an attempt to evoke some type of emotion within yourself – anything but the nothing-but-numbness you've been feeling for so long. When this is all tearfully confessed and you have assured them that they are not one of the aforementioned tarts, these optimists look at you with a raw mixture of pity and fright in their eyes. Beware, it is good to be afraid, you tell them.

There are some, though, who are not afraid. After such a confession, their looks verge more on a compound of disgust and steely resolve. They will overcome the same pitfalls which have felled you. These are the ones who are not only hopeful and idealistic but who also fervently believe themselves talented and sometimes even are so. With them, you enjoy being your most cruel and damning. You laugh openly. You just want to give them a little advice, you say. Everybody wants to think that they're special, talented. Destined for greatness. Harsh reality is that none of us are special, *none*, and the sooner we realise it, the less pain we'll suffer from the fallacy. The best any of us can hope for is to be a little bit luckier and richer than our neighbours. And to have a great sex life, you add with a grin – sex is the saving grace of an otherwise dismal existence.

You turn back to the lads now to hear that the conversation has progressed to classic chat-up lines. They're already bantering around some of your more successful ones and are begging you to recount a particular story.

You quickly acquiesce. 'Okay, okay. So we were at the pub and it was a good hour or so before closing, but I was wasting no time. I went up and said to this babe, "Get your coat, you've pulled." She looks me up and down and is, of course, more than satisfied with what she sees, but still starts to protest. "I'm with a friend," she says. So I say, "Fine, both of you get your coats, you've both pulled." So they did.'

The lads laugh and Giles asks, 'So which one did Martie end up with?'

'Neither.' They all laugh louder in a say-no-more kind of way. You assume an air of reminiscence which assures them you are replaying the evening in your mind with fondness. In fact, neither of those women ever spoke to you, or probably each other, again. In your experience, that's often the case in such tussles. You don't usually set out to destroy interfemale relationships but you're just never satisfied with the one woman you're with at any given moment. And why is it that pretty girls always have even prettier mates or sisters or other relations? Once, you even made a pass at the mother of two sisters you were dating. You brought a whole family to its knees. Takes a certain talent to do that sort of thing.

The lads continue to catalogue and score the most effective chat-up lines and you throw in for consideration the gem you'd thought up for tonight, in honour of Giles's bachelor party – 'My mate's getting married. Want to make it a double wedding?' That little ditty earned you your first kiss of the evening.

'Pete, old man,' says Martin. 'I didn't think you ever said the M-word, even in jest. You're not actually starting to think you may want to share more than your pillow with some lucky little lady, are you?'

You consider telling them the truth. That you have con-
templated having a more in-depth relationship before. Not
marriage, not by any stretch of the imagination. Not everything, not nothing, just a very nice and passionate
*some*thing. You keep going out with all these women hoping
that one of them is going to surprise you. You're only asking
for perfection and can't understand why none can deliver.
There were a couple of times when you thought you might
have met someone to fit the bill. One in particular, just a
couple of months ago now. This beautiful, blond, intelli-
gent prize named Rebecca. She really could have been it and
you were just on the verge of that meaningful something you
were hankering after, when she dropped the bomb on you
by showing you a scar she had branded across her body. In
the snap of a finger, this beautiful, perfect woman meta-
morphosed into something wretched. You'd never been so
disappointed. Besides, that had been a messy situation,
another case of coming between friends. Perhaps it was ear-
marked for failure.

Still, marriage banned from your vocabulary? 'Whatever
works,' you tell the lads. That's your philosophy at its core.
It doesn't matter whether or not you speak the truth; it only
matters whether or not they believe you. Whatever women
believe is what works. That's why nothing you say is ever
totally new or spontaneous, nothing is ever honest for the
sake of honesty, sincere for the sake of sincerity – words and
information, for you, are merely serviceable, more or less
appropriate for the current situation, adapted and tweaked
as necessary. The rehearsed word is much more convincing.
Recycled and rehearsed. Today your sister is dead, yesterday
she was alive, tomorrow you'll have a brother who never
existed before. Your childhood, your family, your friends,
your views on politics, religion and the meaning of life,
who you voted for in the last general election. All things are

recyclable. And why not? It makes sense – it is infinitely more economic and efficient. Why waste time and energy delving deep, searching for new and different truths to talk about with a person? Why not just use and re-use to perfection the same half-truths to talk about with many different people?

'Talk is the great aphrodisiac,' you tell the lads. 'You've just got to know the right things to say. It's an instinct with me now, but any bloke can manage it. Just takes practice. Remember those weekend breaks we used to take in Amsterdam? Those infuriatingly multilingual Dutch. I remember watching one young street vendor. He was only selling doughnuts from a trolley, for fuck's sake, but he seemed to speak all the languages of the United Nations. People would come, money in hand, to buy their doughnut and he knew before they even opened their mouths what language to address them in. One old man even sounded like he was speaking Russian or Polish or something. No problem. The doughnut-man knew, just looked at him, and knew what to say, without skipping a beat.

'Well, it's kind of like that with women. You can tell a lot just by looking at them, closely. But I find the real trick is to get them talking first. May seem like a bit of a cop-out but it's quite effective. Listen carefully, make them feel important and interesting, like you're hanging on their words. And then you'll know exactly how to play it, what story to recycle and how to spin it out.

'And another trick we can learn from our friend the doughnut man,' you continue. 'Learn a few sweet nothings in all the major languages – including American.' Chuckles all around. 'It makes the exchange students feel at home and every woman, no matter what her nationality, is impressed by a worldly man.' You drain the dregs from your pint and add it to the tower of glasses already close to toppling off the single knee-high table set amidst the box seats. 'Remember my friends, words are an aphrodisiac.' You pause to let that sink in. 'Another round? Let's make them doubles this time.'

When the drinks arrive, you toast to propaganda, great sex and Giles's monotonous afterlife. Scanning the club, you pin-point Emmy, with a fresh R&DC, still on the mezzanine (does she ever dance? you wonder) and Louise and Hillary in a corner off the dance floor just tucking into their bottle of house white. They raise their glasses to you in cheers.

'Time for a dance,' you tell the lads. 'Who's game?' Martin in tow, you thread your way down to Louise and Hillary. They thank you again and offer you some wine which you quaff straight from the bottle to a chorus of giggles from the girls. Down here on the ground floor, the music is throb-bingly loud. Wine sloshes around in the girls' glasses of its own accord and is in grave risk of being up-ended com-pletely by the wandering bodies that continually collide with your foursome in the path to and from the dance floor. You make a knock-it-back gesture with your hand and point out at the sea of dancers. You can just barely read Hillary's lips as she screams that they've just come in, but Louise nudges her friend along. They dump their glasses on the floor and bring the bottle as they head out again, with you in the lead.

The beat of the music and the parade of slammers are taking over your body. You start to march to your own beat and your fellow dancers automatically clear some extra space for you. You wave your arms madly, drop to the floor and spin around on your knees, stand up again, twirl like a whirling dervish and sashay left, right, left, right a few times. Louise and Hillary are laughing and trying not to get in your way. You grab Hillary by the hand, spin her like a top and then bend her body back into a dramatic dip. She looks up at you, dizzy and breathless, as you brush your lips across her cheek and then release her. Louise hands you the wine bottle and you take a swig and then start to dance with it, too. Another girl – a redhead who you haven't met yet – takes your free hand and offers herself as your new partner. Passing the wine to Martin, you seize the mystery dancer and spin and dip her accordingly.

Your hands weld themselves to her slim, bare waist. She is short, compact and lightweight. As you lift her off her feet, she kicks her heels in the air, causing her mini-skirt to flutter. Her knickers glow neon-white at you in the fluorescent lighting. You imagine plucking those knickers off between your fingers. Talking, talking, talking to your petite pirouetter as you did so, folding her back into submission. You make a mental note to track her down later for a phone number.

When you bring her back to earth, the mystery dancer bops back to her friends who have formed their own circle to your left. You quickly skim the crowd to mark what other heads have turned your way. You wave up at the balcony for the rest of the lads to come down. You don't dare raise your eyes to the mezzanine, but you know that Emmy is still there with her friends, watching you, wondering what you're up to.

Two hours and several increasingly expensive rounds later, you're back, seated dripping and exhausted next to Emmy. She's still nursing the same R&DC you had sent up over an hour ago; several later ones sit untouched and watery on the floor at her feet. You got here just in time. You had to extricate yourself at top speed from the dancers when you caught a glimpse of Emmy out of the corner of your eye. She was packing up to leave – you stopped her before she could go through with it. Giles is nearly comatose and the lads are taking him home in a taxi. Before they left, you pulled

Martin aside and reminded him that, if you showed up back at the flat with Emmy, your sister died when she was nine.

Now Emmy seems fed up and irritable. You're going to have to invest another good hour or so before you can convince her that you weren't really having fun, you were just dancing for so long because, as you said, it was Giles's bachelor party and he wanted it so, and anyway those girls came up to you, not the other way around. Yes, you were still distraught from your earlier conversation and it didn't seem fair that you should even have the opportunity to have any fun, even potentially. But you weren't really having fun at all, it only looked that way, and it was such a chore and wouldn't it have been so much nicer if you could have bonded with Emmy the whole night instead?

Finally, she is starting to soften again. Her friends want to go home now but you tell her that you can't bear to cut your meaningful conversation short. You beg her to stay; she gives in and says goodnight (and good riddance!) to her gaggle. Later when the club is closing and the bouncers begin ushering the stragglers out, you tell her again that you don't want to stop. You invite her back to your flat – the two of you can stay up all night talking, you suggest. She hesitantly accepts, paying a passing nod to coyness. As she collects her coat – American, psychedelic ski-jacket, from-a-catalogue fashion – you map the rest of the evening's dialogue out in your head, including when and how the words will progress to heavy petting and, all going to plan, something more. You hope that she'll permit you to leave the lights on.

Out on the street, all is deserted except for the handful of other final club-leavers. A premonition of winter has grabbed hold of the night. The escaping atmosphere of the club poofs into steam as the doors close behind you, and the open night air splashes abrasively against the film of post-dancing sweat coating every inch of your skin. You shiver. Thank God you managed to find a parking space close to the entrance; you wouldn't want to go searching the streets for your car at this time of the night, or rather morning. Fish-hooking your keys from your pocket, you head round to unlock the passenger door first.

Emmy stops short as you hold the door open for her. What's the matter? Women always love that polite, chivalrous crap. Maybe she's a staunch feminist and you just haven't wheedled it out of her yet.

'Is this your car?' Emmy asks, glaring at the navy BMW. Yes, well, obviously it is your car. 'You aren't really going to drive us somewhere in this, are you?' What the hell, is she a feminist anti-capitalist or something? She didn't mind your display of wealth when it was buying her drinks. Maybe she's some kind of made-in-America zealot.

'What's wrong with it?'

'Nothing's wrong with it, Pete. But you can't honestly believe you're okay to drive. You must not be thinking straight. Don't you remember all those slammers?'

Oh shit, not that. You look up and down the street but there's not a taxi or even a minicab depot in sight. It is late and cold. You want to get into your car, you want to get into your bed. Quickly. 'Emmy, there's no other way.'

She points at a few of the club-leavers huddled on the corner at a bus-stop, stamping their feet and waiting for the night bus. 'We can do like them.'

You laugh. 'Jesus fucking Christ, Emmy, you don't really expect me to wait out in the cold all night for the bloody night bus when I've got my car right here?'

Crossing her arms and narrowing her eyes, she tells you, 'Pete, all I expect is that you wouldn't make the same stupid mistake as that murderer who killed Viola.'

Viola? Fuck Viola!

Emmy leans past and swings the passenger door shut for you. 'Go kill yourself and someone else's sister, someone else's father, if you like,' she says. 'I'm getting the bus.' She storms off towards the bus-stop, stamping her two-tone, trainer-clad – sorry, *sneaker*-clad feet as she goes. (A sure sign of an American, even before they open their gushing mouths or pull on their ridiculous overcoats. Haven't they ever heard of DMs?)

There is no way you're following this madwoman, you will not be a party to freezing your balls off. Grumbling, you walk round and climb into the driver's seat. Put the key in the ignition, turn and let the motor idle for a few minutes. Impatiently, you switch the heater on and cold air blasts out on to your feet. As it warms up, you scout the bus-stop surreptitiously via the rear-view mirror. Emmy, sleeves pulled down to mitten her hands, has already started chatting to her fellow sad idiots and is showing no signs of disengagement.

You pop a tape into the stereo – Richard Thompson. Rewind to the song you were playing on your way to meet the lads earlier, a ritual to get yourself mentally prepared for the hunt ahead. Thompson warbles out at you, 'I feel so good, I'm going to break somebody's heart tonight . . . I feel so good, I'm going to take someone apart tonight.' As you pull the car out into the street, you honk your goodbye to Emmy.

Perhaps you'll call her tomorrow. Certainly this week. You'll need to win her over before she takes off back to home and country for her Christmas break. You know exactly what to say. You'll apologise profusely for your behaviour. Then you'll tell her what a horrible person you are. Start off with the lost ideals, going through a self-destruct mode number. That one always sounds so convincing. You'll agree that she was right to walk out on you, then follow up with a most sincere warning that you are no good for her and she's better off without you. Like the others, that will just make her more eager – she won't believe you, you're just feeling overly guilty, or she'll admire you for your honesty and think, as bad as you are, it's okay because she'll be the one worth reforming for. Maybe you could even throw in your autocratic, alcoholic father for good measure. There is no end to how far you can take this one. Women are so gullible.

CHAPTER THREE

BEWARE THE DWARFS

Sunday 3/1/93

I have always detested the apparent futility of New Year's Resolutions and, for the most part, gave up on them long ago. So I hesitate to call this a resolution, I prefer to think of it as an experiment. Charlotte is willing, she assures me that she wants to help so I'll let her. Also, I think she wonders what I'm doing all the time, what I'm scribbling about. Or rather, what I used to do all the time, what I used to scribble about. She can't help but be like everyone else, always wanting a peek inside.

For as long as I can remember, I have kept a journal. An entire row of my bookshelf is filled with these multipatterned, hard-bound notebooks. The notebooks are filled with multicoloured, cramped pages of writing. The writing filled with multicoloured, multipatterned, multifaceted thoughts and memoirs. Through every period of my life, the highlights and the lower-than-lowlights, my journal has been my most consistent and faithful companion, a patient receptacle for my tirades. Many people have asked me how I find something, so much, to write about so regularly; they ask what I write and why I write and if I find it helpful; they ask for just one peek at the most 'salacious details'.

When they ask me why I write, I invariably say because I am a writer. Of course, I do believe that everyone can benefit from keeping a journal; a pacifier for their worries, a conspirator for their fantasies, a textbook for their lessons as they are learned, a testament to their lives. But as for me, my journal is the key to something much greater. I've always considered it as given, and most biographies of the literary greats and not-so-greats support this, that writers keep journals. A journal is designed to keep one's mind free-flowing, and to keep one's hand and will disciplined to the task of writing. Most times, I do find that it helps; my journal acts as an inspiration for the stories and (someday) novels that I soldier on at every day. Now is not one of those times. Even the journal page stares at me with such a blank and yawning expression; it is taking me hours now to write even these few paragraphs.

That's why Charlotte has volunteered to help. I don't know if this type of experiment has been done before but it is certainly unprecedented for me. Charlotte and I will be co-authors of this journal.

The rules are simple. We both write whatever we want: details of our day, our innermost thoughts, reactions to what the other has written, favourite quotes. Absolutely whatever. We never discuss what is written or tell anyone else what we're doing. We have the right to be brutally honest. We do not take offence.

I pray that this experiment will work and that 1993 will be the year that I rediscover my writing ability. In any case, I am determined to start writing – something, *anything* – again. I suppose that is a resolution after all.

Sunday 3/1/93

Hi. This is Charlotte here. God, am I just supposed to write about any old thing? Okay, let me think. I'm twenty-three and I work as a PA in a financial services firm down in the City. I hate my job and my boss who is podgy and middle aged. He chain-smokes. I wish I made as much money as the traders I see in the streets every day. But I don't want to wear those stupid headache jackets which make them all look like Philip Schofield understudies.

I share a flat with Harriet and Liz. Liz is my best friend – we've known each other since we were kids. Harriet (hi, Harriet!) is a good mate too, of course. Liz's boyfriend Alex is long-time mates with Harriet's long-time boyfriend Edward (I think that's how you first met us, isn't that right, Harriet?). Liz works at another City firm. She's not a trader but she makes a lot more money than I do. She does stuff with computers. She's very smart. So is Harriet. Harriet is an editorial assistant on a magazine, a fishing magazine I think (right, Harriet?). She's also a writer, not just on the magazine but for real. I've read some of her short stories and they're really good (honest – are you listening?). Liz thinks so too.

So it's Harriet's idea to do this joint journal thing. I'm not sure what I'm supposed to do (is this right?) but it sounded like fun and I wanted to help Harriet. She seems sort of depressed lately (are you?) and hasn't brought us any stories to read for a very long time. She says this writing project with me will get her going again. I'll be her source of inspi-ration, she says. I've never been a source of inspiration before. (Does that mean maybe you'll include me in one of your novels someday and make me famous?) Plus, Harriet says the journal will help me sort my life out. Sounds good to me.

So I agreed to all the rules like she wrote above. The only thing I feel really weird about is not telling Liz. Like I said, she's my best friend. Also, I feel a bit silly going on about a 'journal'. It seems more like a diary to me – can't I just call it that, Harriet?

Tuesday 5/1/93

Physical description of Charlotte:

Medium height, about 5ft 7in. Shoulder-length brown hair, cut in a bob with fringe, naturally wavy, soft, thick, some streaks of red (she dyes it occasionally). Eyes a very deep brown. Surprisingly fair skin, the kind that one would expect to freckle but doesn't. Straight, white teeth (she wore a brace as an adolescent) but with a small hairline gap between her two front teeth. A largish bosom but she hides it, no tight-fitting or patterned tops. Tends to slouch.

On the whole, the right side of pretty. Wears a bit too much make-up. Dresses passably well. Short skirts that just brush the tops of the knees are most flattering, but well-worn jeans are a staple. Vivid colours suit best, deep greens and reds. High heels for the office, DMs otherwise.

Wednesday 6/1/93

Well, that was just like staring in a mirror! Is that really what you think I look like? Do you really think I go overboard on the make-up? And don't you think I'm fat? I sure do feel fat. I've been trying to lose weight but I can't afford to join a gym or buy a bike and I hate jogging. I bought an aerobics video but every time I try to do it at home (when you and the guys aren't around to gawk!), the downstairs neighbours use it as an excuse to complain. Still, you didn't say fat in your portrait of me, so maybe it's not too bad. Weird. Can I add something else to that description?

Charlotte: She doesn't have a boyfriend although she's been looking for the right guy for ages. Peter, the last man in my life who could qualify as a boyfriend, did my head in pretty badly and I didn't get over it so well. What a little shit he was! He and my ex-friend Rebecca still populate my nightmares. (Although, I do have them to thank for living with you guys now. So the consequences weren't totally bad.) For a while after him, I swore off men completely but that was no fun. So I'm back in the running now, I haven't given up. I've met a few guys recently, some who seem pretty nice and sufficiently opposite to the disaster that was Pete. But then, as he taught me so well, you can't always trust first impressions, or even fifth impressions, when it comes to men. I mean, really.

Anyway, it's difficult these days not having a boyfriend, especially when you live with two girls who are happy halves of partnerships. (Harriet, are you going to talk about Edward at all?) Yeah, Edward and Liz's Alex are always around the flat. Don't get me wrong, Harriet, I like them both just fine. They're really nice guys. Although I do think Alex is just a tad possessive of Liz's time and affections. Just occasionally, you know. But don't ever tell Liz I said that. Still, the four of you make lovely couples. Seems sometimes like everyone has a boyfriend. Even our friend Joyce who is . . . well, let's just say she's folically challenged. But even she's got a boyfriend now. Liz and I were talking about this just the other day. Neither of us could recall Joyce ever having a boyfriend before, not all through school. Don't know what happened with her off at university but she certainly never talked much about men and nookie between hitting the books. I don't even remember her having many dates. But now she's got – what's his name again? Do you remember? Nick, I think. Don't know him too well yet but he's really cute as I recall. Yep, Joyce who didn't have a single, measly date all through school now has a man, everyone's got one. Except for me – but that's not for long.

Maybe we can all go on a triple date sometime soon once I decide who to go out with. Which is what my main New Year's Resolution is all about – find a boyfriend by Valentine's

Day. I don't have a very good track record in this department. In the past, I was either so single I couldn't pass the Noah's Ark test if I was an ant, or I was involved in relationships that broke up mysteriously at the end of January – maybe due to post-holiday blues. But not this year, and that's a promise. I want a man to lavish attention and presents on me to make up for all those he missed out on giving me this Christmas. And also, for once, I want to feel something better than subhuman on the 14th of February.

At the moment, the odds are looking pretty good in my favour. I've got several possibilities, including three top-runners. The number one sterling choice is Garret, of course. He works with Liz and Liz hates him, says he's real trouble. But he's been awfully nice to me and we've sort of been seeing each other – we were before the holidays anyway – and I really like him. Then there's this trader Louis I met at the pub on New Year's Eve. He works for the Deutschebank but he's not German. He's English and he's real cute. I'm sure he'll call soon. And last but not least is that bloke William from the Royal Navy. Remember him? He was so sweet last time he was in the country. I got a postcard from him a few months ago. I think his ship (and mine too?) is coming in before long – hopefully before the middle of next month. I'm sure he'll ring me soon, too.

Friday 8/1/93

Sometimes I think that I will never be a successful writer because I am not insane enough (so many of the masters being such sad suicidals) and other times I think the fact that I want to be a writer so badly is proof that I *am* insane, utterly and completely, beyond any hope of recovery. This is my greatest strength and my greatest weakness: wanting it so fiercely and fearing so deeply that I might never achieve it. I am passionate and I am petrified because this thing, my writing, means more to me than I can express. (Rather ironic for a person who considers herself a weaver of words.) If I cannot achieve this in my life, if I cannot find the words to clarify my life, the words that will reach out to others in their lives, I know that I will never achieve true meaning in whatever I do. If I do not succeed at this, at this one thing, then I have failed at everything. I have failed myself and my life. This is why I say that I'm insane, maybe insane enough to pull it off. Nothing else matters and I will go to any lengths to succeed. But still, isn't it insane to stake your entire existence on a gamble?

Saturday 9/1/93

Do you always go in for such heavy stuff, Harriet? That's seriously heavy stuff. But don't be silly, you're not insane, you're just a little intense sometimes. Very focused, like an X-ray lens. (Me, on the other hand, I'm about as focused as a still-wet, Impressionist painting.) Stop worrying so much, you're a great writer and you can make a success of it. It must be nice to know so much what you want to do with your life. I know I don't want to do admin stuff for ever but I don't know what else there is. Maybe I could get into personnel or something. That has a nice sound to it. But all I really want is to meet my perfect Valentine and be swept off my feet. Then I'm sure the rest will take care of itself.

I know you know all about this already, Harriet, but I thought maybe I should explain about New Year's Eve and how I met Louis the Trader. It's kind of funny and I can't think of anything else to write about and I thought I'd better write something to hold up my end of the bargain. Okay?

Anyway, unlike the board executives who we haven't smelt a whiff of since well before Christmas, we PAs actually had to work last week, including New Year's Eve. It wasn't so bad, though, because we paid for a crate of wine from the petty cash box and got to knock off at half-day. The King's Arms around the corner was having an all-day-long New Year's happy hour for the skeleton crew left in the City, so we went there and continued to get pretty pissed. Louis was also at the pub but I didn't really notice him or anything. In fact, Wendy and I were sizing up one of his friends. Louis saw me looking in their direction and waved so I gave back with one of my Princess Di waves – elbow, elbow, wrist, wrist, wrist – and later I stopped him on his shuffle to the loo. He wasn't gorgeous, not like his friend or anything. But as Wendy put it, 'No disfiguring marks, no obvious handicaps. He's okay.' Plus he bought me a drink which earned him a few Brownie points. We talked some, he bought me some more drinks and we hung out until City closing.

There were still several hours to go until 1993 so Wendy and me and some of the other girls trailed Louis and his friends – including the gorgeous one named Derek – to a pub in Chelsea. We figured if we stuck close to Louis, we'd also have a good chance of snogging Derek when the clock struck twelve. Well, it was a good plan and worked for Wendy but not for the rest of us because by the time midnight came around, she'd already made off with Derek to God knows where. It was okay though, because I discovered that Louis – and several of his friends for that matter – were pretty good kissers. For me, the first few minutes of the new year were a smorgasbord of lips and beer- and wine-coated tongues of many flavours with Auld Lang Syne playing loudly on a jukebox in the corner. Not bad. Sometime later, Louis invited me to go with him and the remaining traders to a night-club in Fulham. I hate clubs – I met Peter in a club – but I was tempted on this occasion. Wendy had deserted me and I didn't have any better offers (who am I kidding? I didn't have any other offers at all). Plus, Louis said he lived up near Camden so, not to worry about the distance, that we could split a taxi ride back. This was the big decision time – a choice between catching the last Tube home with the other PAs who were pretty pooped by then or drawing out the experience with a group of pissed, pin-striped men. I chose the pin-stripes and looked forward to the luxury of taking a black cab home.

Well, as soon as my friends vamoosed, Louis started humming another tune, saying how I would just crash at his place. I kept saying no way. Then he got really annoying and kept trying to grope me. By the time we got to the club, I just wanted to go home. I said I was leaving, he said I wouldn't 'dare' (quote unquote) leave him and so, of course, I bolted. Unfortunately, the Tube was well and truly closed. So first I had to find a taxi – not such an easy proposition on New Year's Eve, a minor detail we had missed in the earlier planning. Finally, after waiting in a scummy office for an hour, I got a minicab home with a mad Pakistani driver and shelled out fifteen pounds for the privilege. That expense nearly wiped me out for the rest of the weekend.

Understandably, I was furious and never expected to hear from this bloke again – Louis, that is, not the Pakistani. Not only because I couldn't care less but also because I was certain that by the end, when I got really bitchy with him, he was no longer interested either. So I was shocked when he called me around noon the next day, apologised and asked if he could see me again. I hadn't even remembered giving him my phone number. He came around that very afternoon (you remember, Harriet, I introduced you to him in the kitchen?), hung around for a tour of the spread (all two minutes of it!), several cups of tea and stale Tesco mince pies left over from Christmas, and some conversation. It actually turned out to be quite relaxed and fun. Now he's called me nearly every day at work this week. I'd say he's pretty keen.

I'm not sure if I'm keen, but maybe, who knows. He's gone up to his parents in Norwich this weekend but he said he'd call me next week so we'll see.

Hey, did I tell you that Garret finally rang on Thursday? I'm going round for dinner tomorrow night.

Monday 11/1/93

Story idea: Charles's mother was stark-raving mad. Everybody knew it, especially after the day she danced nude through the aisles of the Sainsbury's singing a medley of Beatles' tunes. Charles never talked about it but everybody knew. Just like everybody knew that Mary's father was an alcoholic who routinely pummelled Mary and her little brother and their mum. Mary never said a word but everybody knew.

Tuesday 12/1/93

Great, so what happens with our Charles and Mary? And where do they live? It must be some neighbourhood where absolutely everyone has lived for absolutely all of their lives – must be, if they all know what's going on in everyone else's kitchens. Let me guess, they live in cute terraced houses somewhere up North? Just five minutes' walk to Coronation Street. Am I right?

Well, I haven't got any story ideas so I'll just give you the latest on the boyfriend hunt. I think I may have mentioned that Garret finally called. I don't know what's up with this guy.

I first met him a couple of months ago when I joined Liz and her office gang at a pub near Liverpool Street after work. A lot of the guys had taken off for a real City lunch and had been drinking all afternoon so they were pretty pissed by the time I arrived. Liz had told me about Garret beforehand, and what an unstable bastard he was. It seems he is the favourite subject of company gossip. He's much older than me, about thirty-five, and divorced with one kid from his marriage and another illegitimate son from a receptionist he bonked at the company. I think he actually left his wife for her, the marriage-wrecking tart. Liz says he promised the woman that he would marry her if she had the baby and now he's left her high and dry. The company gossip-mongers renamed her the Receptacle, you know, instead of the receptionist, for being such a willing bin for all his bull-shit and sperm. How grim. Anyway, being totally pissed didn't really improve Garret's personality when I met him. I took an instant dislike to him, all his cruelly sarky comments and his plummy accent. I remember asking him if he practised being horrible and smarmy in front of the mirror at night with a bowl of fruit.

At the next pub night out about a week later, I was sort of looking forward to continuing this verbal swordfight with him. He loves to take the mickey out of people but doesn't always perform so well on the receiving end so that can be fun to watch. He was pretty funny about it all really. Anyway, we talked a lot and I remember thinking that he fancied Liz and was trying to hit on her. I asked him if it was true, if he was trying to pull Liz. I was going to warn him about ball-and-chain Alex, you see. But Garret said no, that he was trying his hardest to try and pull *me*! I was gobsmacked and couldn't help but laugh. He said, 'Charlotte, don't you know what an incredibly ebullient and attractive woman you are?' (This is God's honest truth, word for word.) Well, no, I guess I didn't know that but him saying it changed my whole opinion of him. What a smoothie. At this point, Liz was getting concerned that we were talking for so long and she tried to pull us apart. She told Garret to leave her friend alone. Maybe this spurred him on or something because the next time she left my side to go buy a round, he grabbed me and hustled me out of the pub. Next thing I know we're in a taxi heading back to his flat in Mayfair. (Can you believe that – a flat in Mayfair!) When he was in the kitchen brewing some tea, I thought, just to pass the time, you know, I'd look up 'ebullient' in one of the many dictionaries he had lying around his lounge – a couple of bilingual ones for languages with letters I didn't even recognise. Of course, I already pretty much knew what it meant – although pronouncing it was another matter – but I just wanted to confirm it in black and white, sort of reassure myself. That's when I decided that I might stay the night – because of the compliment there in print, that is, not just because he obviously knows three-and-a-half times as many alphabets as I do.

I almost changed my mind when the Receptacle called while we were having our second cuppa. They talked for a long time which made me feel rather awkward. I think she still wants him to marry her. In fact, she has a knack of calling every time I'm there, like she knows or something. Miss Radar more like it. I think she even asks him if he's got somebody with him because usually about half-way through the conversation about baby Nigel and the day at the office, his answers become single yeses and nos and he turns his back to me. These awkward moments occurred often in late November and December. But even such momentary pangs didn't ruin what a fabulous era that was. With the lead up to Christmas, there were informal parties and piss-ups just about every other night. I started to pack a fresh blouse and an extra pair of knickers in my handbag just in case. I was hoping that Garret would even invite me to their company's black tie Christmas do, but he took the Receptacle instead. He said he felt obliged to since she didn't get out much, what with the baby and all, and I said I understood. Besides, Liz says they didn't act like a couple or look like they were having any fun or anything. Liz my loyal spy in the midst.

Garret asked me not to talk about that first night together, or any of the nights after that, with Liz or any of the blokes from his office – he said discretion was necessary, his was a delicate situation and so on. Of course, Liz knew when I didn't come home that first time (remember how she questioned me the next day?) and she kept warning me off him and stuff. But she promised she wouldn't tell anyone else and I didn't of course. Then Liz told me everyone knew anyway because Garret himself had gone around blabbing and telling all the guys how hot I was for him. I don't know why he does that. Sometimes, I think he must hate me but then he'll suddenly call and treat me to dinner like on Sunday or he'll want to take me home after the pub, and he's so nice and we have so much fun together. I guess the bragging is just a part of his badboy front. I can see past it of course, but I don't think everyone else can and I wish he'd stop it all the same.

Wednesday 13/1/93

'To achieve great things we must live as though we were never going to die.'

Vauvenargues

'Far better it is to dare mighty things, to win glorious triumphs, even though chequered by failure, than to rank with those poor spirits who neither enjoy much nor suffer much, because they live in the grey twilight that knows not victory nor defeat.'

Theodore Roosevelt

Thursday 14/1/93

Nice quotes, here are some good ones I just read in an interview with Michael Caine:

'Be like a duck,' my mother used to tell me. 'Remain calm on the surface and paddle like hell underneath.'

'And remember my motto: The flogging will continue until the mood of the crew improves.'

You see, I can fight quote for quote with the best of them – 'my name is Michael Caine.' I especially like the one about the duck. That's how I feel sometimes, except I find it really hard even appearing calm because I'm too worried about drowning. I never have been much of a swimmer. (What do you think, Harriet? Do I seem like I'm sinking or swimming most of the time?) You know, I really like Michael Caine. I don't know why no one takes him seriously. Okay, maybe he's getting on a bit now and maybe he hasn't always been so choosy about his films, but at least he's rich. And why is everyone always picking on Kenneth Branagh and Emma Thompson for that matter? I think they're pretty talented and obviously very much in love. Am I the only person in the world who enjoyed *Peter's Friends*? And who wouldn't go to Hollywood given the chance?

Would you go to Hollywood, Harriet? If someone asked you to write a screenplay about Charles and Mary and they were going to pour big bucks into it and make it a block-buster and you were entitled to so much of the earnings? Do you think Charles and Mary would make a good film, who would play them – maybe Ken and Em? Or would you write some other story for the screen? What would you write? And why don't you ever write much in here? You never write anything about your own life, about Edward or your job or your weekends, you hardly write anything at all. Are you keeping some other journal you haven't told me about? I'm sure you're not. It's okay anyway. I know the whole point of this thing is that you're having trouble with your writing and you need help (am I helping?). Besides I'm sort of

starting to enjoy this, it does help to write things out sometimes. You swear you're not ever going to show this to
anyone, right? That would be too embarrassing if people
really knew the bizarre things I thought about sometimes.
People might think I was obsessed with men or something –
a fatal case of penis envy.

In fact, there's only one man I'm obsessed with at the
moment. I'm ashamed to admit it, I know I shouldn't be,
but I've been thinking a lot about Garret lately. I keep thinking about the nights I've spent in his bed. Before meeting
him, it'd been such a long time since I'd had sex. And, you
know, it wasn't the orgasms so much that I missed –
although, let me tell you, Garret definitely knows how to
deliver on that score! The real thing was that I forgot how
nice it can feel just to be physically close to a guy, to have
the weight of his body on top of you, to enjoy the warmth
of his skin, to be kissed tenderly, to be touched and caressed
in all the right places. And, best of all, just to be held, to
have someone's big, warm, bear (and bare) arms wrapped
around you. At the end of the day, that's what it's all about
for me.

If it weren't for times like that, I think I could get over
Garret – because, in truth, outside the bedroom or the company of two, he really can act like such a tosser. But I know,
deep down, he sincerely cares for me. Honestly, Garret really
likes me and enjoys being with me – he's told me as much.
Maybe he even loves me. But he's got some major hang-ups
about us coming together (no, I didn't mean it like *that*!).
First there's the age difference thing – I think by being so
much younger than him, I make him feel old, but I don't
think he's old at all, just sophisticated. Second, he says his
life is too complicated – what with an ex-wife, an ex-lover,
two kids, alimony, palimony and all these father-type responsibilities – and he thinks I'm too young to understand or

have a place in it. He thinks everyone wants something from him. But I don't want anything *from* him, I just want to be *with* him.

And then there's his flat of course, that's another reason I'm determined to keep seeing him. I love his flat and I love spending time there. You wouldn't believe how posh it is and absolutely all the mod cons you can think of – an amazing telly, video and stereo system, washing machine *and* drier, microwave, computer, central heating, an espresso maker, the works. And super plush carpets and original paintings in frames and loads of bookshelves (filled with books!) and even a separate dining-room. I feel more important just knowing someone who lives in a place like that – and to actually be there is a *real* buzz. I mean, how often do people like me actually know someone who lives in Mayfair? It puts our little matchbox flat to shame. It makes every other place in my life just seem dingy. Dingy, dingy, dingy.

Maybe I can buy him some candlesticks for Valentine's Day. I'll cook him Chicken Kiev and we can have a terribly romantic candlelit meal while exchanging cards and chocolates and flowers. And maybe I can finally give him his Christmas present. It's nothing much, just one of those peek-aboo picture frames with cardboard cut-outs for several different shots – I thought he could put pictures of Nigel and his daughter Phoebe in there, and maybe one of us if we ever had a picture taken together. I've got several frames like it myself – you know me and my photos. Of course, I wanted to give it to him for Christmas. I wrapped it up in festive paper and bought a totally non-mushy card and everything. I carried it around in my bag with my knickers for a week or so in December but the time never seemed right to give it to Garret and then, before I knew it, he was gone for the holidays which he was splitting three-ways between Phoebe and his ex-wife, Nigel and the Receptacle, and his own parents.

Besides he obviously hadn't bought me anything and I didn't want to seem too keen or scare him off by giving him a gift when he hadn't got one for me. You know that kind of scene. I mean, we were sort of seeing each other, but you could never have called him my boyfriend, it wasn't serious. So it's understandable that we didn't exchange gifts but still it would have been nice. Anyway, I could give him the candlesticks and the frame (rewrapped in new festive paper, of course) for Valentine's Day and he could buy me something terribly expensive and romantic – maybe a weekend in Paris or Venice, with him of course?

Jesus, I've just realised it's only one month to go until V-Day! Just thirty-one days and a measly four weekends until *the* weekend. And since it's now past midnight, he's already missed the deadline for asking me out for this weekend – he always either calls by Thursday or waits until the following Monday. He'd better call soon.

Sunday 17/1/93

Story idea:

Sarah is a screenwriter. She has seen every single side of a sentence and still she cannot sift the sense out of the words. She edits them to death. The punctuation, perfect. The grammar, great. The vocabulary, visionary. And yet . . . Where is the vision? Where is the greatness? Where is the perfection? What is the point?

Perhaps the point she ponders is her own. Perhaps if she plunked pen on paper, played with some ideas, plotted them out, proved there was a point. Perhaps.

But Sarah is scared. In spite of her sincere soul-searching, in spite of her passionate ponderings, in spite of her feeling that she will explode or implode or disintegrate slowly in some way like Alka Seltzer dissolving in water unless she gets it all out, unless she squeezes some great something out, Sarah fears that she will find in the end that she has nothing to say. And so now, before she will let herself begin, before she will ever draw up to the half-way mark, long before she will ever reach the nearly-there point and certainly far from the ribbon-tearing record-breaking grand finale finish, Sarah is sad and saddened, seriously and sincerely and soul-searchingly sad. And maybe, she thinks, she resigns herself to thinking, because it is so easy and also so soothingly, stoically, seriously sad, maybe there is no point anyway.

Monday 18/1/93

So you have thought about screenwriting before, hey Harriet? That's great. And I can see that you subscribe to the 'authors always alliterate' school of thinking. That's cool. Does that come off well on film?

Anyway, Garret still hasn't called me – yet! It's only been a week since that Sunday night we went out to dinner and played water polo in his bed (I 'accidentally' knocked over a large glass of water while tickling him and he thought I was behaving very childishly) and that Monday morning when we shared the Central Line from Bond Street into work. I even kissed him goodbye and told him to have a good day (should have said week, or month maybe?) when we went our separate ways at Liverpool Street Station. Why does it seem so much longer than a week? Anyway, it still is only a week, a mere seven days. And it's okay because I know he'll call me soon. I know he's interested in me and finds me attractive. And I know that he will call. Right now he's probably just trying to play it cool. That's fine. I can wait. I can play it even cooler. He once advised me never to suck up to a man. Well, I'm taking that advice. I won't suck up to him or any man ever again. I will wait, and he will call.

So I'm not going to dwell on Garret any more. I'm a new

positive-thinking woman. I'm going to take control of my life. As part of this new era, I decided to give Louis the Trader a ring. Remember him – he was the guy I met on New Year's Eve who really fancied me? Well, I haven't heard from him in a while although I do keep hearing about him. Wendy actually started dating Louis's hot friend Derek after that strange night. So she's seen Louis a couple of times and says he's asked about me. Wendy thinks he's still really keen. Probably, he just stopped calling because he thought I wasn't interested since I've been so wound up with Garret or, I don't know, maybe he was shy or lost my number or something. Anyway, I called him and he seemed really glad to hear from me. We've arranged to meet tomorrow night at Swiss Cottage, go to the cinema and maybe have a few pints. I thought a midweek rendezvous was nice and safe and innocent. I don't want him to get his hopes up in case I don't feel the same way.

Wednesday 20/1/93

I'm sorry, Harriet, I know you haven't had your entry yet, but I couldn't wait my turn. I'm so livid at the moment and have just got to get it all out. Last night I met up with Louis the Trader – or Louis the Traitor as I should now refer to him. To be honest, there were no fireworks from the start. Out of his pin-stripes he wasn't impressive at all – not only physically speaking but financially as well. It was like he'd had both a brain and wallet transplant. I mean, I know these are post-revolution days and I did ask him out but I didn't expect him to be quite such a cheapskate. I'd bought the cinema tickets before he'd arrived (30 minutes late!) so that was no big deal. Once inside, though, he actually waited until I returned from the loo – quite a wait since there was quite a queue – to send me off to buy a big tub of popcorn, drinks and Maltesers.

Afterwards, when we went to the Tavern, he didn't even offer to tackle the bar mob himself, just yawned until I asked what he wanted. And worse than that, he drank like a fish – I couldn't keep up with him and I was only drinking half-pints to his pints – and he made a production of turning his glass upside down and looking bored until I waitressed him another. Cheap, cheap, cheap. I didn't know what was going on here – I mean, I am just a lowly PA and he's a trader who makes about a million times as much as I do. And what happened to the guy who drowned me with drinks on New Year's Eve anyway? Maybe his resolution for 1993 was to never pay for another beer. To top the whole disastrous evening off, I realised that, underneath it all, Louis was a really boring and self-important git. Underneath and bubbling right up to the surface actually. Like an oil slick. Despite my inner seething about him being such a tightwad, I did try to grease the wheels of conversation. I asked him about his job and was rewarded with endless waffling about antics in the pit, exchange rates, derivatives and futures and all sorts of market rubbish until I was reeling from the weight of the boredom. When I tried to tell him a little about my job and my hopes to get into personnel, he just laughed. How dare he!

By the end of the evening, I had decided that this was going nowhere fast and was very happy to say goodnight. I knew we wouldn't be going out again, but I figured if I did run into Louis with Wendy and Derek sometime, I could at least be cordial and we could have a laugh about derivatives over a Dutch pint or two. No tears wasted. But then, this afternoon at the office I got the shocking news from Wendy who'd met Derek for lunch. Apparently, the reason Louis the Traitor was acting kind of weird was because he didn't know how to act because he didn't want to encourage me.

He thinks *I* like *him* just because I asked him to that stupid film. That makes me *so* angry! Wendy says, according to Derek, that Louis has just revealed that when he went back to Norwich the other weekend, he had a mystical reconnection experience with an old childhood sweetheart – apparently he's kept it kind of hush around the boys because he didn't want them to know he was smitten. He and the unfortunate female are already negotiating marriage and he's feeling sensitive about being unfaithful so early in the game. So why didn't he just say that, if that's really the truth? (And for that matter, when did going to the cinema with a non-romantic interest suddenly become an act of infidelity?)

I mean, I never liked him as more than friends (except maybe for a few seconds after my tenth pint on that first night when I thought he was *sort of* cute and probably not even then) and don't think I ever did anything to make him believe otherwise. Why are men so arrogant that way? Why must they assume that they know how I feel? It seems that no matter how I feel – whether I don't like the guy at all or whether I do but am trying to play it cool – he'll think that I like him. Why do I even bother, the end result is the same nine-and-a-half times out of ten – scratch that, the end result is always the same, full stop. No wonder I worry about what guys are thinking if I so much as have a conversation with them or call them for some reason or ask them out to the fucking cinema. I'm not just being paranoid, they do always get the wrong idea. Men are the pits. For half a nanosecond, I actually liked Louis the Traitor, I thought he might be different and that maybe we could enjoy being good friends. But he's ruined it all now.

And another thing, how is it that men always manage to turn the tables? I mean, the Traitor started this whole thing and just three short weeks ago I had him wrapped around my little finger. Now my finger's snapped off at the knuckle and I feel rejected. *Rejected*, for God's sake, by a man I never even fancied! By a man who willingly wears a Joseph dreamcoat in public. That's pathetic.

Thursday 21/1/93

'Keep away from people who try to belittle your ambitions. Small people always do that, but the really great make you feel that you, too, can somehow become great.'

Mark Twain

Friday 22/1/93

Or as my mum always used to tell me – if you want to be admired, get a dog.

But I hate dogs. Men are dogs and I hate them too. Louis the Traitor is just so stupid anyway – if he had any idea how much I couldn't give a toss about him, how all I think about is Garret, how Garret is the only man I could possibly fancy at the moment and how lousy Louis in loud loser jackets (see, Harriet, I can alliterate too!) doesn't hold a candle. Well, if he knew all that, he'd feel pretty foolish to say the least. And so would I, I suppose, since man-of-my-dreams Garret still hasn't called – and now he's missed the deadline for another weekend.

It's Friday afternoon now and I've taken a sicky. I just couldn't face work today what with Derek coming in to collect Wendy and thinking that I've been doormatted by his loser friend. I stayed in bed until almost noon which was nice but then I realised it wasn't nearly as grey outside as it could be. I thought I'd better get out and enjoy the few beams of sunshine while I could. So I'm sitting in the park now and all I can see everywhere I look is couples. I don't know why none of them are at work, maybe they're skiving too or maybe they've just got especially long lunch breaks.

In any case, they're beginning to disgust me because they look too damn happy for their own good. It really is amazing how much a person's looks improve when they're happy. I mean, that dough-balled woman over there for instance. My bits and bobs are better proportioned than hers – which isn't saying much, of course, but I definitely do have nicer hair. Not that nice hair is the final, end-all determinant of romantic success – Joyce, God help her, is living proof of that. Still this woman here, this poor woman. I mean, talk about bad haircuts – she must have gone to the Vidal Sassoon school on first-timers' day. And I'd never dream of going out with someone as homely as her gangly, spot-ridden boyfriend. And yet, together, they just look gorgeously happy – all hand-holding and cooing and gazing deeply into one another's eyes. Happy = beautiful. Happiness found in being one of two, half of a whole. Completeness. I wonder if I've ever looked that beautiful in all my life.

I remember once feeling so happy that I could have been the most beautiful woman in the world. One night with Peter, it was. Seems like centuries ago now, but he didn't think I was beautiful so that happiness didn't last long. There have been times with Garret that came close, for limited periods when we played wrestling games in his flat. God, these men, why the hell can't I get them out of my head! They're like squatters that you can't evict for anything. And why the hell hasn't Garret called? I know he must be struggling over whether or not he can handle another 'complication' like me in his life right now. But if only I could talk to him about it – that is, if he would ever listen, if he would take it in without trying to twist it around and turn it back on me, redefine my motives and leave me scurrying to defend myself, warding off an attack. Always the verbal swordfight.

But perhaps he has come to his decision, the one he'd

already half-concluded in his mind from the very beginning. He'll decide that I'm too young and naïve and inexperienced, that he's too old for me, too cynical, that his life is too complicated, that he doesn't want to hurt me, that there is no room, no room in his life for anyone else, for me, for any complications. He'll decide to end it all before it ever really got started. God, I wish I could be with him right now, to change his mind or to stop him before he makes that decision, to remind him – remember this is me, *me*, Charlotte, not just a situation, but me who you care about and enjoy being with, Charlotte who is so god-damn ebullient (ebullient! however the hell you're supposed to pronounce it) and talkative and childish but so awfully goddamn fun, me who 'enlivens' you (his words, I swear), who fascinates you, who you like *so* much, me, remember it's *me*! 'Don't leave me,' I would tell him. 'Don't give up on me, don't say I'm just a situation or a complication. Just look at me and think about me and remember how much fun you have with me, and then stay with me, tickle me, seduce me, make love to me, be with me. Jesus, just notice me and don't forget! *Please!*'

Wonderful, now I'm crying and the beautiful ugly couple have stopped staring goggle-eyed at each other to stare goggle-eyed at me. I feel like such a plonker. Plus the sun is playing hide-seek-and-never-find-again. Maybe I'll climb back into bed with a Horlicks. God, maybe I should just get it over with and call Garret. What do you think?

Sunday 24/1/93

'Many have the desire, some have the resolve, few
      have the talent.
If you have the desire, you have the ability to ache for it.
If you have the resolve, you have the courage to reach
      for it.

If you have the talent, you have the power to possess
it.
If you have all three, it is yours.'

I have nothing. What can I do?

Monday 25/1/93

But what happened to Charles and Mary? And what about
Sarah the screenwriter? And what the heck is going on here
anyway, Harriet? I don't think this little experiment is working at all. I thought we were supposed to react to each other
and you hardly ever react, you never write anything. I'm
pouring my heart out here and getting nothing back.

You want to know what to do? Try picking up a pen for a
change – write something, anything. Isn't that, supposedly,
what you want to do, after all? You could have fooled me.
Why don't you write some more about your stories instead
of just a few lines? Why don't you write about your real
life? I mean you have Edward, this great boyfriend, this
great relationship, and you never talk about it. Jesus, Harriet,
do you have any idea how jealous I am of you? I'd kill to be
in your position. A relationship, a career kind of a job, a goal
in your life. I'm sick of this, I don't want to do this any
longer, it's stupid. I'm not going to write any more unless
you put some effort into it too.

Besides which, what's new – that bastard Garret still hasn't
called!

Thursday 28/1/93

You want a reaction, Charlotte, you got it. The reason I don't
write about anything is because there's nothing to write. As
regards my personal life? What's there to say? Edward and I
have been together for nearly three years now. He's nothing
like perfection. He tells ludicrously unfunny jokes – over

and over again – and doesn't understand why I never laugh. He eats too much garlic, wears too much cheap aftershave, and wouldn't know Jane Austen from Jane's Addiction. Oh, he's all right I suppose – generous and attentive certainly. But, for the most part, he's just *there*. I suppose that I may love him, but basically I'm simply accustomed to having him around. Relationships are habitual like that sometimes, no longer exciting, just comfortable and steady. And, if truth be told, most of the time, downright tiresome.

You're jealous of me because of what I do. That's hysterical. I positively despise my job. Do you have any idea what an editorial assistant on a magazine like *Fishing Digest* does? Basically, I have the privilege of handling all the dogsbody dross that no one else could be bothered with. Every day, I go through stacks of tedious, poorly written press releases about fishing equipment for God's sake. From these, I get to compose the weekly 'Fisherman's News' section. Sometimes, I get to write the features no one else wants (i.e. the ones which involve no trips or freebies) – incorporating exciting topics like 'Best Bait of the Year'. I also have the immense responsibility of organising our regular readers' competitions which means I get to wade through hundreds of entries (even more poorly written than the press releases) on 'what fly fishing means to me'. Poetry to J.R. Hartley's ears, but not mine, I'm afraid. Really. How rivetingly inane – I never even *eat* fish let alone *catch* it! Oh yes, and lucky me, I get to answer the phones and make tea for the editor and his puerile deputy ten times a day.

You're jealous of me because you think I know what I want to do with my life. Jealous of what exactly? Since childhood, I've had this vague aspiration of becoming a great writer, of composing tremendous masterpieces of literary fiction. But I can't write any more. Perhaps I never could but at least I once thought I could. Now I can hardly think properly, let alone write properly. All day I report on tackleboxes and wellies until my brain starts to atrophy so that when I come home I don't even have the energy to scribble a few sentences about something that might actually matter.

How exactly do you want me to react, Charlotte? All I can say is please don't stop writing. Honestly, what you're doing is helping. This is my last hope. And besides, you're not missing out by my omitting the details of my daily grind. Your life is much more interesting than mine. Trust me.

Sunday 31/1/93

Okay, okay, Harriet, I didn't mean to upset you. I just wasn't sure this was going anywhere for you. I'll keep writing if you promise to do the same. Anyway, if I didn't do it here, I'd just have to shell out for another notebook of my own. This writing thing is really habit-forming, you know.

So the latest is that I called Garret. Big mistake? Who knows. All I know is that I had to do it – it's been three weeks now from our last date and it's just fourteen days, a mere two weeks and a single full weekend remaining until V-Day. I suppose it was only a matter of time.

Before caving in, I'd taken to planting myself where I thought I might 'accidentally' bump into Garret. You know, like walking around Liverpool Street station about lunch-time. This is suspiciously far from my office near Cannon Street but I rehearsed the explanation of how I was just delivering something urgent for a client. Then I found myself going to Mayfair after work and one or two pints, casually strolling down his street like I always took drizzly-evening promenades around there. This weekend I went by there again, nearly marched up and rang the bell but I could-n't bring myself to do it. In the end, I walked to Green Park and called him from a phone box. Said I was shopping on

Oxford Street, was only a few minutes away, maybe I could come around for a cuppa. But he said it wasn't terribly convenient – he was on his way out or something. So then I swallowed hard and just went ahead and did it. I invited him to see *Blood Brothers* with me on Thursday night. Everyone's been raving about what a great play it is, plus I love musicals and I thought he'd enjoy it. He said he could probably come, if he didn't get a better offer. He's so funny sometimes.

Wednesday 3/2/93

Remember that writing workshop I used to go to? That was the last time I had a story I managed to see through to completion. At the time, I thought the story was half-decent, or at least salvageable. I had to read it aloud to the group one night. They obviously didn't understand it. After I finished, they just sat there looking puzzled for a few minutes until the instructor finally broke the silence with a heart-warming comment about my writing lacking structure. She never liked any of my work.

Why is it that I can have so much structure, to the point of distraction, in my life but not in my stories?

Home, office, Edward. Wake, eat, work, sleep. With breaks for good behaviour and screwing on the weekend. I'm structurally impaired and creatively comatose.

Thursday 4/2/93

Well, that instructor is a stupid bitch. Remember Mr Twain's famous words:

'Keep away from people who try to belittle your ambitions. Small people always do that, but the really great make you feel that you, too, can somehow become great.'

Whatever you do, Harriet, steer clear of life's dwarfs. Words to live by, words to live by. I only wish that I could live by them, but I'm feeling rather dwarfish myself today.

I guess Garret got a better offer. I still can't believe it, but he actually stood me up. He tried to corral Liz into being the messenger but she was having none of it, although she did call to warn me about it. A few minutes later, as if on cue, he called and played the sarky bastard performance to a tee. He went on about his complicated life and how I was just too young to understand. So predictable. I snapped back that if he didn't want to see me, then he shouldn't have said yes in the first place. He agreed – in hindsight, he probably shouldn't have. Other memorable snippets from our ghastly conversation include . . .

Me: I don't think you've been very fair to me.
Him: Who said I had to be?

And later,

Him: Look, I'm sorry! (Heavy on the sarcasm, i.e. 'I couldn't care less, you silly cow.')
Me: That's okay. (I was about to let him off, but then . . .) No wait a minute, that's not okay at all. I'm not going to let you get off this phone and feel good about yourself. I'm not going to give you any forgiveness. I hope you can't sleep tonight or tomorrow night. I hope you sleep horribly the rest of the week thinking about it. I hope you take up smoking again and die an early and horribly painful death from cancer.

He wasn't even fazed by this. He calmly thanked me for my 'well wishes', told me to 'have a nice life' and then rang off. What a tosser! Anyway, now I had these two tickets and no one to go with. You said you already had plans with Edward and Liz ummed and ahhhed, said she'd promised Alex to watch some documentary with him, but she went with me in the end. Another big mistake. Throughout the first act, I knew she was dying to tell me 'I told you so'. Instead, at the interval, she bought me a Magnum and started in on 'Now, I'm not going to tell you "I told you so".' Which is of course just as bad. I let her spout off while I ate my ice-cream, and I didn't say anything because she was probably right and I think she feels guilty for ever introducing me to the bastard. The whole time, I was just dying to get home and write it all down.

Anyway, the upside – there is always an upside, well, usually anyway – is that Liz and I did actually enjoy the play. But I don't think Garret would have appreciated it that much after all – Willy Russell's not plummy enough for him, you know. Liz and I went halves on the soundtrack.

Saturday 6/2/93

Sometimes we confuse the ability to hate someone with the inability to understand them.

Sunday 7/2/93

If that's aimed at me, Harriet, the only thing I want to say is that that is complete bullshit. You know, Liz knows, you've all known from the beginning that Garret was slime. It just takes me a little longer every now and again. I can completely understand him and yet hate him at the same time. I can only swallow so much shit – he never meant to hurt me, he's been hurt himself before, can't handle commitment, no more complications, blah blah blah blah. Boo fucking hoo for poor old Garret.

I remember at the beginning he said to me, 'You have the potential to hurt me and I have the potential to hurt you.' Like that was okay if someone got hurt as long as we started out on equal footing. But if the ground's so even, how come I'm always the one who ends up thrown for a somersault?

Either I keep meeting men with a lot more potential than me or I just haven't got any potential of my own whatsoever or I'm having trouble finding it or something. Still, at the end of the day, all men are amoebas!

Goddammit, a week from today and I will be officially Valentineless.

Tuesday 9/2/93

I apologise, Charlotte. But you shouldn't be so sensitive. The comment wasn't aimed directly at you. The thought simply occurred to me whilst reading your entry and I wrote it down impulsively. Besides which, I thought you wanted more reaction from me.

Sunday 14/2/93

Sorry I haven't written all week – I've been too wrapped up in my cosy state of depression about the arrival of today. Plus, I suppose, I was secretly hoping for some miraculous turn of events in my love life to stave off the inevitable.

But oh, as Doris would say, *que sera sera*. It's officially Valentine's Day and, once again, I'm officially alone on the most romance-ridden day of the year. I suppose I could have gone out and found someone in a pub or, worst case, some sad wino on the streets who I might have convinced to go to dinner with me. As long as I was paying. But I'm not that bad, I'd rather be by myself than with someone I don't want to be with. But then I'd much much rather be with someone I do want to be with than by myself. I don't understand why it's so difficult to find someone I want who wants me back. Other couples make it look easy – mutual attraction, romance, love, making that connection.

Well, anyway, it's just gone midnight now so I've officially survived V-Day 1993. I guess that's an upside. The down-side, on the other hand, the worst part will be tomorrow in the office when everyone's talking about their weekends and asking about mine and then I'll have to admit that I didn't get a single card or flower or chocolate. I suppose it's better than the years when Valentine's Day falls on a weekday and I have to sit there trying not to bawl when all the other PAs (and even my chain-smoking, podgy boss – doesn't he know V-gifts are meant to go in the other direction?) are receiving deliveries of red roses and heart-shaped balloons all around me. How agonising! Why do I have this completely ineffectual effect on men?

Maybe New Year's Resolutions *are* futile. Still, I've survived. Valentine's Day is now behind me and I've got 365 days to work on hunting down a boyfriend for next year. What did you and Edward do this weekend, Harriet? Please tell me.

Tuesday 16/2/93

Edward planned a surprise weekend away for Valentine's Day this year. We left early Saturday morning and drove to a charming B&B in a village just outside Stratford. On Saturday night, we went to see the Royal Shakespeare Company performing *As You Like It* which was quite good. The next morning he took me for a sumptuous Valentine's brunch at a nearby estate. When we arrived, there was a single red rose and a gift-wrapped package laid out on the table waiting for me. I still cannot figure out when Edward had a chance to deliver the present. We exchanged and unwrapped gifts over champagne cocktails. I gave him a couple of CDs that he's been wanting and a cashmere jumper. He gave me an enormous flask of perfume and a gold necklace.

Thursday 18/2/93

Maybe you shouldn't write any more about your private life after all, Harriet. It's distressingly depressing for me.

But it's no time to be depressed. I have good news. Up, up, upside. William, my Royal Navy man, has finally blown back into my life. Sadly, his call yesterday came three days late to qualify him as my Valentine, but then maybe it can be counted retrospectively (or is it retroactively, I can never remember). We're going to meet in the West End for dinner on Friday night.

I'm really looking forward to that. I'm not sure how I feel about him. The truth is I don't really know him that well. We met about a year and a half ago at a friend's party. He was very nice and, as military men so often are, extremely well-groomed and polite. After that, he'd pop up on sort of a six-monthly basis for a couple of dates and some nice good-night snogs – okay, yeah, and maybe a grope or two – before another wave bye-bye. I wasn't really sure where I stood. Then, the last time I saw him, which was last summer, he invited me for a weekend away in Brighton with him and several of his Navy mates. That was great fun. He and all his friends made like it was completely normal and expected for William and I to be together. He acted very couplish and territorial, even in front of his mates, and that was a nice feeling, almost like being someone's girlfriend. This time when we said goodbye, he promised to call and to write.

Well, over the past eight months, I've received two post-cards from him but no telephone calls. Until yesterday. And again, I'm not sure where I stand with William. Every time he goes away, I prepare myself to never see him again. Then he comes back and surprises me – like a semi-annual bout of flu. Albeit a very enjoyable one.

Friday 19/2/93

Contrary to what you may think, Charlotte, a relationship does not instantly solve all of life's problems. Nor does it mean you become an overwhelmingly fulfilled person overnight. A partner, no matter how good or bad, cannot do or be everything for you.

Edward, for example, doesn't seem to understand me at all most of the time. Rather than listening to what I have to say, he expends most of his conversational energy trying to put me to sleep with a litany of bad jokes. My beloved harbours a desire to be the next Ben Elton but has about as much capacity for humour as a Conservative Party Conference. When I do try to elevate our talks, they inevitably go right over his head. During our terribly romantic Valentine's weekend, for instance, we had a conversation about my writing (or lack thereof at the moment). I told him about my story idea for Sarah the screenwriter. He scoffed, said it would be a horrible story and asked why I didn't write something people wanted to read about. The rest of the discussion went something like this . . .

Harriet: But you haven't even read it – I haven't even written it yet. How do you know whether it's good or not?

Edward: I've read some of your stuff (only about half a story a couple of years ago!). It's not what people want. It's too high brow, too literary.

Harriet: So what do people want to read about?

Edward: Sex, especially sex with famous people, coupling in ways that shock. Like – 'Oh heavens, is that the Queen Mother and Pope John Paul II across the street, having dinner in the Prima Pasta? Yes, it is. And yes, she's got that self-satisfied Cheshire cat grin. They've definitely been shagging.' Then the Pope dribbles spaghetti bolognese down her pearl-clad chest and licks it up. Get the idea, Harriet? That's what people want. Sex. Good and raunchy.

Harriet: That's nothing but tabloid, bodice-ripping rubbish. I wouldn't read that. Would you?

Edward: But you read, Harriet. You read more in one
week than most people read in a year.
(Probably true, compared to you, my beloved
illiterate fool, Edward.) You need to write for
people who don't read! That's what sells!

Inspirational words from the love of my life, don't you
think?

Saturday 20/2/93

Whatever you do, don't ditch Edward – you may regret it.
I'm telling you, it's hell out here. No, better to just run
roughshod over his dwarfish tendencies. Write what you
want and tell him to clam up.

Well, more news from the front. Last night and William
were a real disappointment – and so bizarre! I think he may
be a little unbalanced or something after all those months at
sea. The chief topics of the evening – completely
unprompted by me, I swear to God – were relationships and
marriage. The institution of marriage in general terms and in
very specific terms – he, me, us. How long did I want to wait
until I got married? What was I looking for in a husband?
Where would I want to live when I was married? Marriage
and careers, marriage and the military, marriage and kids,
marriage and in-laws, marriage and life. He said the words
'marriage' and 'marry' so many times – I counted three times
when he actually 'proposed' to me, supposedly in jest – I
thought I'd be sick. By the time we received our starters, I
nearly was sick. When he said the M-word once again, I
had to put my fork down and say in exasperation, 'You
know, William, you're talking an awful lot about marriage.
Are you anxious to get married or something?'

I suppose he was rather taken aback by my straightfor-
wardness but not nearly as taken aback as I was when he
said that, yes, he was anxious to get married and asked if I
was open to the 'proposition' (note, not proposal). I guess
that I'm a prime candidate since I've seen him a grand total
of five times in the nineteen months since we first met!
According to him, that makes us terribly serious – news to
me, considering I didn't even know where we stood as of the
day before. He seems to think that just because we have
known each other over a long period of time, we know each
other well. What a load of bollocks!

I asked William why he wanted to get married. He talked
in circles but the basic gist seemed to be that he was afraid of
being alone for ever. He explained to me what it was like
being in the Navy – the military isn't a nine to five job, he
said, it's a life and you have to buy into it 'hook, line and
sinker' (quote unquote, honest). But it wasn't easy – especially when he came home and saw his friends, saw them
getting on with their lives, involved in serious relationships,
announcing engagements. He wondered what he was missing out on. Plus his mum is pressuring him to find a nice girl
and tie the knot – she wants grandchildren and now.

I was beginning to feel bad for the guy. But then, in the
course of this conversation, it accidentally emerged that
William was at home in Kent for Christmas. In fact, he's
been in the UK this whole time since the holidays, including
Valentine's Day. I asked why he hadn't called in all that time.
He made some feeble excuses about family commitments,
exercises in Portsmouth, officer exams and so on. But I still
thought it was pretty ridiculous that in two whole months
he couldn't find two minutes to ring the girl he supposedly
wanted to marry. Has he been trying this line on every bar-
maid and waitress in the south of England and now he's just
scraping the bottom of the barrel with me?

Anyway, I told him I wasn't ready for a husband, I just wanted a boyfriend. And he said he'd see if he could work on that, with an eye to the future of course. But I think it's pretty much too late – he really weirded me out with all that marriage talk.

God, I don't know. Am I meeting all the wrong people, or all the right people and just finding things wrong with them? Anyway, the upside here is that some man wants me, even if he may be certifiable.

Monday 22/2/93

'To my mind the most interesting thing in art is the personality of the artist; and if that is singular, I am willing to excuse a thousand faults.'

'The writer should seek his reward in the pleasure of his work and in release from the burden of his thought; and indifferent from aught else, care nothing for praise or censure, failure or success.'

W. Somerset-Maugham, *The Moon and Sixpence*

Don't worry about me, Charlotte. I know now what I must do. You won't like it. I don't like it, if truth be told. But it must be done.

Tuesday 23/2/93

'When I'm by myself, nobody else can say goodbye.'

Edie Brickell, *'Circle'*

A thousand faults, a thousand faults. Too many to start counting now. Anyway, had to add my own quotation for good measure.

What must be done, Harriet? Whatever it is, don't you worry, you've got my support. And Liz's and Joyce's too, I'm sure. That's what friends are for. The support from you guys is about the only thing I've got left! Liz is Liz and Joyce calls often, and you've been great, too, letting me hog the journal like this when I know you want to be writing stuff. Thanks, really, I appreciate it.

I'm experiencing more than my share of dwarfism these days actually. I've taken another sicky from work. I didn't go in yesterday either. I don't think I'm really physically ill or anything but I could probably get myself there. The truth is I just didn't feel like going to the office. In fact, I don't feel like going anywhere, haven't done since Sunday when I climbed into bed after trying to call William. I wanted to talk to him because I felt kind of bad about how we left things on Friday night. I didn't want him feeling rejected, because I know how horrible that is. So I tried calling him at his parents' house. His mum answered and said he'd already left – on another six-month tour. He never said anything to me about going away! Plus, his mother didn't even know who I was. The girl he said he wanted to marry and his mum had never heard of me. Right! All that talk about marriage – he just wanted another easy shag.

Anyway, I haven't ventured out of my bedroom much except to the loo and the kitchen (for more comfort food – lots more). It's now got to the point where I'm almost afraid to leave the flat at all, even just to go to the high street. It takes too much energy I guess to drag myself out there on to the grey, wet streets and it's so warm under my duvet. Liz keeps bringing me cups of cocoa, coming into my room to sit on my bed, gabble and try to cheer me up. Until Alex hauls her away, that is. I think he's jealous of the little bit of time he leaves Liz to spend with her friends, plus I'm sure he thinks I'm wacky. A bad influence, being single and all. (Like it's catching.) Men! Still, I know I'll have to pull myself together quickly, because the office will want a doctor's note if I'm gone much longer.

Thursday 25/2/93

'When you look at it closely, all life is unbearable. That is where you draw your strength.'

Edward Bond, *The Sea*

'It takes so little, so infinitely little, for a person to cross the border beyond which everything loses meaning: love, convictions, faith, history. Human life – and herein lies its secret – takes place in the immediate proximity of that border, even in direct contact with it; it is not miles away, but a fraction of an inch.'

Milan Kundera, *The Book of Laughter and Forgetting*

All in good time, Charlotte.

Saturday 27/2/93

I think I'm within a hair's width.

I just need to meet someone, some gorgeous man who's going to save me from all this, from this shitty February weather, from my going-nowhere job, from myself. Liz says she wants to introduce me to Alex's brother – but I don't know how wise it is to get involved with that family. Besides, I don't think I can handle blind dates right now. I don't have the stamina to endure any more disappointments. It's incredible really to feel like this. I can't believe that just two short (but hellishly long) months ago, I thought I had it made – so many choices, so many men. Now I feel more alone and rejected than ever. And it's not really William or Louis or the boss or Alex. It doesn't matter that *they* don't want me, only that *he* doesn't. They're all just part of a sideline Chinese water torture – that keeps drip, drip, dripping away when

I'm already drowning in a pool, a sea, an ocean of misery called Garret. It has a name.

Jesus, I can't stop thinking about him. Garret, Garret, Garret, what have you done to me? Maybe the hard nugget of truth is that he never cared about me in the least. Maybe he was using me all along. That would be absolutely the worst. I don't want to believe it because then there really would be nothing of me left inside. But maybe not. I don't know. All I know is that he doesn't want me now and that feels bad enough. He's even stopped going to his own company's regular pub for beers after work – just in case he might run into me. How humiliating.

Garret and I are never, *never* going to happen. It's over. It was over that moment, that precise moment when he put the phone down on me after I told him to smoke himself to death and he uttered that death-knell – *have a nice life*. He meant it, he meant 'sort it out for yourself, babe, 'cos I have no fucking intention of sticking around to see what happens to you'. And 'by the way, frankly my dear, I just don't give a shit' – damn, whatever. That's what he meant.

God, Liz tried to warn me about him. Why didn't I listen? Probably for the same reason I'm playing deaf to the chorus of people who are now telling me that I need to get over it, get on with my life, that at the best of times he was nothing but poison for me. And there's no future in poison. Okay, so I admit it, it's not going to happen. But admitting it is not good enough. Why is it so much easier to admit than it is to accept? Because I keep thinking and remembering and *wanting* so much.

I keep telling myself all these things – nothing's going to happen, he doesn't want you, he's poison . . . And still I dream about him and think about him all the time and remember the weight of his body on top of mine – I am tempted to rip the phone out of the wall to stop myself from calling him again.

Calm down, calm down, Charlotte. Think about something else. What about you, Harriet? What's up with you? I've been so self-absorbed these days, seems like I hardly ever get the chance to talk to you any more. My fault, I know, I'm just not taking the time. Are you working on a new story? I don't mean to be nosey, it's only that I've noticed you've started burning the midnight oil, as it were. Is that what you meant by you knowing what you had to do? Just get on with it, eh? Good attitude, I admire that. So what's the story about?

Monday 1/3/93

'The fool doth think himself wise,
The wise man knows himself to be a fool.'

Will Shakespeare

'The trouble with common sense is it ain't all that common.'

Will Rogers

You'll know soon enough, Charlotte. I promise.

Friday 5/3/93

What? What will I know? The suspense is killing me. Though something else may well beat it to the finishing line.

It's Friday night and the rest of the world is out with their mates or partners at the cinema or the theatre or maybe at the pub making sure they get their money's worth before last call, maybe debating which curry house they'll opt for tonight. I am at home listening to an hour's worth of London's Love Songs on Capital – *by myself*. Curled up in bed with the radio propped next to me, listening to either the decade's most romantic or most wrist-slashing songs – depending on your perspective. I think you know mine.

As if on cue, my mum called me about half an hour ago. (When the phone rang, I raced to it thinking, maybe, maybe, maybe. How silly.) I told her about my man troubles. She just sighed and said, 'Charlotte, I think you were meant for a different purpose in life.' Say what? In other words, no my dear, not for you love and happiness – think again, set more realistic goals. God, even my mum has given up on me. Maybe the whole thing is hopeless after all.

You know I was just thinking about what would happen if I died. I used to think about this sometimes when I was a kid, when my brother and I had a blazing row and my parents always sided with him. And I would think, just wait, they'll be sorry. If I suddenly died, hit by a lorry or something, there my mum and dad and little brother would be at my funeral. They'd be crying their eyes out, feeling as guilty as hell and wishing they could take it all back. So now I'm thinking about that again, except I'm visualising Garret at the graveside, looking sad and remorseful, vowing to put that nasty lorry driver behind bars. Or even better, what if I actually killed myself, then he and all the others would really feel like shit, so much guilt. They'd all be thinking, Did I drive her to this? Am I responsible for her suicide? Arrogant bastards to the end. But they *should* feel guilty, every one of them, for the rest of their lives. It would serve them right. Garret, William, Louis, and everyone before them, including and above all, that god-damn philandering pissant Peter. Each time I thought, well this one's different. But they're not different, they never are. Men are much of a muchness – dwarfs and amoebas one and all!

You guys will all be there too, of course. All my friends. At the funeral. But I'll try to give you some kind of sign. Let you know I'm all right. If I'm all right. If you care.

Sunday 7/3/93

'Razors pain you;
Rivers are damp;
Acids stain you;
And drugs cause cramp;
Guns aren't lawful;
Nooses give;
Gas smells awful;
You might as well live.'
Dorothy Parker, *'Resumé'*

Monday 8/3/93

Where the hell do you get all these quotes, Harriet? Do you just spend your journal-writing time thumbing feverishly through the Dictionary of Crap and Condescending Quotations? Have you got nothing better to do? I haven't, not tonight anyway, but you still don't see me resorting to second-hand reference books.

I mean, are you trying to cheer me up, or what, Harriet? I don't think so. You're in cahoots with the rest of them, aren't you? Perhaps this is paranoia, but my 'lack of self-confidence' seems to be a topic of great discussion recently. Alex, as always. But now also Joyce, Wendy, my parents, you and Liz – you even seem to have corralled Edward into it. I heard him in the lounge last night, cracking jokes and you all tittering until I came in the room. It's getting to be a little (read incredibly) embarrassing. I mean, doesn't anyone else have security problems? And don't you people have anything more important to talk about? Or perhaps that's what makes being in a relationship so much fun – you can laugh at and pity those who aren't so lucky.

I know I must seem pathetic because I moan about men all the time, but I wouldn't say I'm suicidally depressed.

(Okay, yes I've thought about suicide in a what-if kind of way, but I haven't actually thought about *doing* it!) I'm just frustrated – emotionally and sexually. I want so desperately to be going out with someone (as opposed to most of the time when I just think it would be pretty damn nice) and experiencing the joys of sex again instead of only hearing them through the paper-thin walls of this damn flat. (Yes, that's right. *I can hear youuuuuuu.*) As much as I want that to happen, it seems destined not to. And it's difficult (read impossible) to ooze self-confidence and have faith in my own sexual appeal when nothing ever works out.

Sometimes I also think if I have no self-confidence it must be because I'm trying to subconsciously balance out the massive egos of all these prats. I swear if I even look at a man, he thinks I'm trying to pull him and then he goes boasting to all his mates how I'm totally hot for him. This actually happened with another guy from Liz's office – and he was gay for God's sake.

So all you do-gooders, my dear friends, keep telling me that I must find some self-confidence. It's like Rebecca. She always used to say 'attitude' was the thing, it was all about attitude. As if it's as easy as paint-by-numbers. Maybe for her, maybe for you, but not for me. How exactly am I supposed to *do that*? You can't order self-confidence and attitude at the local take-away, with chips please. And what good would it do anyway? You know, I've been down this road before. I remember after that heartbreak over Peter and Rebecca. I moved in with you guys to escape and tried to starve and aerobicise myself to physical nirvana. (I might have got somewhere too if it weren't for jammy dodgers, McDonald's take-aways and those tossers downstairs banging their broomsticks on the ceiling every time I did so much as a sit-up.) Meet new friends, make a new life, manufacture a new me. And throw myself back into the fray. It's no different now. You all keep assuring me it's okay to be single, being independent is what's most important. But that's bollocks. It's just a word game for you. It's like when someone says 'Oh, she's a really nice girl' when what they actually mean is she's as ugly as a box of toads. It's a euphemism, isn't it? That's the right word, I'm sure of it, I just looked it up. A euphemism: 'the substitution of a mild, indirect or vague expression for an offensive or unpleasant one; also the expression so substituted.' Independent is just a euphemism, another word for alone. And alone is just another way of saying sad and lonely. Euphemistically.

No, the fact is there is only one real replacement for a man, only one way to restore my self-confidence, and that's another man. Where the hell are all the good ones?

Tuesday 9/3/93

'You needed love so badly you hugged the shadow of it.'
Bill Goodman, *Fragments of Lear*

Q: What are you really afraid of?
A: I'm afraid to die and I'm afraid to live another minute.

Wednesday 10/3/93

I'm not stupid you know, Harriet. I know you're trying to get at me with these ram-it-down-my-throat excerpts from your literary store – other books, other people's work, things *you haven't written*. I'm not paranoid either.

It's not paranoid or crazy after all, the way I've been acting. It's just a situation in search of reclassification. In fact, it's you beautifully happy couple types who are the crazy ones. At least that's what I read in *Time Out*. There's this guy, Dr Richard Bentall, who wants happiness to be classified as a mental disorder. He says, 'Happy people are less rational than depressed people . . . the truth is that your friends *are* really saying things behind your back.' He's a doctor, he should know.

So what are you guys saying about me anyway? I can just imagine the heyday you're all having – Alex must be loving it. You wouldn't tell Liz and the others about this journal and what I've been writing about, would you, Harriet? You promised you wouldn't do that.

Thursday 11/3/93

Character study:

My problem is that I want too much. My problem is that I am too keen, too desperate. My problem is that I don't know what I want. My problem is that I care too much about what other people think. My problem is that I'm too fat, too short, too stupid. My problem is that I have spots, my breasts are too big, my teeth are too crooked, my feet are too smelly. My problem is that I am too trusting and naïve and ignorant and innocent and immature. My problem is that I am overstressed and undersexed. My problem is that I want everyone to like me and to want me and no one else. My problem is that I hate myself. My problem is that I'm lonely and tired. My problem is that I have too many problems.

Friday 12/3/93

What's this 'character study' bullshit, Harriet? That's not you, or some character you made up – that's me. What's going on? What are you up to? What have you done? Liz wants me to go home to my parents for a while. I need to know – have you told her about the stuff I've been writing in here? You have, haven't you? I thought this 'experiment' was our secret. I don't understand.

Saturday 13/3/93

I have always been aware of the way words sound. Words fascinate me, the ways that one can string them together, the many many ways. When I write, I seek not just the best way to say something, but all the ways. I love the words, I have always loved them. But I sometimes wondered, I worried, whether I had just one story to tell. Many words, many ways to work them, but only one real tale.

And so I couldn't write. It has been so long since I even had enough inspiration to pick up a pen. Why? Was the material dead? Was the inspiration dead? Was the art dead? Was the world dead? Dead and buried? No, we were just waiting – for the right story. Perhaps it is true, perhaps each person has only one story. That's not fair. It's not enough, I tell you. Luckily, different people have different stories.

Sunday 14/3/93

Please Harriet, please don't do this. It wasn't supposed to be like this. It's us against the amoebas, us against the dwarfs, remember? I can't write any more, I can't think straight, I can't stop crying. You can't do this.

Footnote

When people discover that you are an aspiring writer, they often start to screen themselves, parts of their personalities or lives that they're not very proud of. They preface confessions with disclaimers: 'But of course, you can never write about this,' they say. They ask to be included in your work but only their good sides. (As if the writer is a photographer in a portrait studio: all soft lights, flattering angles and an airbrush.) They want to be immortalised but not humiliated. Unfortunately, for the writer, the blemishes make much better reading.

Perhaps that is, in fact, more unfortunate for the writer's subject. Poor Charlotte, I never told anyone anything. She did all the telling, and all the writing, for me. Great writing it is, too. At least that's what my agent tells me. In an amateurish though endearingly frank fashion. Truly inspirational.

Book Proposal

Synopsis

A young writer (Hannah) is having problems finding inspiration for her work. She proposes to her flatmate (Colette) that they share a journal. The journal will be an open space for both of them to describe the details of their lives, jot down quotations, work out ideas, etc. As the journal develops, the flatmate reveals more and more of her sadly sordid love life. She is in a race to win a boyfriend by Valentine's Day and sinks further into depression when the fateful day arrives and passes without event.

Character Outline

Description of Colette:

Medium height, about 5ft 7in. Shoulder-length brown hair which she dyes auburn and wears in a bob. Eyes a very deep brown. Surprisingly fair skin, the kind that one would expect to freckle but doesn't. Straight, white smile but with a small gap to the right of the two front teeth. Overweight, with a largish bosom which she tends to flaunt. On the whole, passably pretty but ruins it by wearing far too much make-up and dressing much too revealingly.

She is desperate for a boyfriend and a regular sex life and will go to ridiculously sad lengths to obtain these. She never does.

Note to agent

When did you say the advance would come through?

Do you think there's film-rights potential here as well? I would enjoy trying my hand at screenwriting. I could see Julia Sawalha playing Colette though she'd have to gain some weight. Do you want to check with her people if she's available?

Do let me know.

Regards

Harriet

CHAPTER FOUR

IT COULD HAVE HAPPENED

It could have happened. Just like that Rachel Nickell woman down in Wimbledon. Except that this is not Wimbledon and things like that don't happen here. Even though it did, or it could have. There were other differences to that Nickell incident, of course. It hadn't been the afternoon for one. And it's May not July. And Charlotte is no model – former or future – either. She's not got a body like Rebecc . . . Rachel, rather, Nickell ever had – nearly her birthday again and Charlotte hasn't lost an ounce since the last one. And most importantly, Charlotte is lucky enough to be alive. Very lucky, considering the circumstances. She was there, alone, by herself at night, walking through the park; it was dark, she had to pee, she dropped her pants because she couldn't wait a second longer, she thought she heard a noise, a rustle. It could've happened that way. And no one was home when she got here. That American girl Emmy was probably at some club or a cultural 'happening' and lord knows where Liz was. Maybe she decided to stay at Alex's place. No one was around when Charlotte came in in such a state; there was no one around to say one way or the other, to know for certain whether it happened or not. No one here, not even a light on next door at Bonny and Joyce's. The whole place seemed deserted. Maybe Charlotte was the only living soul left on the planet or at least in Hampstead Garden Suburb or at the very least in Oakwood Road.

Later, Charlotte hears Emmy bustle in, humming, sounding purposeful. She hears her turn on the TV. Loud American accents arrow up the staircase, unmistakable even after the blunting of distance and walling. Emmy must be rewatching one of those crappy, middle-apple-pie-belt, teen-angst videos from her John Hughes collection. Charlotte is tempted to join her downstairs on the sofa where she sees Emmy cracking open a pre-bed snack of American delicacies that her 'mom' shipped over in twee care packages. 'Cookies' or some sort of good old American crackers. Charlotte is tempted, but she resists. At this point, she is in need of more than calories. Some time later, Emmy's fast-food and flick fix satisfied, the house grows quiet again as Charlotte's anxiety gathers momentum.

Relief arrives around 2 a.m. when she hears Liz come home. At last. Liz is trying to be quiet but the front door gives her away. She opens it slowly but it still squeals as though drawing in a sharp breath of too-cool summer air. She hears a muffled laugh. It is deep. Of course Liz would bring him home with her. There is a soft thud, Liz swatting him to shut up, followed by a moment of silence and then sucking wet, kissing noises. Charlotte can imagine them, standing in the foyer, embracing – Alex stroking Liz's long wavy hair, slobbering all over her neck, then thrusting his tongue deep into her mouth. And then more intimate whispers. They climb the stairs and someone stumbles, probably Alex in his haste, tripping over his trousers which are already down around his ankles.

They must be able to see the crack of light under Charlotte's door but they don't stop to say goodnight. Perhaps they think she has passed out with her bedside lamp on again. In any case, they obviously have better things to do. They pause for a bathroom break. The tap starts to run and the toilet swooshes and clanks. Charlotte buries her head under one of her pillows. She can see them in the bathroom together, brushing their teeth, swallowing paracetamol, poising on the toilet. She doesn't understand how Liz can find Alex attractive after watching him have a shit. Or vice versa. Charlotte hears him at the toilet now – one long, hard, continuous stream – he has definitely been drinking. It flushes again and they move through to the bedroom.

Charlotte tries to close her ears to the sounds that follow – each smack, each grunt, each tumble, each moan. Alex is easing Liz back on to the bed, telling her he loves her as he climbs on top. Liz runs her fingers through his blond, tangled chest hair. The bed begins to creak, picking up a steady rhythm.

Later, when all is quiet, Charlotte is running away again, away from the park and all the things that could have happened. The tears begin to squeeze themselves from the corners of her eyes. She knows the crying will wake Liz and Alex. She sobs even harder, her breath coming out hard and ragged, laboured. If they are in fact asleep. Even if they aren't asleep yet, they will stop what they are doing to come and check on her. She sounds urgently distressed. They will worry. Perhaps Alex will think she's just faking, stirring up some melodrama again to explain away another Friday night's drunkenness. He'll regret these unkind thoughts when he learns how serious it is. Charlotte is in pain. She gasps for air, clutches a pillow to her chest and curls herself tighter into the corner of the bed where it wedges itself against the wall.

Liz has heard Charlotte now and had time to pull her robe on. She knocks lightly on Charlotte's bedroom door. 'Charlotte, honey, are you all right?' No answer. 'Charlotte, can I come in?' she asks as she cracks the door open. Charlotte raises her head to see Liz standing in the doorway. Liz is wearing her forest-green, terry-cloth bathrobe. Big turned-up collar, too long sleeves and too wide cuffs – the robe hangs heavy and full from her slim shoulders down to swish around her ankles.

Charlotte will let her come in and is about to tell her so when she notices Alex looming behind Liz in the hall, clad in his Bart Simpson boxer shorts. And behind him, Emmy, Medusa-haired, who's been drawn from her ground floor slumber by Charlotte's outburst. Shrieking, Charlotte buries her head under her pillows. The pillows – the five matching full-sized florals and three muted pastel-coloured throw cushions – overwhelm her single bed. Sometimes they are festooned artfully around the mattress, fluffed up and resting against the wall at crafty angles, but more often they are piled carelessly high and mountainous at the end where a headboard should have been. When the rest of her room is tidy and Charlotte is looking at the bed, she prefers the artful display which makes the bed look more like a plush sofa and her tiny bedroom like a small sitting-room. But when she is in bed, she likes the mountain, she likes to be beneath the mountain and to feel the weight of the pillows pressing down gently on the back of her neck. As it does now. Under the pillows, she feels safe, sheltered, as if all of her body and world were captured there. It is warm and muffled. The faster she breathes and harder she cries, the steamier and smaller and safer it feels there.

'Jesus, Charlotte, I hate it when you do that,' Liz is saying. 'Can you even breathe under there?' Charlotte hears but Liz sounds very far away, the gulf is too wide to warrant a reply. She senses whispering and other noises not meant for her ears. Emmy is probably indulging in a full-action, full-volume yawn, rolled-shouldered, wide-armed gestures and all. Alex is probably telling Liz to leave Charlotte alone but, if so, she seems to ignore him.

Liz pads across the room to the bedside. Charlotte doesn't so much hear the footsteps as feel them. The floorboards are old; they bend and reposition themselves and Charlotte's mattress quivers beneath her in response.

'Come out, Charlotte, honey. Come out and talk to me – please.' Liz peels away the top layer of pillows. Blue floral pillow two, pastel pillow three. The nape of Charlotte's neck tickles as the pressure is relieved.

Charlotte grips the two remaining pillows over her head. 'Tell him to go away, Liz,' she whispers. 'Make him leave. Don't let him look at me. And Emmy too. Please.'

Charlotte is grateful that Liz doesn't ask why. There are more whispers above the pillows and then the comforting click of the door as it closes. A few minutes pass before Charlotte surfaces. Liz is sitting on the edge of the bed next to her, her arms folded across a creamy yellow throw-cushion. Charlotte notices how much the pastel pillow pales against the forest-green backdrop of Liz's robe. A stab of possessiveness. She wants to take the pillow away from her friend but she says nothing.

'Emmy wants to know if you want anything to eat.' For once in her life, Charlotte doesn't and says so. Liz crosses to the door, opens it just wide enough to pop her head into the corridor and mouth something to their flatmate. She closes the door and returns to Charlotte's bedside.

'Emmy's worried about you, you know, Charlotte,' Liz

says. 'So am I.' Interesting that she doesn't mention Alex, thinks Charlotte as she grunts in acknowledgement. 'Don't you like Emmy?'

Charlotte shrugs. 'She's young.'

'She's not that much younger than us. Only three years.'

'She's a student.'

'And you wish you weren't still?' Well, yes . . . no . . . exactly the point.

'She's American.'

'Is that bad? She can't help that.' Liz regards Charlotte with a patient, school-teacher stare.

'She's got a stupid name.'

'What's so stupid about it?'

Charlotte sits up straighter and flounces another pillow into her lap. 'Emmy? Come on, what is that? She's named after some stupid Broadway theatre award.'

'Those are the Tonys actually. The Emmys are the awards for American daytime television.'

'Even worse.' Charlotte rolls her eyes. 'What's it short for anyway? Emma? Emily?'

'Neither, I don't think. I think it's just Emmy.'

'That is so stupid,' Charlotte says again, more irritated.

'This isn't like you to be so nasty, Charlotte. What's wrong?' Charlotte wishes it wasn't like her, but she's been feeling nasty inside for so long, she doesn't think she could possibly be like anything else. Her eyes start to brim with tears as her hands reach instinctively for another pillow.

Liz stops her, squeezing her fingers lightly. 'Do you need a hug?'

Charlotte nods as Liz embraces her. She rests her chin in the hollow of Liz's right shoulder where the robe has slipped down some and the skin is exposed. She leans her cheek against Liz's neck. Liz's skin is cool to the touch, especially cool against Charlotte's cheek, hot and puffy and red from tears and the enclosure of her pillows. The wide collar of the robe rubs dryly against her other cheek.

Beneath this robe, she is completely naked, Charlotte thinks. He has touched every millimetre of every inch of this small naked body beneath this robe. Her skin still tingles and burns with Alex's fingerprints, her thighs still slick with her own excitement. Charlotte's lips brush against Liz's shoulder, she inhales deeply. This is him. This is his smell. She recognises Alex's aftershave, Drakkar Noir. The dampness of his sweat. She licks her lips and tastes the salt of his skin on Liz's skin. Liz squeezes her hand. More moistness. Her hands still syrupy with his semen.

Again, Charlotte starts to cry. Liz cradles her. They rock gently back and forth on the creaking mattress as Charlotte tells the story. The pub, the Tube ride, the walk home through the neighbourhood, the dinner party she watched through someone's front window, the short-cut through the woods, the pee break, the man, the button-fly jeans, the rocks in her back, the escape, the arrival home, the fear. The rape.

Liz stays with Charlotte that night. Alex sleeps by himself in the room next door, or rather he lies in the bed, duvet tossed to one side, and he listens to them talk. He cannot distinguish the words but he hears the murmuring: Charlotte's high-pitched, agitated; Liz's soft, soothing, smoothing over occasional sobs from her friend. The voices buzzing into one, weaving together tighter and tighter as the night stretches on and his feet grow cold and he is pushed farther out of their circle.

The next morning Liz returns to him, still in her robe and her woolly grey socks tugged up to her knees. Pulling the duvet over them both, she cuddles up spoonlike against his backside. When she runs her hands across his chest, her fingertips are somehow cold and foreign. He turns to face her, her red and tired eyes, her tousled hair, her slightly acrid morning breath, her lips stained brownish orange from the cups of coffee she's been sipping through the night while sitting up with Charlotte. She whispers the explanation: Charlotte's story, the rape.

'God, that's terrible,' says Alex, hugging her, running his hands up and down her terry-clothed back. 'Has she called the police yet?'

Liz shakes her head against his chest. 'No, she wasn't up to it.'

'Jesus, we'd better call now then.' Alex pulls back to receive the nod, his leg muscles tense slightly, readying themselves for a leap into action. 'Would you like me to do it?'

'No, thanks Alex, but Charlotte's not ready for that yet. She's hysterical. She says she doesn't want to report it at all.'

'Why on earth not?'

'I think she'd just rather forget about it right now.'

'But that's ridiculous. I mean, a crime occurred here –'

'Yeah, I know, I know.' Liz's head sinks back to rest on his chest. A few static hairs cling to his face, tickling his nose. 'We're both aware of that. We've been up all night discussing it. But she's really scared right now and –'

Alex reaches a hand up to iron her stray hairs back into place and out of irritation range from his face. Once smoothed, he lets his fingers rest at the nape of her neck. 'But Liz, if she doesn't report it, the guy might never be caught. Surely that's the scarier option.'

She tosses her head impatiently. 'Look, Alex, you don't understand. We've been through all this already. She just doesn't want to report it, okay?'

'Okay, okay, I was just trying to help.' He pauses and then ploughs ahead. 'She is going to see a doctor, though, isn't she? I'm assuming that her rapist wasn't exactly a safe-sex advocate.' He attempts a smile.

'Very funny.'

'Sorry, but you know what I'm saying, she is going to make sure everything's all right down there, isn't she?'

'She's thinking about it. Of course, I'm strongly encouraging her to do so, but, well, she's a little hesitant. Like I said, she just wants to forget about it.'

'I'm sure it'll be much harder to forget about down the line if she finds herself pregnant, or worse yet, if she's caught some disease. Jesus, Liz, have you seen what happens to AIDS victims? It's terrible.'

Liz brings her arms up to her chest, crosses and locks them into place between them. 'Alex, Charlotte and I are both well aware of how the female reproductive organs work and we too watch the news. But really, this is for her to decide and if she's not ready right now, she's not ready.'

'What does Emmy think?'

'What does it matter what Emmy thinks?'

'Well, she's always got an opinion, that girl. I'm sure in this case she'll agree with me. Go to the professionals, go to the police, that's what she'll say. Two all.'

Liz sighs. 'Really, Alex, this is not a contest, no one's keeping score. And, unlike you, *I'm* sure that Emmy isn't going to pass judgement on the situation. She's just going to be supportive, of Charlotte. That's who we need to be thinking of here. We can't push her.'

'Hmmm, sure, of course not.' Alex falls back on to the mattress, slipping his right arm through the gap between Liz's pillow and her neck. He gives her shoulder a little squeeze and Liz, softening, turns back into the curve of his chest and arm. Her head bobs gently with his own breathing. Liz is upset, she's tired, she's worried about her friend. Alex can understand that. He'll just hold her for a while, comfort her in her turn, play the strong but caring, sympathetic boyfriend she is craving right now. He can do that.

He wants to keep his mouth stapled shut, and he's trying. But he has doubts, grim doubts that are shimmying up his vocal cords in search of a voice. The doubts fold themselves into more questions that Alex can't control – they eke out, still in soft whispers that blunt the sharper corners. He hopes. Was she at the pub last night? How much did she have to drink? Why didn't she catch the bus home? Why was she walking in the woods at that hour when she knows better? Was she bruised at all? Can't she remember what the rapist looked like? Was he wearing a mask? What colour were his eyes? Were there any witnesses? How exactly did she get away?

No, Yes, Don't know. Do not know! 'Charlotte is frightened, Alex,' Liz tells him, exasperated. 'She is very hurt and very embarrassed right now, she can't remember everything clearly, it was dark after all.'

'Liz, all I'm saying is that if this is what really happened then –'

'What do you mean "if"?' Liz shoves away, looking him sharply in the face. 'What are you suggesting? God, Alex, why do you have to doubt everything Charlotte says? Especially something as serious as this. How can you?'

'I'm just trying to be practical; I'm just trying to get the story straight.' The faintness drains out of Alex's voice. 'Besides which, why do you have to believe everything she says? So blindly, so unquestioningly.'

'Because she's my friend. She needs me. She's so shaken up right now. I mean really shaken, poor girl –'

Alex reaches to circle his arm around Liz again. 'Come on, sweetie, admit it. It's not like this is the first time Charlotte has acted a little strange. I mean, all that stuff with Harriet at the old flat –'

'I'm not so sure about that, Alex. We don't really know what happened there.'

'Come on. We know what happened. Charlotte freaked out, she couldn't handle life. You and Harriet tried to sort her out, but she was having none of it. You should have made her go home then. You should have got rid of –'

Liz's own arm flies up, batting his out of her way and throwing the duvet back in one motion. She jumps out of bed. 'That's enough! That's much more than enough. Thank you very much, Alex, for being so terribly understanding. You couldn't grasp this sort of thing to save your life.' Liz picks his rumpled jeans and jumper from the floor and tosses them on to the bed. 'You know, I think it's probably better if you go home right now. There's nothing you can do for us here today. These are desperate times, Alex, delicate times that need to be handled caringly and tactfully. At times like these, particularly times like these, women don't need men around, they need other women, they need their friends.' Boxer shorts, one sock, then another come sailing on to the bed. 'So, right now, I think it's best for everyone if you just leave, give us all a little distance for a while. Okay?'

'How long is a while?'

'I don't know. A while. As long as it takes.'

'As long as it takes. Geez, Liz, what about me, what about us? You can't be here to save Charlotte all the time. You need to think about getting on with your life too, our life together. Like we were talking about before, a place of our own –'

'I don't want to talk about that, Alex! Now is not the time to be thinking about you or me or us. Right now all I want to worry about is Charlotte. She needs me to be here and here is where I'm going to stay. So as I was saying, I think you'd better go home. I'll call you later.'

Alex considers protesting but now Liz is picking up one of his steel-capped DMs and he thinks better of it. He hustles out of the bed's target range and takes the shoe from her hand.

'Fine, no problem,' he says. 'I was going round to Edward's for some footie today anyway.'

Charlotte, awake next door, pillows scattered across the carpet, listened to the initial quiet of their intimacy through the wall. Soon after Liz left her, her bedroom began to lighten with the first attempts of the morning sun. Charlotte closed her curtains and pretended it was still night and she had no reason to worry about getting out of bed. Still, the persistent, watery sunbeams wriggled through the cracks around the curtains' edges and suffused the chinks in the material itself, bathing the room in a greyish half-light. Sinking back under her duvet, Charlotte piled a few pillows on top of her head and erected another night-time world.

Again, she sees herself exiting Golder's Green station. Walking up the Finchley Road, she passes the pizza place and the teeny-bopper disco under the train tracks. At Hoop Lane, she turns, passes the crematorium and slips into Hampstead Garden Suburb at the western edge amongst the ritzy semi-mansions. She must wend her way through the residential streets to her own dilapidated, former servants' shoebox on the eastern Suburb border. Thankfully, it isn't raining. She isn't drunk either, not at all, just a little tipsy from that last pint, and still annoyed that Wendy went off again with Derek and left her with his stupid friends, all of them cracking jokes about her long-ago, non-existent crush on their fool friend Louis and treating her like a contagion that was safest not to touch or even get within breathing distance of. And then Garret had come into the pub with his bandwagon of drunken buddies. He pretended he didn't see her, but she knew better. At closing, she caught the Tube home alone and couldn't even manage to strike up a conversation with the pot-bellied banker in the seat next to her.

So here Charlotte is, by herself again, walking these deserted streets home. As she passes the big, lawn-fronted houses, outdoor sensorised security lamps flash on to illuminate the façades, as if spotlighting the life that she's missing. And the homes themselves seem to withdraw, away from the glare and her, closing in on themselves and their occupants, retreating behind locked doors with brass knockers and shuttered, draped, bay windows. Except for one house. Twenty-two Heathgate – shamelessly emanating light and laughter and music through the windows nudged ever so slightly open to the late spring evening – assails her as she rounds the corner. She lingers on the pavement outside the house, watching the action within through the proscenium arch of the nearly floor-to-ceiling windows which stretch the length of the house's front room. The remnants of dinner on the abandoned table; guests in fine clothes, holding wine glasses, sitting and standing around a civilised string quartet. How terribly sophisticated. Charlotte turns away and walks on. She quickens her step along the neighbourhood's central square, her bladder beginning to weigh heavier against the jostling movement of her legs. This walk always takes so much longer at night, especially with a full bladder. She may burst before she reaches her toilet. She turns off Northway to take a short cut through the woods.

Once swallowed up within the densely overhung trails, Charlotte realises she has made a mistake. The woods appear different at night, wilder and less friendly. Streetlamps are few and far between – she never noticed their deficiency during her afternoon strolls – and the betweens are very dark indeed. Though she tries to aim for the direction of Oakwood Road and where she knows her house to be, the path wants to wind itself in ways that aren't familiar to her and fork more often than she remembers. The faster she walks, thinking that she will surely break through the perimeter soon, the bigger the forested park becomes, and the further she distances herself from the last streetlamp. And the heavier her bladder becomes as well. She clenches her buttocks together as she accelerates but this is not helping. She must pee. Right away. With no one else around, there's no need for modesty or further seclusion. Just speed. That decided she halts, unfastens her belt, rips open the button-fly of her jeans, yanks them and her knickers down to her knees and squats at the edge of the path.

Relief shoots hissing on to the matted forest floor. She sighs and reaches for a low-hung branch, for a leaf to wipe herself with, when she hears the noise. What was it? A snap of a twig, a rustle of branches; is there someone there? She tries to stand up but her left foot slips on a stone, she loses her balance and falls backward instead. Moss and the skeletons of orphaned leaves weaving into her hair, rocks poking into her vertebrae, the knobbled points of fallen branches digging into the flesh of her buttocks, her jeans dipping into her own puddle of piss. Is there someone there? Someone who will leap out from behind this tree and throw himself on top of her as she fumbles helplessly on her backside? She can't distinguish the outside noises from the ones she's kicking up around her. Scrambling urgently now. Dirt everywhere, staining the palms of her hands as she pushes herself back on to her feet. She pulls her jeans on, top-buttoning leaf corpses, trampled moss, scurrying ants, a film of dirt and the last spray of urine into her drooping knickers. The ends of her belt slap against her thigh as she runs away.

It wasn't until she at last made it back to her empty house that the real terror began to sink in. Charlotte relinquished her soiled clothes to the hamper, hid herself under the pillows, and launched into a series of return trips to the forest, exploring the dimmest corners of what could have happened.

Once she imagined herself to be her own rapist. A medium-height, thickset man wearing blue jeans, a black bomber jacket and a khaki Balaclava. Overdressed and over-cautious for the weather. He's been waiting there all night, leaning against the trunk of a pine tree, letting his eyes grow accustomed to the dark and sweating dark rings into his armpits. He hears someone racing along the path towards him, then a young woman, a girl really, appears. She brakes suddenly on the path, just a few feet away from him. Perfect. He peels off a strip of bark and waits, watching the girl as she crouches and finishes her business, then he makes his move.

On the next trip to the park, Charlotte is her foolhardy self again. She is scrambling in the dirt of the forest floor and the man is on top of her. He pins her arms down as she tries to thrash about. There are the rocks in her back, the broken branches tearing at her exposed buttocks, the soil staining darker and deeper into the pores of her hands and the knit of her clothes. There is the smell of stale beer, cough syrup, fading Drakkar Noir aftershave and second-hand smoke. And there are these two hard eyes staring out at her from the peepholes of a khaki Balaclava as a hand gropes towards her still damp vagina.

That was the way Charlotte remembered it. Or at least one of the ways. On other trips to the park, she manages to free a hand and tear the mask off. She sees the face of her rapist. Sometimes it is just a face, blank and undistinguish-able. Sometimes it is a face she knows – her ex-boyfriend Peter, or her ex-lover Garret, or Louis or Derek or one of their stupid friends from the pub. Sometimes it's Alex, laughing at her as he tweaks her nipples; sometimes the banker from the Tube who can't even stand to look her in the face. All the men who have ever betrayed or mistreated her, or just any man at all. And occasionally, on other trips, she imagines again that she is her own rapist. Pinning down a body that does not struggle so very much. Peering out through itchy peepholes at her own expression of pain.

Charlotte is having trouble breathing now. She digs herself out of the pillows to find the grey half-light a shade brighter and the sound of footsteps thundering down the stairs. Good. Liz is making Alex leave. Liz understands what Charlotte is feeling. She says she'll call and explain things to Charlotte's office on Monday. Wendy will understand too. All Charlotte need do is sit back and try to relax. The week stretches ahead of her in comfortingly long and empty hours and days. If the sun is persistent, she'll sit out in the garden – Liz will clear a path through the knee-high grass and strip the worst of the rust off the single deck-chair. Whatever the weather, Charlotte will fill her days with languor – sleeping in late, watching Richard and Judy in the morning and the Aussie soaps in the afternoon, scoffing house meals in the evening with the girls. Friends who will understand, sympathise.

Because, after all, it could have happened that way, the way that she told Liz in the small hours of the morning. Charlotte was there, alone, by herself at night, walking through the park; it was dark, she had to pee, she thought she heard a noise, a rustle. It could've happened. And no one was home when she got there, no one was around; there was no one around to say one way or the other, to know for certain whether it happened or not. So as far as she was concerned, and as far as Liz was concerned – as far as everyone would be concerned – it happened just as she said it did. Maybe some people – people like Alex, men – maybe they would say she was asking for it, that she wanted it, foolish as she was for being there at that time, alone. And maybe some people, maybe the same people would say they couldn't believe it anyway, just couldn't believe that any man would want to rape her. Unless he was blind. After all, Charlotte was no Rachel Nickell. Maybe they had a point. But what did it matter? She was raped. She was. Just like Rachel Nickell, just like down in Wimbledon, but Charlotte is lucky enough to be alive.

Charlotte hears the front door swing open and Alex's voice raised in objection. There's a silence, Liz talking too quietly for her to make out. Then the door clangs shut, firm as a vault, just a few decibels short of a slam, and Alex's determined stride on the pavement outside. Liz will be back to comfort Charlotte some more soon. She promised to return as soon as she disposed of Alex. She will bring hot cocoa with marshmallows, she'll blow on it and stir it with a tarnished teaspoon and so will Charlotte. Ordinarily, this would not be the time of year for cocoa. But this is not an ordinary time, this is a time when Charlotte needs cocoa, duvets and plenty of pillows. And friends too. Liz will call in the troops, get Joyce and Bonny over from next door, organise a girls' night in. Maybe even a whole day, a luxuriant, all-female pity-party at which she will be the guest of honour. Charlotte pulls out another pillow and fluffs it. It's a commemorative needlecraft pillow from the Royal Wedding. She was only just turned eleven when her mum gave it to her. Just a kid. She places the pillow at the summit of her pile and waits.

CHAPTER FIVE

THREE TUBS OF HÄAGEN-DAZS AND A BOTTLE OF DIET COKE

6.30 p.m.: The Coast is clear. Alex dashes home after work to swap clothes before heading out again for his five-a-side match with Edward and his workmates. No sooner has his goodbye kiss dried on your cheek than you're on the phone to Joyce and Bonny. 'The coast is clear,' you announce. After a moment of whooping, they decide they'll make a quick trip to Sainsbury's and come round about 8.00 p.m. Slip into something more comfortable – like your tattered, ten-year-old sweatpants and one of Alex's hand-me-down, worn-around-the-seams, long-sleeved jerseys. Downstairs, Emmy has cranked her stereo up to an invitingly loud level. Aretha Franklin crooks her finger, hooking you by the ear-lobe, and bounces you down the stairs on your tapping toes.

6.45 p.m.: Provisions. Quick dash to the corner shop to stock up on supplies. Emmy's silver star contribution to the evening's menu is Häagen-Dazs Strawberry, yours a delectable tub of Cookies 'n' Cream. Praline Pecan wins as the third joint choice. Once home, Emmy refires her stereo and drags both speakers out into the lounge. Aerobics was never like this. The two of you jitterbug around the coffee table, in the centre of which you've placed the tub of Strawberry. Defrosting is essential, otherwise you might break a tooth on a rock-like, real fruit chunk. Serenade one another in truly off-key fashion, point and laugh derisively when the other forgets the words. Mimic the bump-and-grind movements of an on-stage Madonna as she cums into the microphone.

With a slam of the door and an icy gust, Maxine arrives home. She storms through the hall into the lounge and shouts at you to turn down that blasted music or else. Emmy pulls a face but trots back to the controls in her room. You bring Maxine up to date on the last-minute girls' night-in agenda and invite her to join you. Shrugging her shoulders, she declares that you might in fact be lucky, she hasn't got any other plans. Yet. She stomps up to her room to slip into something more comfortable – like a fresh mask of make-up, spray-on jeans and a skin-tight, midriff T-shirt.

7.05 p.m.: Bad day. Maxine trudges through to the kitchen and returns with a bottle of red wine and one flute-shaped glass. Just in case anyone was confused as to who owned said bottle of wine, there's a name tag with inch-high letters spelling out MAXINE pasted across the decidedly unvintage label. Uncorking the bottle, she immediately pours herself a glass and takes a big slug. So much for letting it breathe. Offers to share are not forthcoming.

'Sooo, Max –,' Emmy ventures before she is interrupted.

'Max*ine*!'

'Sorry, Max*ine*. So, Max*ine*,' Emmy starts again all sugar-and-spice like, 'good day at work?'

'No shitter than usual,' she barks.

What a great start to the evening.

Aggro alert. Incoming. Phone call from Emmy's mum this time – another non-starter. Emmy's still a student. She spent her junior year here in London at LSE, but classes have finished now and she's got to go back for her final year. You can't remember the name of her university. Somewhere on the east coast of America. Virginia or West Virginia. Are they two different states? Wherever it is, Emmy doesn't want to go. Her mum, grandparents, even her aunts and uncles have been taking turns, calling transatlantically to bitch at Emmy down the telephone. They want her to come back now, get a job for the summer, something that'll look good on her CV for the milk rounds. They started pestering about midterm for her to book a flight.

'No, Mom, I'm not yelling,' Emmy yells out in the hall. 'Just a bad connection. Can't you hear that static on your end?'

7.15 p.m.: To tire of London is to tire of life – *not*. Emmy returns from battle in deflated mood. Only a flesh wound but the mood is contagious. You twist the lid off the ice-cream tub, rip back the plastic seal then hand tub and spoon to Emmy in order to initiate the ground-breaking ceremony. Since what there was of summer has shrunk back under the grey cloud from whence it came, the ice-cream is in no hurry to melt and the defrosting efforts have not been overly successful. This is more like boulder-breaking; a pneumatic drill would not go amiss. Without one, Emmy wrestles to shovel out a decent first scoop, the handle of her spoon warping backwards with the force of her effort.

You glance at your watch. 'Hey, it's kind of early for the call, isn't it? It's only midday there. Shouldn't she be at work?'

'They're redoubling their efforts. Mom's now decided to call during her lunch hour.' Passing the ice-cream back, Emmy launches into a full-blown verbal dissection of just how unhappy she is about her imminent repatriation. Not wanting to interrupt, you listen, lingering over the ice-cream, chipping away at it while she talks.

'I'm really going to miss this place,' Emmy says. 'I mean, how can I go from the most exciting city in the world back to the University of Humdrum in Bumfucksville, USA?'

Maxine snorts. 'I'd hardly call London the most exciting city in the world.'

'Well, you're wrong. Just look around you – all these people, people from everywhere, from every nationality doing all sorts of amazing things. It's like, like . . . like having your finger on the pulse of the world. And so much history. You've got Tube seats older than my college here. It's all so old and yet so modern, so hip, so very . . . very . . . well, really . . . relevant at the same time.' She lurches on, 'And God! So much culture. The clubs and the museums and the galleries and the . . . the theatres. I mean, the theatres alone are enough to make me want to renounce my US citizenship.'

Maxine has doubtless been to her share of clubs (a carnivore quickly sniffs out the meat market), but she doesn't look the type to appreciate the theatres or their red, velveteened seats and, judging by her dismissive response, Emmy's argument is holding no sway with her. Admittedly, you don't go to the theatre so very often yourself. You used to go sometimes with Charlotte. She loved a theatrical night out and was especially inclined to the big flashy, West End musicals. She would sometimes save up for months to afford the top-price tickets and a nice after-show meal. Emmy, on the other hand, likes the real dramatic plays. She digs through *Time Out* with a highlighter pen to find all those little Fringe venues tucked above pubs – iron-weighty, avant-garde fare where men kiss each other and talk like they've just back-flipped off Shakespeare's quill pen. Emmy frequents this one theatre nook in Hampstead and every time they've got a new production on, she'll show up with exact change and her student ID. She talked Alex and you into accompanying her once, but when the lead actor dropped his pants in the first act, Alex refused to stay on after the interval. That was curtains for your theatre-going days. Emmy's also pretty much given up on you for a clubbing excursion. With Alex in tow, it'll just never happen. Maybe with just the girls, someday. How Emmy has time for both hip and highbrow is a mystery to you. You don't seem to have time for either, let alone both.

7.30 p.m.: Paradise. Between lollipop licks of her Strawberry spoonful, Emmy continues to wax lyrical on how lucky you are to be British and how much she loves your little Atlantic archipelago. You are in fact grateful when Maxine interrupts to say what you've been thinking yourself all along.

'Why on earth are you so bothered about staying in this place? I'd give anything to be able to go to America, to be able to live and work there for a while,' Maxine tells her. 'Even a holiday would be good enough. I have an aunt who ran away to Florida before I was born and I've always dreamt about running after her. I don't know where she lives or what she looks like or even what she's calling herself these days. She hasn't been in touch with our family in over twenty years. But I keep imagining it would be easy enough to find her. I'll just walk down this long, sandy white stretch of beach until I bump into her lounging on a towel. Then we'll order daiquiris from one of those beachside waiters and we'll go and sip them in the shade under a clump of palm trees.'

The words describe something warm and dreamy, but they're as misleading as a Michael Fish weather forecast. There's nothing soft or far-away in Maxine's voice as she utters them. Her hands are bunched into fists and she punches at the threadbare rests of her armchair as she spits this dream out like a big gob of vengeance. Maxine is an odd girl. Not someone you or Emmy would have willingly chosen for a housemate. But the assortment of outcasts that responded to the advert placed by Landlord Lurie – or Lurid as you call him – was truly depressing. For weeks they swarmed through here, inspecting Charlotte's old room and the rest of the house and you. Many decided against the place – maybe because of the jungle garden or the threateningly low sag of the kitchen ceiling or the dribbling faucets or the clunking loo. Or maybe because of the weekly rent – multiplied by 52 and divided by 12 to equal a monthly sum much greater than one would first imagine. How does Lurid get away with it? You certainly would've opted out when you and Charlotte first viewed the place if she hadn't been so desperate to escape your West Hampstead flat with Harriet. As soon as humanly possible.

Other *Loot*-lookers were ruled out unconditionally by you or Emmy. After several weeks, Lurid threatened to charge the both of you for the empty third room if you didn't say yes to someone soon. Mister Miser! So you were forced to admit Maxine to your happy household, the best of a bad lot. She's not *so* terrible, you suppose. At least she hasn't ratted on you about Alex living here. But then, there's just cause for her to pay double-room rates too and chip in a bit more towards the water and electricity bills. She's only been here a few weeks and has already paraded no fewer than five of her male colleagues past the late-night cocoa inspection line. Each on overnight, fly-in and fuck-off visits. (Even Alex has joined the game of scoring them by servings of the powdered drink mix. 'He's a definite three heaped tablespoons – what a mug of cocoa, that is!' Emmy might say. 'Not even,' Alex would respond, 'half a teaspoon at best.') All take longer than normal showers in the morning, like they're trying to rinse away any hint of Maxine's scent before they return to the office. One of them even nicked your razor, the bastard. Last week's looked older than your father. Had a real father-like name too – Brendan or Bertram or Bernard. Something like that. You think he may have been her boss and definitely married, probably had kids tucked up in bed as he tucked into Maxine. You caught him half-dressed in the hallway, on the phone to his wife, making some pathetic excuse for his absence from the home-fire. Computer problems at the office – right, and the cheque's in the post. You hoped the old lady didn't buy it, but you're not asking any questions. What an old tart, that Maxine.

And bitter about it. Maxine is a bitter, bitter pill. Emmy can't stand her. Likes to call her Max, which Maxine can't abide, just to wind her up. Behind her back, Emmy has even more fun with it. 'I'm totally *Max*xed out,' she'll say when she's had too much of the girl, or 'I've exceeded my *Max*imum dose today.' The girls' nights are certainly different with Maxine around, sitting there all lemon-lime sour and brink-of-a-yawnish. When she deigns to join you. You wouldn't invite her at all, but sometimes it just can't be avoided. She does live here after all. At least Emmy's joviality serves as a good distraction. You could sit all night and listen to her cultural and 'philosophical' observations and tales about life in America. She's young, you know, but sweet, insightful even sometimes. And she means well. You don't know what you're going to do once she's gone. Hopefully, you won't have to take pot-*Loot* again. You're hoping Rebecca might save you.

'I don't know why the British are so fascinated by Florida,' Emmy is saying. 'Florida is nothing but a dumping ground for geriatrics, unemployed *Miami Vice* extras who don't realise the pastel-jacket eighties are over, and vacationing fags. If it were up to the rest of America, I think we'd just as soon break the tip off below Orlando. Maybe keep the Keys. Why the hell do Brits want to go there?'

'Grass is always greener,' Maxine chides.

'Paradise is nowhere,' you add because you feel you should say something too. You don't really believe it. No one pays any attention which is just as well.

7.45 p.m.: Life Philosophy I. 'Heck, it's not so bad,' Emmy semi-concludes one of her unscheduled trains of thought. 'After all, better unhappy with my life than with myself.' She eyes Maxine pointedly.

'What do you mean by that?' Maxine demands, thumbs pressing fingers palmward again.

'It's just one of my little life philosophies,' Emmy explains. 'There's a big difference between being unhappy with your life and being unhappy with yourself. In my opinion, the former is much more constructive. You can work towards changing various aspects of your life, but it's much more difficult to change who you are.'

'Little life, little philosophy or both?' Maxine scoffs but nevertheless prompts Emmy to elucidate further. The sides of the Häagen-Dazs tub are now slippery and sweaty in Emmy's hands. The frost on the outside has all melted and you can see that inside, the strawberry ice-cream is getting mushy around the edges. Emmy puts the carton on the floor, lays her spoon face down in the lid and wipes her hands on the lap of her jeans. You tear a cottage-print kitchen towel off the roll in the middle of the coffee table and, using it as a mitt, grab the tub before Emmy has a chance to knock it over. You turn your attention to skimming away the thawing edges. Maxine pours herself a third glass of wine.

'I've always thought of it as having a relationship with my life. We are a couple, like you and Alex, Liz,' she nods towards you, 'except we're never apart. We're always with one another, everywhere, through everything, no matter what.' Emmy adopts a sing-song tone; she's launching into the longer version of a speech you've heard many times before. It's a good philosophy, you think, it makes sense, so you don't fault her for repeating it. You do, however, marvel at how she knows it by heart, never a word out of place, without notes or anything. She must have written it down somewhere, rereading it often, even rehearsing the various hand movements. You wonder if the words are all her own or if she's borrowed from one of those American self-help guides for the terminally normal. You prefer to think that they are original, if oft-repeated, notions.

'We're inseparable, my life and I. Together. Sometimes we're happy, sometimes we're sad,' index finger traces a smiley face in the air then turns it upside down. 'And sometimes we're very happy and sometimes we're very sad. Up and down like a roller coaster, the Sooper Dooper Looper,' her hand spins wheelies in the air, 'three monster 360s and what a drop,' the hand plummets floorward – good thing you moved the ice-cream – then shoots back up. 'Up and down like an elevator, a steel capsule hurtling to the 100th floor and back to the lobby, stopping on the 29th, 57th and 62nd,' fingers flash rapidly, not quite corresponding to the numbers cited.

'Tip to the little Asian operator in the monkey suit, thanks very much; up and down like a flag on a flagpole, good ole Stars 'n' Stripes,' hand clutches chest, 'what emotion, watch out here comes Taps now, the bugle is sounding,' half-opened fist touches lips, 'hand over your heart, take off that hat,' back to chest, flip at the forehead, then general flapping about. 'Up and down, up and down, up and down like any self-respecting, fucked-up relationship worth its weight in tears,' index fingers pull courses down from the corners of her eyes, 'and laughter. Up and down. My life is no easy partner, not so easy to get along with, to put up with day-in day-out, night-in night-out, around the clock,' shows you her palm, then the back of her hand, then skims round a circular clockface in the air.

'Sometimes my life bores me and sometimes it makes me so mad I want to scream and sob, I do scream and sob. But this is it with us. Sometimes it's good and sometimes it's bad,' flip-flopping gesture again, 'but we keep trying, we have to, because breaking up is not a possibility, an end to this relationship, an end is not an option,' her head wags furiously in one direction as her hand counters like a dysfunctional metronome. 'Checking out, giving up, just won't work. Not for me. Not for my life. We are together for ever,' hands now gripped together in front of her, fingers laced. 'For better, for worse, for always. My life and I.' She pounds the coffee table with her doubled fist for final emphasis.

Wow. Should you applaud? Or hold up a score card? (Much better than the last performance of that piece, if anyone cares to know your opinion.) Maxine doesn't think so – she stares at Emmy, mouth agape. 'I'm exhausted just watching that. That Zen crap's enough to make me want to vomit,' she says as she uncrosses and recrosses her legs, karate-kicking her feet up so high you're afraid somebody will end up with a bloodied nose.

'Well, you asked,' Emmy huffs.

Stay out of this, your instincts holler. Good advice. You look down at the emptying ice-cream tub and work at the excavation of one of the last diamond-sized strawberry chunks.

8.05 p.m.: Back-up arrives. Saved by the bell. Jump up to answer the door. It's Joyce and Bonny from next door and

none too soon. They arrive laden with Hobnobs, two volu-
minous bags of crisps – air-packed means they pack in more
air, not more crisps – and two bottles of Diet Coke. Excellent.

Joyce and Bonny are the only other twenty-something
tenants on the whole street, also captive to Slumlord Lurid.
You've known Joyce for ever, since before even you and
Charlotte and she were all in school uniforms together. She's
been living in this street for a couple of years and was the
one who first tipped you off on the availability of your current abode – but you try not to hold it against her. Joyce's
flatmate Bonny is a little dippy. Or not your average
Einstein, as Emmy might say. But she's good entertainment
value. You've all bonded while banding together against the
neighbourhood association about the state of your gardens.
The middle-aged, Mondeo-driving, bring-Margaret-
Thatcher-back homeowners are always complaining,
insisting that you trim the bushes and mow the lawns, but
you tell them to speak to your landlord. The damn lawns
were overgrown long before you moved in and now they're
too out of control to tame. One weekend in the spring,
Charlotte took a rake and shears to your front garden but,
even after two full days of work, she didn't achieve a noticeable difference. All she got for her trouble was a collection
of thorn scratches and weed rashes – not a word of thanks
from Lurid. As if.

Their kindness to Charlotte during the rape incident also
helped to further endear Joyce and Bonny to you. That was
when this whole girls' night-in habit really took off. You
manufactured it for Charlotte's sake but then discovered you
all really enjoyed it. So you've kept it up now, even though
Charlotte's gone. You keep planning a raucous, get-those-
beers-down, grab-unidentified-men's-bums, girls' night-out
as well. Emmy says she knows just the club for it. But it hasn't
come off yet. It's hard enough to find time for the slob-out,

gorge-yourselves-silly, girls' night-in gabfest, particularly since Alex moved in.

You escort Joyce and Bonny to the lounge where they flop down on the sofa next to Emmy. Clear away the depleted Strawberry carton, pay a reconnaissance trip to the kitchen and return with more supplies. A tray loaded down with mismatched glasses, chipped bowls, an ice bucket, the second tub of Häagen-Dazs – oh yes, oh yes, at last, the Cookies 'n' Cream – and extra spoons. Now that the relief forces have landed, the serious eating can begin.

As you pour out glasses of Diet Coke, careful not to let the foam overflow the rim, Joyce cracks open the Hobnobs and offers you one from the top of the pack. Slide it off between pours and pop it into your mouth.

'How's Nick?' you ask her. It's the courteous thing to do. Nick is Joyce's boyfriend but he's a real Prick with a capital P, ending in -rick. Nick the Prick, that's what you all call him now behind his back, and hers of course. Joyce never says a word against him when she comes round, but by the way she talks, it's evident. Especially when she says things like the thing that she says next.

'Okay.' She frowns, her forehead rippling up into little bands of embarrassment. 'I haven't seen him so much this week. He's been a little under the weather and doesn't want me to catch it.'

Yeah, right, you think. Prick. You don't know why she puts up with that guy.

'Oh, yeah, right,' hurrumphs Maxine. 'I don't know why you put up with that guy.' Maxine always says – and does – the things you wouldn't dare even though you might like to (though you don't like to admit it, even to yourself). But you're both right in this instance. You all know it, even if you don't vocalise it. Why is Joyce with such a tosser? Maybe because he's the first and only boyfriend she's ever had. And maybe, probably, she believes he's the best she'll ever get given her, well, um . . . handicap. Morse code. Bracket, unbracket. *Joyce is going bald.*

That's a taboo subject, though, and no one ever puts it that bluntly even when Joyce isn't here. Still, despite Joyce's sparseness of hair, she is a good friend, an honest-to-goodness, girl-next-door type (who also happens to actually live next door now) and, you all think, she deserves a lot better treatment than she gets from Nick the Prick. You wish Charlotte could have stuck around just a little bit longer so she could have seen how unhappy Nick was making Joyce these days. She took it pretty bad when the two first started going out. 'Now *everyone's* got a boyfriend,' Charlotte had wailed. 'Even Joyce!' But if Charlotte could see Joyce now, maybe she wouldn't have been so desperate for a boyfriend herself. She'd probably swear off men for good. For real this time. (Joyce probably should, heaven knows.) You tried to tell Charlotte, Emmy told her (not that Charlotte ever liked listening to her), even Harriet told her for God's sake, that a man was not the answer to all her prayers. But she wouldn't listen. And you should know, after all. Even at the best of times, Alex is no prince – not even with a lower case p, ending in -rince.

'Yeah, Nick's a bastard,' says Bonny, not thinking as usual until she clocks Joyce's miserable expression. 'Oh, but he's really cute, Joyce. Dreamy. He actually reminds me a little bit of Mel Gibson. Don't you think?'

8.10 p.m.: The Arts. Proceed to rate and pant over Hollywood's dishiest dishes. Johnny Depp. Keanu Reeves. 'Phwoar!' roars Bonny. Patrick Swayze. Woody Harrelson. Brad Pitt. 'The whole fucking tin of cocoa,' cries Emmy.

'What does that mean?' asks Maxine.

'Oh, nothing. Just yummy.'

Michael J. Fox. Christian Slater. 'Wey-hey!' you hoot. Harrison Ford. Denzel Washington. Charlie Sheen. 'Totally drool-worthy!' screeches Bonny. Sean Penn. Sylvester Stallone. Paul Newman. Robert Redford.

'Eeek!' squeals Bonny like she's swallowed a prawn pierced with a rusty nail. 'Paul and Rob are, like, grandfather material.'

'So what?' challenges Maxine. 'They're still sexy. I sure wouldn't kick them out of my bed.' But then who would she?

'What about you, Joyce? What do you think?' you ask.

'I don't know.'

'Oh come on, Joyce,' prods Emmy.

Joyce shrugs. 'You've said just about everybody.'

'Give us a name, just one name.'

Joyce hesitates and casts her eyes about the floor as if the bloke was going to pop out from under the sofa. 'Woody Allen?' she suggests.

Puh-leeze. Couldn't she try harder than that? 'Are you serious?' gawps Maxine. 'You can't really be serious.'

'I couldn't think of anyone else,' cries Joyce. 'You guys already said everybody there is.'

Oh really. How about River Phoenix, Emilio Estevez, Nicholas Cage? 'I think I'll faint!' swoons Bonny.

'You see, Emmy,' you say, 'you've got a lot going for your country.'

'Oh, sure,' she replies, 'but you guys have got loads of hot English movie stars, too.' English? Movie stars? She starts to read off the enormous roll-call. Hugh Grant, Alan Rickman, and, wait for it, wait for it – Kenneth Branagh. Oh, God. You wonder why Emmy and Charlotte never got on. They have so much in common. A fondness for philosophy, a theatrical streak, a soft spot for Ken and Em.

Emmy moves deep into theatre lovey territory – 'talk about hunks,' she says – but is mercilessly shouted down.

Maxine pulls another bottle of wine from out of some cupboard. Where has she been hiding this inflatable wine cellar and when does she find the time to scribble all those labels? The rest of you raise your glasses of Diet Coke and toast to Californian vintage hardbodies.

8.25 p.m.: Gotta hate her. Speaking of hardbodies. The conversation is interrupted by the doorbell again. You know who it'll be and let Emmy get it this time. A second later, in breezes Rebecca. For a beat or two, the whole dynamic of the room changes. Rebecca's staggering beauty cannot be ignored. It's something you've got to make room for, something so big and in your face. Subconsciously, you all suck in your breath at the sight of her, clear some space for it. Even if you see her every day, a beauty like that will always make you suck in your breath. It's shocking. There are other reactions too. Bonny drops a handful of Hobnobs, looking guilty; Maxine glowers with a bit more purpose and readjusts the seam of her crotch; Joyce brightens and pats the sofa cushion next to her invitingly.

And you? You just sigh, inward-like, not so anyone would notice. If Charlotte could see you now, she'd feel betrayed. That you could be here gorging yourself with someone who had betrayed her so terribly. But Charlotte isn't here any more and she can't see you. When she was, when she could, you hadn't dared associate with Rebecca or speak of her, even though you'd grown up with her. You took Charlotte's side in the whole matter of that man, Peter, the mythical devil whom none of the rest of you had ever met. You took Charlotte's side and that meant acting as if Rebecca no longer existed.

Joyce, on the other hand, had stayed in touch with Rebecca, though she never mentioned it to Charlotte. Joyce idolised Rebecca, no matter what Charlotte said she did.

Once Charlotte left, Joyce started pestering you about re-admitting Rebecca to your circle. Charlotte-less, your defences weakened and now here you all are. And, aside from the momentary pangs of guilt, you don't really mind. Rebecca has never done anything to you and she isn't so bad really. Even if she is too beautiful for her own good, for anyone's good. You reach for another Hobnob.

8.30 p.m.: Health, hair and diets. Other miscellaneous but essential chit-chat is raked over for the benefit of the recently expanded audience. Who saw who where, with who, doing what. Office flirtations, workloads, new hair-styles, the cost of highlights, crash diets, latest supermodels. And, of course, the shitty weather. Sufficient defrost time having elapsed, Emmy arranges the bowls on the table, scoops them full of Cookies 'n' Cream and distributes them around the group, except for Maxine who has declared once again her abstention.

'Oh, I really shouldn't either,' says Bonny. 'It'll absolutely ruin this week's diet. But I do love this Cookies 'n' Cream. It's my favourite flavour. I suppose we can't let it go to waste. Waste not, want not and all that.' She seizes her bowl and raises a mountainous spoonful to her lips. 'Here's to paying for it tomorrow.'

'Or puking it up tonight,' Maxine mutters and then goes into a spasm of fake coughing. You're beginning to wonder if Maxine has some sort of vomit fixation. She's Kate Moss thin. Maybe she's an anorexic who yearns to be bulimic but is too vomit-phobic.

Emmy leans over and claps Maxine hard on the back. 'Careful, don't choke on it, Max.'

'Max*ine*!' she splutters. Her residual coughing is soon sti-fled, washed down by a gulp of wine.

'Don't worry about it. It's a proven fact,' Rebecca informs

Bonny, in a hearty attempt to be 'one of the girls' with normal girl problems, 'that Diet Coke counteracts ice-cream calories.'

'Really?' she beams.

'Ummmm . . .'

'Yeah, really,' interjects Maxine. 'And the earth is really flat as a saucer. And the sun never sets on the British Empire. And Hitler didn't really gas all his Jewish mates. And . . .'

'Oh, you're kidding,' wheezes Bonny. 'Gosh, zero calories, I wish!'

Rebecca offers a Hobnob to Emmy but she declines. 'It's too bad we don't have a pack of real Oreos,' Emmy says. 'That's one thing I miss for sure. I do love Oreos.' She lowers her spoon. 'But then, it won't be long before I can have all the truckloads of Oreos I want. At which point, I'm sure I'll be missing Hobnobs like crazy.' She forsakes her bowl of ice-cream and swipes three biscuits out of the open pack.

'What're Oreos?' Bonny asks.

'That's the cookie in the Cookies 'n' Cream,' Emmy tells her.

'I always thought it was just dough.'

'No way. It's a chocolate sandwich cookie with white cream in the middle. The trick is you've got to twist it apart without breaking either half, lick all the cream out of the middle and then eat the chocolate bits. It's very messy and sticky and you usually have blackened fingers and blackened tongues and lips by the end of it.' Emmy closes her eyes and licks her fingers to demonstrate the point. 'But it's delicious.' Sigh.

'Many monks will die,' you mimic in your best Sean Connery voice.

'Huh? What monks?' Joyce asks.

'Come on, you know. Sean Connery and Christian Slater. *The Name of the Rose*.' Joyce and Rebecca stare at you blankly. You've obviously been through Alex's video collection once too often.

'Oh, so it's just another biscuit,' Bonny realises.

'No!' exclaims Emmy. 'It's not just another biscuit. It's America's favourite *cookie*.'

'Oh, yeah right, cookie. Anyway, it's great in ice-cream.'

You have to agree with that. Unlike Bonny, you're familiar with the famous Oreos and Emmy has described the ritual of eating them to you before. She promises to send you a pack once she's back in the States. In the meantime, you content yourself with the Häagen-Dazs. You stir the ice-cream in your bowl, whisking it into a Mr Whippy consistency. The Strawberry residue gives the resultant gloop just the slightest tinge of pink.

8.45 p.m.: Media bullshit. Analyse the Häagen-Dazs cinema advert. Half-dressed couple on a table, eating each other alive, have a brainwave that a tub of sinfully delicious Häagen-Dazs would be a better antidote for their hunger.

'I mean, I love Häagen-Dazs as much as the next girl. But what kind of sensory overload is that?' Bonny queries. 'Me, I'd rather just make do with the man on the table, ice-cream or no ice-cream.'

'Like you'd ever have a choice,' zings Maxine, sending Bonny into a slump. You don't dare voice your preference for the Cookies 'n' Cream and delicious spoonfuls of semen-free calories.

Emmy probes into the open fridge scene from *Nine and a Half Weeks*, and describes a personal attempt to recreate the steamy, roll-in-foodstuffs foreplay. 'Okay, Kim Basinger I am not,' she admits, 'but what a disaster. Have you seen the kind of crap guys our age have in their frigidaires these

130

days? How can you get your rocks off dribbling browning guacamole, half-eaten kebabs, frozen chips, rancid yoghurt and beer over naked bodies? Talk about sticky. Not to mention the goosebumps you get from those cold metal shelves welding into your exposed skin.'

You have visions of Alex and you in bed with fruit salad detritus scattered on the sheets. So true, sticky is an understatement. Usually, Alex and you just squabbled over who would be nudged into the wet spot after sex, but on that occasion, there wasn't a dry, non-Velcro-ised patch big enough to rest an elbow on. In the end, you had to strip the bed and duvet. Just another scene from your ongoing charade of trying to spice up your sex life.

Joyce says, 'I wonder if movie stars actually have better sex in real life as well as on the screen. I mean, they've got better bodies, more money, better-looking lovers.'

More hair, you think sinfully.

'They do have all the advantages,' agrees Rebecca, pretending as if she didn't. Which as you and Joyce know, she doesn't really, underneath it all.

Emmy shakes her head. 'Nah, it's not for real on the screen. Those steamy scenes are thanks to the directors and cameramen and lighting folk and a hundred hours in the cutting room. The actors don't do anything. They've even got doubles to sweat for them. Media bullshit. In real life, those guys have no advantages; they're no different from the rest of us.'

Bonny narrows her eyes, maybe envisaging Keanu Reeves having trouble trying to get it up. A little Hollywood smog of disappointment settles across her face.

'Even for movie stars, sex is never like in the movies,' you say.

'Or even in the adverts,' sniffs Bonny.

Maxine refills her glass. 'Speak for yourself.'

9.00 p.m.: Sex, sex, sex. As expected, the conversation degenerates into a no-holds-barred, detail-by-delicious-detail sex gabfest. Sex lives of the rich and famous. Sex lives of the not-so rich and not-so famous. Confession sessions on each and every one of your personal sex lives. 'Non-existent!' wails Bonny. Even cranky Maxine contributes a few salacious titbits – the wine must have loosened her lips. You are less than truthful when it comes your turn. Why bore them with the predictability of so-called sex on tap? Why spoil the myth? Latest pill scares, different brands and their side-effects. Novelty condoms. Vibrators and other toys. Favourite positions, favourite places, most intense orgasm experiences. 'Non-existent!' Bonny cries again. Sex, sex, sex. On the bed, on the sofa, on the kitchen floor, on the boardroom table, on the television, on the beach. Sex. On the brain.

The third pack of Hobnobs is unsealed; Rebecca inaugurates the crisps. Sweet and salty taste sensations are circulated in opposite directions around the group, bypassing Maxine with each orbit. Emmy sprints to the freezer for the Praline Pecan. 'These tubs are simply not big enough,' moans Joyce. Gorgefest Round Two.

9.30 p.m.: More sex. *More!*'s position of the fortnight. 'Difficulty rating five!' Bonny shrieks. 'Not even Mary Lou Retton could manage.'

Every episode of Margi Clarke's *Good Sex Guide*. 'Did you see the one where all the blokes played pin the clitoris on the donkey?' says Emmy. 'Talk about male incompetence. No wonder orgasms are so hard to come by.'

10.00 p.m.: Relationships. The girls vote to advance into relationship analysis gear. All eyes descend on you. Consensus rules that you are the house expert as the only one present involved in what could be deemed a serious relationship. Occasionally, they turn to Joyce to open the bidding. But that's really just a courtesy and it's too late for that tonight – too many calories under the bridge. Besides, you all know her relationship with Nick is an Ulster bomb waiting to detonate. Alex and you, on the other hand, are the real thing. Or so everybody seems to think.

You don't know what to think any more. You stare out of the window, amazed as you are every summer that it can stay so light, so late. Perhaps your fierce concentration will distract the others? It doesn't. Rebecca, Emmy, Bonny, Maxine, even Joyce. They're all looking to you to say something and suddenly the subject you'd been waiting to discuss seems like another awful, unbroachable taboo. You drain the last dribble of ice-cream milk from your bowl, lizard-lick a pecan flake from the hump of your spoon, take a deep breath and blurt it out.

'Alex is talking about living together.'

'But you already live together,' Maxine says, too acidly for your liking. Alex has rather a lot of stuff, you realise that, and it's impossible not to notice that it and Alex have been all over this tiny house since he and his mates got kicked out of their flat a month ago.

'He says it's not the same. He wants us to get our own place. He's even talking about getting a mortgage and buying, going the full monty.' You shudder to think what kind of 'our own place' you two could afford. A bed-sit or a grubby little studio if you're lucky. Your eyes wander around the lounge – the grimy blank, hospital-white walls; the tattered armchairs; the gnawed, mould-green sofa with the orange afghan carelessly tossed over its seat to hide the holes; the rental TV with the broken remote; the unidentifiable brown hue of the trampled, 70s flashback, shag carpet. The lived-in look of a room people didn't want to live in. A house no one willingly called a home. 'Our own place' could even be, God forbid, worse than this. At least here, there were other rooms to escape to, other people to talk to. Visions of 'our own place' flash up before your eyes. One cramped room for the two of you and all your junk where the only place to go to get away is the loo. Alex doesn't seem to understand that a couple needs privacy, not just from the rest of the world but also from each other. At least sometimes.

'That's too bad,' says Emmy. 'I was looking forward to living together when I come back.' The pregnant pause gives birth. 'If I come back.'

'Hey, hold your horses, it's not like I've said yes yet.'

10.15 p.m.: Devil's advocates. 'What a relief!' exclaims Emmy with what you think is just a tad too much enthusiasm. But her mood seems to match that of the other girls who join her in bombarding you with doomsday warnings about permanent cohabitation, as if they knew anything about it first-hand. You feel yourself turning swings and roundabouts in Alex's defence. What's so bad about your boyfriend anyway?

Apparently, plenty once you sign your name next to his on a lease. The arguments that will follow, according to the collective female wisdom, will involve everything from money to groceries, household chores, clogged drains, shower times, toilet seats and, oh yes, more money. Surely, it must be *your* turn to pay the gas/electricity/phone bill/rent!

'And the sex, of course. That's dead, you just lose that for good,' Maxine pipes in.

Goodness, you didn't know there was much else to lose in that department. You wish you could change the subject, you wish you had never brought it up.

Bonny removes the spoon from the tip of her nose where

she's been attempting to hang it. 'But don't pay us any mind, Liz.' She leans across to touch your arm. 'You're the one with the dreamy boyfriend. And really, Alex is a catch, so cute. He looks a little like Jason Donovan, don't you think?'

'Ugh!' Maxine burps.

'Anyway,' persists Bonny, 'you'd save a lot of money, I bet, in the long run. My mum says you pay tons less per month with a mortgage than if you're renting. Especially if it's a joint mortgage. And with a mortgage you're working towards something. Rent is just vaporised money. Why not go to Nationwide – check it out?' She buffs and blows on the spoon, then wriggles her nose.

You wonder if Bonny's mum has been counselling Alex. That's the argument he keeps using. Screws are tightening. Maybe you could escape with Maxine to find her aunt on a Florida beach. Of course, you'd have to drown her in the homosexually studded surf. Maxine that is, not the American auntie. Although maybe her too, depending on how Max-like or geriatric she was.

10.30 p.m.: Life Philosophy II. Joyce, no doubt trying to be helpful, gears into change-of-topic mode. 'Hey, talk about your blasts from the past. Did you read about Harriet in the newspaper?'

'No,' you reply, 'what about her?'

'God, I should have kept the clipping. It was very weird though. You know, you open the news section and you don't expect the face of someone who you know to actually be staring back at you. Anyway, there she was, our Harriet. She's just landed some huge book deal, got a big advance – I think it breaks some record for advances for first novels. She must be rolling in it now.'

'She always did want to be a writer, didn't she?' says Rebecca.

'Yeah, she did,' you reply. 'Joyce, when's the book coming out?'

'I don't know. Sometime before the end of the year. Get it out for the Christmas rush, I guess.'

'Did the article say what it was about?'

'No, not really. Just that it was kind of a chick book. Actually, no, they said it was a *new* kind of chick book. Love, romance, rejection and stuff – I don't know what's so new about that. I guess we'll have to buy it and see.'

'Yeah, guess so.'

You pause long enough for Joyce to take the conversation on an inevitable tangent – though you'd rather not go there. 'Speaking of all that, Liz,' she says, 'have you heard from Charlotte lately?'

Rebecca fidgets uncomfortably at the question, as do you.

'No, not in over two months.' Charlotte fled right after Alex confronted her and you haven't spoken to her since. Your emotions are still in a tailspin – over both the revelation and her sudden departure. You feel duped by both events.

'Gosh, that's too bad. She was your best friend, wasn't she?' commiserates Bonny. 'Still, I don't understand why she did it. Who makes up something like being raped?'

Emmy springs to your rescue. 'She was lonely, that's all. She'd reached the end of her leather reins in this old relationship rodeo. I can relate to that, can't everyone?' There are a few nods around the room; Bonny's spoon loosens from her pointy nose and drops into her lap. Thoughtful stares into empty bowls.

'Yeah,' slurs Maxine as she unravels the armchair and eyes Rebecca. 'I hear that girl had been through a lot.'

'It's so ridiculous, people and relationships,' Emmy continues. She's on a roll again; her hands wind up into action. 'Relationships are like car-pools. Like when I was younger and my parents were supposed to pick me up from some place. I'd call them well in advance and tell them exactly when to be there, but I'd still wind up waiting for ever – the last kid left. And I noticed while I waited that that was always the case. There were always lots of kids waiting around for parents who were late. And there were always lots of impatient parents sitting in cars, waiting for their kids who didn't show up on time. It seemed like such a waste to have all those people sitting around waiting. I thought it'd make so much more sense to pair up the punctual kids with the punctual parents and then the late-comers could get together. Then everybody would be clam-happy.

'But that wasn't possible. So I'd sit there every time getting angrier at my dad and getting more embarrassed the longer I sat there looking stupid, rejected, uncared for. I envied the kids whose parents would drive up just as they were walking out of the building. I thought these families must share some wonderful secret about timing. But there weren't too many of those types. Someone was always waiting for somebody else, at least for a little while. Like with relationships. People never seem able to get co-ordinated and fancy or love each other at the same time to the same degree. It's just this big game of waiting and hoping the right person will show up and eventually come around to your way of thinking. And feeling. It's so chancey and hopeless sometimes that it amazes me when it ever works out at all. I mean really, Liz,' she says pointing towards you, 'I'm convinced that you and Alex are the statistically happy exception.' You raise your eyebrows. 'In most cases, at least in my own sad experience, it's much more complicated. This boy likes this girl, but this girl likes this other boy, this other boy likes another girl and the other girl has got so many boys she doesn't know who she likes.' Everyone subconsciously eyes Rebecca as Emmy says this. Rebecca, feeling the accusatory glances hot on her skin, inspects her lap. 'It doesn't seem fair,' says Emmy, which is just what everyone else is thinking. 'But that's car-pools for you.'

Joyce, Bonny and you chortle. Maxine says, 'Right. So if life is a relationship, and a relationship is a car-pool, what exactly is a car-pool in your philosophical meltdown?'

'Well, you know, it's just a car-pool,' she shrugs, tipping the salt-doused, crisp dregs into her open mouth. 'Don't be so pedantic.'

'So why are you so traumatised by this car-pool experience,' Maxine presses. 'What, did your daddy leave you sitting out in the cold once too often?'

Everyone tenses – you can actually feel your pancreas, wherever that was, petrify along with the rest of your internal organs – except for Maxine who is oblivious. You know what's coming, you've warned the others. 'Yeah, he left me sitting out there all night once. The night when he was on his way to pick me and some other kids up from the pool and some shit-faced trucker blindsided him and left him for dead.' Emmy emits a humourless laugh, her hands rest motionless and junk-foodless on her thighs. 'Might have been funny too what with all the kids picking on me and complaining like they always did when it was my parents' turn for the car-pool. Might have been funny. Only he *was* dead. My dad was dead.'

The room is silent, silent like only a very awkward situation can be. Even Maxine is stunned. For all her talking, Emmy rarely talks about herself. Not when she's sober and not in real terms anyway, only in fuzzy, philosophical ones. This is as real as it gets. Your eyes are drawn again in embarrassment to the window where the light has finally died. Moths and midges and flies have flown in through the open window to zigzag drunkenly around the tasselled hanging lamp. In the deepest lull of the conversation, the buzz from the insects sounds deafening. You leap up to shoo them out and draw the curtains. The spell is broken.

Maxine clears her throat and rallies to true form. 'Look, here's a real-life philosophy for you. Life is nothing but endless, unadulterated shite. That's it.' All the charm and tact of an alarm clock, that one.

10.40 p.m.: Pizza. The measured group response to this rigorous philosophical debate is simple. More food! Pizza delivery wins the vote; the suggestion makes Emmy brighten.

'Domino's?' Bonny proposes.

Emmy balks. 'No way! Did you know the guy that owns that is a raving anti-abortionist?'

You recommend Pizza Hut Delivery because of their special three-course menus. Round of yeah-yeah-yeahs from the girls.

'Extra large Supreme Pan Special,' chimes Rebecca.

'With a litre of Diet Coke,' says Emmy. 'No, better make that two litres.'

'And the cheesy garlic bread starter,' adds Joyce.

And to finish? 'Another tub of Häagen-Dazs!' you all chorus.

'Shit, live dangerously,' Maxine comments. 'Why don't you tell the delivery kid to stop at the offie on the way? Pick up a few bottles of vino.'

Bonny tssks, 'God, no. Have you any idea how many calories there are in alcohol?'

'Besides,' says Emmy, her eyes sliding contemptuously over the droopy-lidded Maxine, 'we don't want any. Good, old-fashioned, junk food is our fuel.'

Pound coins and other loose change rain down on to the coffee table, from all corners – bar Maxine's of course. You collect and count the kitty, add a fiver to make up the difference and wheelbarrow yourself to the phone to place the order.

11.30 p.m.: **No discussion**. Breather. You, Emmy, Rebecca, Bonny and Joyce are slumped back in your seats, holding your ballooning bellies. Bonny has unbuttoned her jeans as far as they'll go and is showcasing her striped cotton knickers. Strewn across the table is the mounting evidence of your gluttony. Everything is empty – greasy, open pizza box, three cartons of Häagen-Dazs, four jumbo bags of crisps, scrunched Hobnob wrappers, sticky bowls, drained bottles of Diet Coke – save for your full-to-bursting bodies. You listen to the sounds of your bones getting fatter. The deafening rubber-band ping of your gut straining against your elasticised waistband drowns out the tinkle of Maxine's Claddagh ring against her nearly empty-for-good wine glass. Your mind reels drunkenly from overeating – as opposed to Maxine who is just, well, reeling drunkenly.

Louder than an unexpected earthquake, the phone rumbles and suddenly noise and motion re-enter your little, bubble-packed lounge-world. Vaulting herself over the arm of her chair, Maxine lands with a thud as her legs buckle beneath her. She grunts, crawls a few knee-steps then yanks herself up by the doorknob and catapults out into the hall.

Emmy, rousing, shouts after her, 'Hey, if it's my mom, tell her I'm not here. I'm camped out at British Airways at this very moment.'

'It won't be your mom. It won't be for you!' Maxine shouts back just before you hear her pick up the phone and answer breathlessly in a slurred, two-octaves-lower voice.

Collectively, the girls giggle. 'Well, it could have been for me,' says Emmy, 'even if it wasn't my mom.'

'Oh yeah?' you prompt. Emmy has been hinting about a man in her life. Surely, it can't be the velveteened theatre seats alone that are tying her so obstinately to London. You know, in fact, that she's been seeing someone for quite some time now. Real on again, off again. Don't know if that's her doing or his. And you still haven't met him yet. You asked her once why she didn't bring him around; she said she didn't want to.

'Don't you trust us?' you'd teased, not blaming her with the likes of Maxine in the house.

'No,' she'd said. 'I don't trust him.'

Bonny half-moans, half-mews. 'Ooohh, do tell. What's his name?'

'Pete.'

Rebecca sits up, looking startled. 'Peter?' she asks. 'I once dated a guy named Peter.'

'No,' says Emmy. 'Just Pete, I call him Pete.' She clasps her hands, signalling that the short-lived conversation is closed. Rebecca seems relieved to let it drop and the others are too dozey to care.

You brush back your sleeve to glance at your watch. There's not much time before Alex will come straggling home. You can feel the air thinning as he approaches. Hoist yourself up, scrabble for a new topic. Your half-hearted plea of 'Hey, Emmy, tell us again about these sororities you Yanks have' solicits a cacophony of moans. Covering her mouth with the back of her hand, Joyce burps sonorously, blushes and flops back against Rebecca. Bonny struggles to rebutton her jeans, mumbling about 48 hours' worth of aerobics that she'll have to endure tomorrow. Emmy cracks her knuckles and flexes her wrist muscles. This she will talk about. Happily.

CHAPTER SIX

CUE FOR THE LOO

Beds are a wonderful invention, I think as I shiver on the cold, cracked bathroom tiles in the early morning chill. I pluck my beach towel from the small pile of my discarded clothes – night-shirt and knickers – and cover, as much as possible, myself and the dozing body in front of me. I still can't sleep. Instead, I finger his nipples as he earlier fingered mine.

'Does that tickle, Liz?' he had asked.

'Mmmhmmm.'

'It's supposed to tickle.'

I smile at the memory of that sensation and the many others that my body served up under the pressure of his touch. How reckless we'd been. Anyone could have walked in, still could, especially with the bathroom door broken as it is. I listen now to the sounds of the sleeping house. Wary as neither of us was earlier. The electric burn of the unshaded light bulb dangling above us, the sagging decline of the floor and ceiling beneath us, the ceaseless respiration of the other occupants, the rustle of arms reaching out to cold, dented pillows in half-empty beds. Any sounds that might signal an end to this time and this body that I'm now clinging to. The session with the girls seems like an eternity away. Even my distended stomach has been whittled back down from the rigour of our antics. I am hungry again and am wondering how I got here.

There was a queue for the bathroom and I waited my turn at the end of it. Already, Emmy had trooped up from downstairs and both Maxine and her last-minute man for the night had stumbled in and out. I heard Alex bumping around in there. I should have waited for him to come out since I wanted to dodge as long as possible the moment when we'd have to start this conversation, but I was getting impatient, I wanted to go to bed. So I barged in and there he was, sitting on the loo, tapping his feet and poring over *Cosmopolitan*. The toilet, as usual, rattled ominously beneath him.

I waved one hand in front of my face and plugged my nose with the other. 'Geez, Alex, smells like a rat crawled up your arse and died!'

It's a large, if oddly arranged, rectangular bathroom with the crotchety old tank-on-the-wall-above-you loo situated right in front of the door, at the bottom of the two short steps you need to walk down into the room. Alex parted his legs to either side to let me pass.

'It wasn't me!' he exclaimed. 'It must have been Maxine or that fella of hers.'

But I knew Alex's telltale pong anywhere. 'Yeah, right.' I marched on to the sink at the other end of the rectangle and grabbed my toothbrush, still pinching my nose between two fingers.

He put the magazine down. 'So, how was your girls' night?'

'Gluttonously gorgetastic.' I turned sideways to model my expanded paunch for him. 'How was your match?'

'A draw, 1–1. But I made an excellent goal to equalise.' Alex fancies himself the next Teddy Sheringham.

'Great.' Squeezing a worm of toothpaste on to my brush, I started to clean my teeth with quick, short, up and down strokes. 'So drinks were on you then?'

He grinned apologetically. 'Umm, yeah. The first round.' He didn't need to add the parenthetical 'of many'. 'You gotta have a few beers with the lads. Just to be polite, you know.'

Alex hesitated for a minute then asked, 'Soooo. What did you gals gab about?'

'This and that.'

'Yeah, yeah, what this and what that?'

Spitting, I told him, 'You know, just the usual – diets, hair, men, sex, diets.'

'Uh-huhh. And?'

'And they asked about Charlotte.'

'Oh.' Long pause this time. 'Right, yes, but what did they say about the other?'

I reloaded my toothbrush. 'About what other?'

Shifting position precariously, he unwound a huge mop of loo roll and reached down to wipe; I kept my eyes glued to my own reflection in the mirror. 'You know. What did the girls say about our plans to get a place together?'

'Oh, that,' I accelerated my brushing.

'Yeah, of course that. What else?'

I spat out another gob of Colgate froth, took a sip of water, gargled and spat again. 'They thought it was a very serious step.'

'Well, of course, we both already knew that. But did they think it was a good idea?'

I located the Neutrogena in the cabinet, squirted some in my hand and lathered up, requiring me, unfortunately, to at last uncork my nose. Yikes. 'There were mixed reactions, I think. Bonny thinks like you – it's cheaper than renting, a good investment, all that –'

'I always liked that girl.' It wasn't worth the bother to contradict him; he'd never had a good word to say about Bonny before now.

Alex gave himself one grand finale swipe between the legs and, at last satisfied, dropped the paper in the bowl. He stood and hauled up his boxer shorts in one motion, then turned to inspect his turd before flushing. An exercise no doubt thwarted by the swirling eels of pink toilet paper. Still, gathering from his grunt and the strength of the stench, it was a rewarding bowel movement.

I tested the water temperature with an index finger. As I bent over the sink to splash and rinse my face, Alex came up behind me. 'We can make this work, I know we can. We need to be out on our own, in our own space. We need to start planning for the future.' He placed his hands on my hips. 'Besides, I can't go on dossing here for ever. Slumlord Lurid is gonna find out sooner or later. And your room is a tad small for the both of us.'

That was true without a doubt, especially with the hoard of crap Alex brought here with him. His clothes and shoes and stinking footie kit and his guitar and all those damn CDs and, God, there was just a helluva lot of all of his stuff, everywhere.

He squeezed my waist and added, 'I wannabe in our new place before the start of the season.' I bet. A place of our own to invite all his mates round to for yob parties to cheer the Spurs on during away games. Alex says this is the year Tottenham's going all the way. And if not? A home for hooliganism and despair, that's what we'd have.

I stood up and knocked his hands away from me. 'Alex. Please. Don't touch me until you wash your hands.' Granting my beloved a thin smile, I side-stepped him and made a dash for my bedroom. 'And don't forget to brush your teeth before coming to bed.'

As I pulled the duvet up to my chin, I continued to listen to Alex bump around in the bathroom next door. God knew what was taking him so long, but I wasn't complaining. And I wasn't going back in that toxically polluted place to check on him. The odour of his footie kit decomposing in the corner came as a blessed relief after the Chernobyl that was the bathroom. I sucked down huge gulps of the comparatively clean bedroom air. Charlotte used to tease me about Alex and I using the bathroom at the same time. It can't possibly be sexy to watch someone else take a dump, or a piss for that matter, she said. It cannot be healthy for your sex life. Well, maybe she had a point. I swilled another lungful of bedroom-flavoured oxygen.

Charlotte had been gone nearly two months now and I missed her. Especially with her birthday coming up. She'd be twenty-four in one week, 3 July. I had a card all signed and ready for her but nowhere to send it. I supposed I'd have to send it to her mum and hope she passed it on. Hope she'd let Charlotte know how miserable I was without her.

There was a hole that Charlotte left behind and it wasn't healing over, it was getting bigger. It was a gaping hole that neither Alex nor Emmy nor Joyce nor Rebecca nor a hundred girls' nights could fill. I couldn't even seem to talk to anyone about it. Certainly not Alex. He never wanted her around in the first place. I begged her to stay, but she couldn't face me or Alex or the girls, any of us in this old life of hers. It was more than the rape, too. I'm sure of it. There was something else too – she had so much she wouldn't tell me, or couldn't. So she deserted again, and left me behind.

The sad, ironic, shitty thing about it all was that Charlotte was wrong, or at least terribly misguided about so many things. She didn't have to lie or make up stories. She *was* liked and loved and fancied and appreciated. She was a wonderful person. The men and relationships she craved so desperately were, based on my own experience, not all that she cracked them up to be. And anyway, it wasn't some personal fault of hers that kept pushing them out of her reach. It was like Emmy said, relationships are a car-pool of chance, lack of co-ordination and unsynchronised watches. Or something like that. Silly Charlotte, she was her own worst enemy. How I wished I could just call her and tell her to stop worrying, stop putting herself down. Charlotte, I would say, we must have mercy on ourselves.

If only I knew how to get in touch with her. But she skedaddled without leaving any number or forwarding address. I tried twisting the news out of her mum, but Mrs Mereville didn't know either, or else she wouldn't tell me. Even though Charlotte was my best friend.

Ho hum, in the heat of foreplay. Alex's face was in my cunt; his butt wagging in the air. I couldn't fault him for trying, he was really going for it, lapping at me like a thirsty dog. And as I lay here, the first thought that popped into my mind was this: 'God, I wish I had his legs!' I admired them, jutting out from below his pimply buttocks. Such perfect legs for a woman, particularly his thighs. So slender and firm and not a trace of cellulite. Even his springy hair was not too offensive – light, doey blond, sparse. Jesus, I scolded myself, I am jealous of my boyfriend's legs.

The second thought that popped into my mind was that in a few minutes Alex would want me to return the oral favour. I tried to psyche myself up, imagined bending over his erect penis. Then I caught another whiff as his bottom wagged closer to my face. The rancid post-shit-session pong. The beer mixed with toothpaste on his breath and the oniony smell of post-football perspiration cloaking his body were bad enough, but this? My own thighs clapped hard around Alex's head until it stopped twitching.

I heard a muffled, 'What's up?'

'Sorry, honey,' I said. 'I'm just not in the mood tonight. You'd better come up for air.'

He emerged with a wet, red face and collapsed back on to the pillow. 'Why, Liz?'

'Sorry, I just feel really tired all of a sudden. These girls' nights wear me out. Too much Häagen-Dazs and pizza. I feel about as sexy as an insurance policy.'

'Great. You should be careful, you know. Too much ice-cream makes you frigid.' He unthreaded a pube from his front teeth and glanced down at my own thighs. 'And fat.'

'Watch it,' I warned him.

'Can't help but watch it; your body fills up my entire field of vision.'

I slapped him on the chest. 'Okay, Alex, that's enough.'

Leaning over me, spewing McFanny and Heineken breath all in my face, he relented. 'Sorry, sorry. But Christ, you might have told me earlier, before I got started.'

I patted his cheek. 'Yeah, well, you probably needed a good flossing. So don't be mad. We both could use a good night's sleep. It is a work day tomorrow, after all.' Then I turned on my side away from him, glad to have that out of the way for another night. Alex curled himself around my backside, his still erect penis cattle-prodding me from behind. But it would soften soon and then wedge its flaccid self between my buttocks. Until we both grew restless and changed positions.

The battle to find a comfortable position was ongoing. We waged it silently, half-wakingly, between each other, the same skirmishes replayed every night. He spooned me until my hair tickling his face became unbearable, then we flipped. I spooned him until my arm under him became heavy with stabbing pins and needles. We snuggled into each other, my head resting on his chest or shoulder, our legs braided; until my face became too cold from the air-conditioned exhalation of his nostrils. I lay on my back and he buried his head into my bosom – like falling into a stack of goosedown pillows, he said – until the feathers in my breasts started to clump and ache. We flipped and flopped, like pancakes, alternating. Him on his stomach, me on my back, his arm draped over me, my leg wrapped around his. He tossed and propelled me into a counter-motion that made him shift once again.

After a while, we gave up trying to maintain a connection, and curled up into our opposite corners of the bed, away from each other. He thought I was hoarding mattress real estate, and reached across me to check how much spare space I had. I huffed and reciprocated the gesture, thereby marking out a line which divided the bed into his side and my side. If one of us edged across the line, the just reward was a swift kick in the shin. The duvet tug-of-war commenced. He wrenched at the top, I wrenched at the bottom, both of us trying to sew our sides tight against any potential draughts. We pulled the duvet so taut in both directions that a shaft was formed in the middle. Cold air blasted down through the shaft and chilled us both. How can this room always be so cold, I wondered; it's June for God's sake. We cuddled back into each other, cemented the shaft shut, and repeated the process.

Until, at long last, one of us fell asleep. Invariably, it was Alex, certainly so on a night like tonight when he'd been drinking. Why was the person who snored always the first to fall asleep?

After a few hours of listening to Alex's honking, stealing more than my share of the duvet from his inert body, and watching the clock eat up larger and larger chunks of my good night's sleep, I gave in and got up. It was only a matter of time anyway as the litres of Diet Coke imbibed earlier with the girls were running another quick course through my body. I might have blamed the insomnia on the Diet Coke too if it hadn't been decaffeinated. I wasn't heartless enough to leave Alex completely exposed. Bequeathing him the duvet (too bad, he wasn't awake to witness how generous I was), I scrabbled at the side of the bed for my bathrobe but couldn't find it so grabbed my beach-sized towel from its drying place on the radiator instead. Then I retreated to the bathroom where, I was relieved to smell, the shit fumes had largely evaporated.

When I sat down on the loo, the whole bowl lurched forward with a clunk. The toilet's forward list had been worsening; one of these days, one of us would up-end it completely, falling on our face with a pool of piss, poo and porcelain on our back. I was sure of it. But, despite our complaints from the day we first moved in, Lurid hadn't done anything about it. I balanced the rocking structure by rolling my shoulders forward and pressing my weight firmly down on to the balls of my feet, straddled in front of me. Thoughts of Charlotte flitted through my head as I emptied my bladder, a high-powered hose release that tapered off to a tinkle. After I had dripped myself dry, I didn't budge from the toilet seat. Where else was there for me to go?

Even the lounge was a no-go zone tonight – one of Alex's footie mates was passed out on the sofa. Before Maxine arrived, I used to go into Charlotte's old room when I needed to get away from Alex or I couldn't sleep. Then, there was still a hint of Charlotte that haunted the place. Her perfume, some stray hairs on the mattress, a few balls of her crumpled-up rubbish in the bin, the bogeys of Blu-Tack on the walls where her collection of photomontages had hung.

Happily selective collages of our lives. Most of the photos had been of us or her family; ex-lovers and ex-friends, like Rebecca and Harriet, having been carefully snipped out of celluloid existence. My favourite was a pic of two lip-glossed pre-pubescents in disco gear. Charlotte and me at a school dance. I remembered it well as the occasion I received my first kiss. From Charlotte. There'd been an older boy chasing me around the dance floor all night. I fancied him but was scared he might try to smooch me during a slow dance, and I didn't know how. So Charlotte took me to the lavatory where we holed ourselves up in a stall for half an hour while she puckered up and demonstrated. By the time we returned to the gym, my prospective dance partner had left and we were in hysterics.

One night while hiding out in Charlotte's deserted room, I found a dusty sandal, two floral pillowcases and a *Les Misérables* T-shirt mummified under the bed. She had packed up so fast on that last day she must've forgotten to look there. But now Maxine had installed herself in the bedroom next to mine, and she'd chased away any trace of Charlotte with her garish duvet covers, outrageous Athena-clearance-sale posters and that sickly sweet burning incense. And of course, the legion of overnight guests, all colleagues from her office. How Maxine could go in to face them *en masse* every day I couldn't fathom. Certainly, she had no difficulty facing them each night on our doorstep – on a, so far, individual basis. The company must have printed our number on the backs of all their business cards or maybe scratched it into the bottom of dozens of pint glasses at their local Red Lion pub. Wherever, only the male contingent had put the number to the test. With a vengeance. These guys had a peculiar habit, which Maxine never seemed to mind, of calling or just showing up at the end of an evening. Like tonight. This bloke called at pub closing time and was here before midnight to have Maxine greet him with open arms and legs. Oh well, to each his own.

I just wished she wasn't around, I wished Charlotte had never left. Maybe if I'd been a better friend, maybe if I'd never introduced her to that tosser Garret, Charlotte wouldn't have needed to rape herself, she wouldn't have needed to invent such a hoax for attention. Then she'd still be here. I tried my best to be that kind of friend, but I guess I couldn't quite pull it off. Charlotte was a very needy person. She needed too much. Not as in she needed many things, but as in what she needed, she needed an awful lot. Does that make sense? Quantity versus quality? No, not quite. More like, the number of needs versus the degree of those needs. Maybe that was it. In any case, the degree of her need was staggering. From me, from men. Maybe from life in general.

Who on earth was she going to spend her birthday with?

As I arched back to stretch my arms, the toilet clunked accordingly. Clunk, click, every trip. My feet were cold so I wrapped the towel around them, as well as my knickers, still down around my ankles, and the rest of my bare legs. I leant forward again, propping my elbows on my knees, my chin balancing on the heels of my hands. Ever since Charlotte left, I'd been thinking about my own needs. I asked myself, what is it that I need? Alex? A mortgage? Marriage? New friends? I hadn't come up with an answer yet; I didn't know.

I thought back to another era. An era where there was Charlotte, and girls' nights out on the pull with Rebecca and occasionally Joyce. An assortment of blokes which constituted crushes, dates, or other fleetingly fanciful moments before the four years that became my relationship with Alex. Other men. The older boy at the dance in the gym, the kid who sat next to me in Geography, the sexy Spanish god I met on holiday, the muscly dough-spinner at the pizza joint where I had my first job, that funky dancer I met while clubbing one night in Soho, a dozen different men in pubs. Opportunities had knocked, some even leant on the doorbell until the batteries wore out, but I'd been too scared to answer. I had wanted to wait for *true love* and I did, and now I had Alex. I mean, Alex and I still loved each other, for sure, but we'd just started wondering if maybe that wasn't enough. I had anyway. Wondering if maybe there should be something else out there.

It went deeper than sex, too, although admittedly that was the first thing on my mind – especially after a raunchy girls' night discussion. Sometimes, even when Alex was in the same room with me, I had to hug myself, stop myself from shivering, as this sub-zero cloud of loneliness descended on me. How could I be in this relationship, how could I spend so much time with this other person, I wondered, and still feel so alone? I knew Alex felt the same way himself sometimes. He thought getting a place together, planning a limitless future, would blot out some of these concerns, would solder us inseparable. Could that be the solution?

Maybe the truth was we weren't so very different from everyone else. Perhaps the foundation for all relationships was nothing but mere tolerance, which verged occasionally on intolerance. One day you woke up feeling that you were madly in love, the next night you went to bed thinking, Oh well, I guess it's better than being alone. Maybe Alex and I, and everyone else, maybe we were all just parasites nibbling off one another. Parasites, yes, it all seemed so obvious now, especially looking at the relationships around me. Joyce and Nick for instance. Nick used Joyce for sex or some kind of sadistic ego trip. And she used him, yes she did, to prove to herself that she was still desirable, still a woman, to convince herself that she wouldn't spend the rest of her life alone. Nibble, nibble, nibble. It's not a relationship at all, not in the real, healthy sense of the word. It's just mutually tolerable exploitation. And that kind of 'relationship', that is the statistical norm. That was what I wished I'd warned Charlotte about her relationship panacea. Enjoy your freedom while you still can, I would have told her if only I could have got her phone number.

And more. Fidgeting on the hard plastic toilet seat, I realised that I did know what I'd been longing for, which might have been the same or completely opposite to what I needed. But since Charlotte was not there to confide in, I announced it aloud to the sink and the bathtub, to the broken shower nozzle and the beach scene plastic curtain which was sprouting fungus at the bottom in the cracks where it gathered when drawn back. 'I long for all the men I knew but didn't screw!' I told them.

As my words reverberated against the porcelain and stainless steel fixtures, the door was thrown open, the flimsy bolt ripped completely off its hinges. 'Oh, Alex, please . . .' I started to say as I looked up with annoyance. But it wasn't Alex. I glimpsed a huge, unfamiliar, starkers, male body loom up in the doorway before it was tumbling down in front of me. On to me in fact. Oh shit! They always forgot about that first step.

I yelped as the face of my intruder landed in my lap, the rest of the body splayed out on the stairs and the floor at my feet. The tumble – with the force of the body hitting the linoleum and the alarming clatter of the toilet beneath us – produced quite a racket and jarring of floorboards. But we weren't crashing through to the kitchen and no footsteps came running as the night regained its composure. Good thing Alex was such a sound sleeper. Like a petrified stump.

The body shuddered, causing the loo to tremble beneath us, and there was a manly moan from the depths of my lap. I couldn't decide whether to be enraged, concerned or frightened. I trembled with one feeling or the other. My heart was fighting to break out of my chest, sending spurts of blood gushing through every artery so that my body felt like one gigantic throbbing, post-high-impact-aerobics pulse. Then, as the head lolled about some more in my groin, I became aware of a not unpleasant sensation arising from the region, and what was once drip-dried began to dampen. Oh, God. What was I supposed to do?

'Ummmm, hey. Are you all right?' I asked, tapping on the back of a curly head of hair.

Another moan. The intruder, struggling to situate himself, managed after some seconds to raise himself on his arms and get a good look at me and where he'd landed. 'Oh shit!' he gasped, clambering to his feet. As soon as the weight was off my lap, I too leapt up, the toilet clanking in response. And so we stood there, frozen. Him completely naked, me in nothing but my skimpy, barely hip-grazing night-shirt, my knickers and towel now trampled beneath my feet. We gaped at each other.

He was taller than my recollection of Alex's footie friend so I assumed this must be Maxine's midnight visitor who I hadn't got a gander at earlier. Now I was gandering aplenty. This one definitely hadn't been past the cocoa inspection line. Not that I could recall and I would have recalled. There weren't enough cocoa beans in all of Ghana to rate this one. Though doubtless another colleague, this was also, without a doubt, not the boss – no grey hair nor a single ounce of middle-aged flab had ever crossed paths with this body. He was very tall really, much taller than Alex, with black curly hair, a pleasantly abashed face, medium-sized muscles, and a nice slowly fading tan, with startling bathing cossie borderlines around his waist and thighs and a lily-white stretch between them to prove it. He'd taken his summer holidays early this year. Oh yes, and there, swelling from a clump of black pubic hair was a large, and ever largening, penis, much larger than Alex's in fact.

Suddenly, realising we should be rather embarrassed by the situation, the two of us started to redden at once. He covered his groin with both hands, trying to nudge his wayward penis back down in the process; I tugged at the hem of my T-shirt.

'God, shit,' he said, shifting from one foot to the other. 'I'm really sorry. I didn't see the light. I was in such a mad dash, and half-asleep, groggy, absolutely bursting for a piss.'

'Sure, uh-huh, honest mistake,' I told him. 'I locked the bolt, but I guess it wasn't very strong.' I pointed my forehead towards the door. The wood was splintered where the bolt had torn off; we both followed the imagined trajectory to where the twisted metal contraption had landed on the bottom step.

'Oh, right. God, I didn't realise I'd yanked that hard,' he confessed. 'God, sorry, I was just absolutely bursting for a piss.'

'Well. Please. Don't let me stop you now.' I shuffled further away from the toilet, kicking my cast-offs before me. As I leant down to pick the towel and knickers up, I saw him limp forward.

'Shit, are you sure?' He turned his back towards me and flicked the lid. 'Thanks. I'm just bursting, you know.' His shoulders dropped as he hunched over his task and let go. The sigh was audibly heavy.

From behind, I stood and watched him. My eyes traced the outline of his back, the crown of his curly head, the tilting slope of his neck, his broad shoulders, the cut of his torso, racing down to the milky-white, blemish-free scoops of buttocks, down his thick thighs and sculpted calves, right down to his big feet which still danced unsteadily beneath him.

The waterfall sound ceased and he shook himself off. He flushed and even remembered to put the seat down. When he turned back around, my eyes, which had commenced the slow climb back up his body, were only at knee level. I noticed the red splotches there where they must have come into hard contact with the floor. Those would surely blacken tomorrow.

'Are you hurt?' I asked.

'Huh? Oh, no, I'm fine. I'll be okay.'

Raising my eyes back to his, noting on the way that his hands were again shielding his groin, I said, 'Well, I hope so. That was quite a fall.'

'Huh? Oh, yeah. Yeah, hey, I'm really sorry about that. I didn't realise.' His eyes darted all over the place.

It was only then I realised that I was still standing there, knickers in hand, naked from the waist down and not bothering to try to cover myself any more. I blushed again and gave a sort of schoolgirl giggle as I bent over, my hair falling in thick, tousled clumps into my face. Stepping back into my knickers, I asked him, 'So you must be Maxine's friend?'

'Maxine's? Yes, well, friend, sort of. Frank, actually, I'm Frank,' he spluttered. 'And you must be . . .'

'Liz.'

'Liz. Of course.' His eyes stopped darting to rest on me and I warmed up like a pasty on a hotplate under his gaze.

It occurred to me that this was not at all normal to be standing there, talking to a naked male stranger in my bathroom. I should probably have said something like, 'I'd better be getting back to my *boyfriend* now' or 'Why don't you knock before dropping in next time?' and then sprinted it back to my own room, my own bed and Alex. But his big frame was blocking my route to the door and I didn't feel much like escaping anyway.

'So,' I said, wrapping my towel around me like a skirt, 'come here often?'

Frank laughed, a bit nervous titterish but nice all the same. His eyes jigged in time with his feet. 'Yeah, well, I don't always frequent this particular venue,' he raised his arms to indicate the bathroom around us, 'and I don't always make such a dramatic entrance,' his left arm swept back to the door, 'but yes, I have been known to answer Mother Nature's call on occasion.'

We both chuckled. He then noticed he'd forgotten to keep his erection covered. As I stared at it, his hands fluttered back to their screening position and we both chuckled harder. Which made my towel skirt loosen and drop which made us chuckle a bit harder still.

I stooped down to pick it up, but it slipped out of my trembling hand which of course fuelled our chuckling even more. I left it where it fell.

Unplanned. Spontaneous. Reckless. So unlike me. I grin again. Bird calls and the remote whine of the early-rising traffic on the North Circular blend with the more immediate purring of the house. I will have to wake Frank soon so we can hug and part and crawl back into our respective beds, slink back into our respective lives. But I'm not ready for the experience to end just yet. Perhaps I'll prod him with a Sleeping Beauty kiss and he'll awaken with my tongue and the taste of his own body in his mouth. A life-giving kiss to make Charlotte proud.

What a story I'll have for the next girls' night in – preferably one from which Maxine is absent. On second thoughts, sod that, she's a silly old slapper. It'd serve her right to have to sit there and squirm while I relish all the scintillating details. *So* unlike me. Rebecca would smile enigmatically, Bonny would gasp, Joyce would blush, Emmy would analogise, Maxine would simmer and they'd all, all of them, applaud and toast to my future as a sex goddess. (Well, something like that though, truth be told, perhaps I'm not quite ready to risk Maxine's wrath.)

And Charlotte? She'll appreciate the tale too; she always liked a good story. Another titbit to add to the catalogue of things I'll confess to her if I ever get her phone number. Or perhaps if, by pure coincidence, we bump into each other on Oxford Street on a Saturday afternoon. I'll grab her by the hand and steer her to a nearby wine bar, sit her down and crack open a bottle of the most expensive champagne on the menu. There's something else you're wrong about, Charlotte, I will say. Watching someone take a piss can be very sexy indeed. God have mercy on us all.

CHAPTER SEVEN

A HAIRY SITUATION

It is a terrible thing. An ugly thing. A terribly ugly thing. Joyce is twenty-three and going undeniably, irreversibly, terribly bald. All of Joyce's girlfriends feel sorry for her, but as much as they would never admit it even to themselves, they enjoy pitying her. They like having her as a friend to compare themselves to so that they can say, 'Yes, well, maybe I have a little cellulite (or my waist is too thick, my nose too big, my breasts too small) but at least I'm not like Joyce, at least I'm not . . . Well, at least I have all my hair.'

But Joyce's friends aren't really so bad, they aren't putting her down all the time and never – no, *never* – would they say anything to her face. They just say these things to themselves, sometimes discreetly to each other in small groups over tea, when they're feeling down, depressed, insecure and fat, as women sometimes do. To her face, they concentrate on the positive – she's got firm tits and a small bum, such a great figure (how does she do that, anyway? She doesn't even belong to a gym! At least she's got the good grace to wear clothes that don't rub it in their faces), a tasty boyfriend (even if he is a prick) and good teeth, too (lots of flossing obviously). They don't actually think about Joyce's baldness very much, or notice it any more because after all she's just Joyce, our good Joyce, their dear dear friend.

Joyce never forgets, though. She started thinning in her teens and hasn't stopped counting her hairs since. She's grown to hate her brush, that offending object which steals her hair, traps it mercilessly between its bristles. For a while she thought the brush was the culprit, that she was using the wrong kind – perhaps a round brush rather than a flat one, a plastic one or a vented one would be better. So she tried them all. She even tried an array of combs and picks. But it didn't matter, it makes no difference. It comes out in anything, everything. Often between her fingers when she flicks her fringe out of her eyes.

And it always comes out with Nick's touch. When they are in bed, it comes out in little tufts and then scatters all over the pillows and the sheets and the duvet. Long strands attach themselves to Nick – his hair, his arms, and somehow a few seem to lodge themselves in the folds of his boxer shorts. 'Fucking hell,' Nick says in the mornings after the nights when she stays with him, 'we need a bloody Hoover to clean this mess up.'

It is everywhere, Joyce's hair, except less and less on Joyce's head.

Nick says she looks old already – old, old, older than the hills, ancient, withered and withering, dilapidated, don't come round here no more, old. And everyone knows there's nothing worse than being old. 'What will you look like when you actually are old?' he asks. 'What about when you're thirty?' He says he wonders why on earth he stays with her, she looks more like his mother or his grandmother, or actually more like his grand*father*, than his girlfriend. He hates how people stare. She knows that he's right and she wonders too. She wonders why he ever started seeing her. Was she wearing a hat when they first met? She doesn't think so. She hates hats – they always sit at drunken, cock-eyed angles on her head and magnetise too many stray hairs to their rims when she takes them off. No, she wasn't wearing a hat, but it wasn't so bad then, she wasn't as far gone. So why is he still here? Maybe it's just a habit now, she's just a habit, an old trick for the old dog. It has been a long time for both of them. Nearly a year. Maybe he's just used to her body, which he still seems to enjoy, although he closes his eyes when he touches her. Or maybe it's because he too feels sorry for her.

Nick thinks more and more about leaving and less and less about staying. Habits are, as they say, hard to break, but everything can be broken, especially if it wants to be, especially if it's full of cracks already, hairline cracks. Joyce is certain that he'll never see her reach thirty or go completely bald, whichever comes first. Sometimes she considers telling him that she's sick – to try to get him to stay. A late diagnosis, she would say. But he'd never believe it. He's been around too many other times when she's denied it. It's something that other people often speculate about. They ask her – sometimes tactfully, more often not – 'Do you have cancer or that, that ageing disease?' 'No,' she says, 'I'm no sicker than the rest of you.' Still, she hears them whisper about her, 'But her hair, and she's so pale.'

Well, who the hell isn't pale in this godforsaken little country? That's what she wants to know. There are only two weather modes – inconsistent and consistently bad. It's nearly the end of August now but Joyce's still waiting for summer to arrive – the only indication of its passage has been the number of people away on holiday at any one time since May. Not including Joyce. She is here, always has been, nowhere else, to see them all go and return, browner and happier and more sexed up. Here to count the paltry number of rainfree weekends – barely enough for one hand. Nick hadn't even suggested a bank holiday excursion in May, not even to Blackpool. Now the August one is racing up fast and he hasn't batted an eye.

Joyce yearns to go somewhere warm and sunny and dry, somewhere to lie on the beach and bake her body honey-brown. She did that once before, with the girls. A package holiday to Ibiza. She'd resisted the trip initially but it was Rebecca's idea and Joyce never could resist Rebecca or her ideas. It had been an okay experience too, lying on the beach, especially when she lay next to her brave, beautiful friend. If Rebecca could have the enormous courage to display her scar to a beach of holiday onlookers, Joyce could hardly chicken out over a little exposed scalp. Of course, the situation is worse now, much worse, and not only because it might be Nick stretched out next to her instead of Rebecca. She has a lot more scalp to worry about burning now.

Hats being out of the question, it is a very difficult dilemma indeed. What to do? Should she rub tanning lotion on to her skull, making what little hair she does have an oily, greasy clump? Or should she burn? Expose that tender, delicate patch of epidermis, set it ablaze under the ultraviolet rays, scorch it screaming scarlet red, until the blisters bubble up and rupture, until her scalp goes dry again and peels, scabs and breaks off in flakes that fall through her thin hair like snowflakes which never melt? What should she do? Maybe it is better to wear a hat. But she hates hats, especially in the sun, with the shadows they cast long across her face, banishing her tanning attempts to two-toned failure. All the options are unpleasant and most certainly so for Nick, lounging next to her. He would laugh and roll over and bury his snickering face into the blanket, letting his full head of hair become sand-filled and wind-blown and salt-flavoured and sun-kissed, lightening to a healthy warm blond.

It's Joyce's birthday. Grey and overcast, what a surprise. Now twenty-four and balding more, she's thinking of ways to spend the Marks & Sparks gift voucher sent by her parents. She could buy five years' worth of socks and knickers with this loot or she could wait for an end-of-season sale, as she usually does, and get all her Christmas shopping done, nice and cheap and early. Have everything wrapped and ready well before Hallowe'en. She scolds herself, she's thinking too small – she must dream beyond the racks and trolleys and linoleum aisles. Yes, of course, why not? Maybe she could cash the voucher in, use the money as a down-payment on a trip for two to Tenerife? A present for both herself and Nick, a chance for them both to get away. They could use some time alone. But, on second thoughts, she knows that's a horrible idea. As much as she wants to mistreat her melanin, inject some colouring into her pale skin to cast doubt amongst the chemotherapy speculators, Joyce will never go to a beach with Nick. It's not worth it.

Happy Birthday. Nick gives her a kitten, ties a tartan ribbon around its neck. Just like yours, Nick tells her while pointing to her drooping hair tie, you could be twins. Joyce likes it, the kitten and the ribbon, even though she isn't a big cat-lover and is actually quite allergic to them, cats not ribbons. Joyce's kitten is small and warm and white and fluffy. She likes it when the kitten rubs up against her, pushes its tiny arched back into the palm of her hand, gnaws gently on her thumb and licks her fingers, its tongue dragging like wet sandpaper across her skin. Joyce thinks it's a very nice kitten, a very nice gift and very thoughtful of Nick to give it to her, even though she swells up and goes red and rashy and sneezes as steady and constant as a train – a-choo-choo-choo – whenever the thing is in the same room.

She sneezes and blows and scratches miserably and counts and arranges these nice thoughts over and over again until several days after her birthday. It's late on a Saturday afternoon and she's at Nick's place and playing with the kitten – who she's named Sniffle – and Nick's in the next room doing something or other. Joyce decides to phone her flatmate Bonny, who she knows will be home at this time, planning out that night's outfit and next week's diet. She picks up the receiver and finds that Nick is already on the other extension. He's talking to one of his mates, laughing.

'Yeah, I bought her this damn cat for her birthday. Thought they could shed together.' Ha, ha, ha. 'Besides,' he says, 'she'll need something to keep her company. I'm not completely cold-blooded, you know.'

Easy, easy, easy and silent, Joyce replaces the receiver before she erupts with another monumental sneeze. She glares down at that damn cat, sitting in her lap, clawing at the sleeve of her jumper. She would like to strangle that cat, she would like to strangle Nick, she would like to cry. She doesn't know what to do. She grabs her kitten and her Kleenex, and shouts to Nick that she's got to go home; she goes home and she cries.

Ordinarily, Joyce doesn't like to talk about her own deficiency with her friends, especially when she spends so much time when they're together watching them play with and talk about their own lustrous locks. Hair, hair, hair – what a lot they do with theirs and what a lot of time they spend doing it. They wet it and wash it and dry it, condition it, curl it, cut it, crimp it, gel it, mousse it, spray it, sculpt it. So much they can do! And still they complain. This one's is too long, that one's is too short. Or too frizzy or too curly or too straight or too blond or too dark. Too much this, too little that. Too much, too much, too too too too much! They're never satisfied. But they have it, don't they, for God's sake? Surely, that is something. And so when they get into their hairy discussions, the trials and tribulations of the well-endowed, Joyce doesn't say much. She never says anything about her own hair. Ordinarily.

But she is desperate. She knows that Nick's going to leave her anytime now. She turns to her friends for advice. It's late in the morning the next day, Sunday. They're all next door at Liz and Emmy's house attempting to read the foot-thick Sunday newspapers. Piles of paper lie strewn across the living-room floor, and the women sit curled up with their sections of choice, fingerprinting their tea mugs with their ink-smeared hands, all except for Emmy who drinks coffee and is fiddling with the radio in search of Voice of America. A few minutes earlier, Maxine staggered into the lounge. Looking crumpled, smears of day-old make-up deeply embedded in her pores, silk pyjamas stained and mis-buttoned.

'Who took the phone off the hook?' Maxine growled though everyone knew the answer. Emmy has been avoiding her family again. All summer, while Emmy has been soaking in the London culture and working part-time, cash-in-hand at the pub down the road, her mother has been threatening to come over and physically strap her into a one-way flight home. No sign of the family posse yet but the phoning is fairly constant. It is only a matter of days before classes begin at her stateside university.

Maxine gulped down some water and paracetamol while her latest overnight visitor exited noisily through the front door, out of sight. Had she managed to trap 'the boss' for an entire night? Unlikely. It was probably yet another. No one asked or commented and, rather than risk any hangover ire,

Rebecca cleared the armchair so that Maxine could collapse into it. Regular newspaper consumption resumed, Maxine stealing the Style and Travel from under Joyce's very nose, until Bonny broke the silence, 'Did you know that experts say Margaret Thatcher had an affair with Genghis Khan in a past life?' (Bonny is an avid reader of the *Sunday Sport*, a tabloid true-believer.) This is followed by several hushes and hisses and a couple of calls for please-may-we-have-some-quiet-to-concentrate-now.

But Joyce can't concentrate. There's an article about something called Gulf War Syndrome on the front page of the *Sunday Times*. Joyce can't read past the headline but is riveted instead to the accompanying photo. Tanks and troops in the desert. Which leads her, quite naturally, to think of sand and sun and sunburn and Nick. She looks up hoping to catch Rebecca's eye. Anyone's eye. But they're all deeply engrossed in headlines, horoscopes and crosswords. So she clears her throat, breathes deeply and says, 'Nick's going to leave me. I think he may be bothered by my baldness. Embarrassed by it. And I don't know what to do.'

This is the first time she's ever said the B-word in front of them. Papers are dropped, tea mugs set down, the radio is switched off, and they all gawp at her as if they've never realised that she had a problem. What is she talking about? Bonny even says, 'Why, I never noticed all those bare spots.' Rebecca throws up her hands and screams 'MEN!', Emmy clucks despairingly and Maxine winces either from shock or irritation at the raised voices (it's hard to tell which). But Liz stands up and walks over to the chair where Joyce is sitting. She walks around Joyce, examining her from every angle, makes her bow her head and shake her hair out. Then she concludes, 'I think it might help if you tried a new style.'

Suddenly, Bonny and Emmy and Rebecca are up and circling her and nodding and saying yes, yes, yes, of course. A new style can do wonders, you know. 'A new cut'll give you a whole new attitude,' says Rebecca. 'It's all about attitude.' Joyce grins admiringly but doesn't dare ask Rebecca what 'it' is and why she should have it. The room is bubbling with suggestions: a bob maybe, or layered, or short and spiked, or maybe a perm, that adds quite a bit of body, or no, shaved a bit in back, shaved and stacked. Yes, that's it, shaved a bit at the nape of the neck, stacked in back, over the ears, short fringe in front. That will make it look much fuller, bouncy, without the damaging chemicals involved in the perm treatment. (God knows she doesn't want to lose any more hair!) Yes, perfect. How chic Joyce will look, how absolutely perfectly hip and modern. Superb.

Maxine watches imperiously from her threadbare throne, a whisper of amusement brushing across her morning-after visage.

'What do you think, Maxine?' Joyce asks.

Maxine shrugs and coughs a harsh laugh. 'Couldn't hurt.' Joyce exhales. 'But then,' under her breath as Maxine eases herself kitchenward to refill her water tumbler, 'what could?'

'It'll look wonderful,' Rebecca chirps, yanking Joyce's attention away from Maxine's backside.

'Definitely,' says Bonny.

'Without a doubt,' says Liz.

'Hipper than a hip thing, voguer than a vogue thing,' says Emmy, fingers fanning, elbows and wrists cocking round her face in Madonna-like contortions.

Joyce is sceptical. She's never been hip before – what if she doesn't know how? And it does seem rather drastic after all. Of course, she has considered a new, less extreme, style before, but she was frightened. She hasn't had her hair cut, aside from a few snips at the fringe, since she first recognised that losing it was a concern. She figured what she lacked in fullness, she could make up for in length. So she grew it and grew it and grows it still, or so she believes though it seems to be quite finished with its growing. Most of the time, she wears it pulled back. It's limp and lifeless and listless but it's long, hanging down her back, held in place by her favourite black-and-red checked ribbon (just like Sniffle's), in a fashion which in fact, despite the name, looks nothing like a pony's tail.

She doesn't want to part with her long hair, but she needs to try something. Her friends have convinced her. Drastic measures for drastic times. Everyone suggests hairdressers and stylists. Liz tells her about a salon that's even open on Sundays, down in Camden near the Lock, so that she could go that very afternoon and get it done, if she wanted. Emmy says maybe that would be a good idea, do it right away, before she loses her nerve, and Joyce agrees but not whole-heartedly. Rebecca offers to come along for moral support but Joyce declines. Her friends mumble words of support as they part, while thinking to themselves, 'Poor poor Joyce, losing her hair and her boyfriend in one go. Thank God I only have to worry about being overweight and unattached.' Except for Rebecca, not at all overweight, who fingers the rough skin at her waist and thinks, 'Well, at least I can cover up my problem.' And Liz who is also thinking, 'Maybe life with Alex isn't all that bad' and Emmy who is beginning to appreciate her ex-pat frustrations and Bonny who is wondering why Joyce got to have such a nice body, when a crap one wouldn't have made any difference. They are all very lucky really, to be who they are and not her, and they know it. Even Maxine.

Joyce is going to do it. She is decided. She leaves immediately for Camden. She's never been there by herself before, especially not on a Sunday afternoon when the market's in full swing. By the time she arrives, the sun has triumphed over the morning haze and everyone's attitude seems revved up at least two notches. There's a festival atmosphere about the place, and it's all much busier and louder than Joyce had anticipated. As soon as she steps out of the Underground station, she's enveloped by the bustling crowd of people. It swarms northward, shrinking and surging into the street as cars try to inch through. Every few minutes she finds herself nudged out into the traffic, confronted by a driver who's involuntarily parked and who is leaning on his horn to voice his anger. She manages to fight her way back on to the pavement where she trips over shuffling feet and makeshift stalls. Vendors have set up shop wherever they could find a spare piece of pavement. Everyone seems to be hawking something or haggling with the hawkers. DMs here, posters and paintings, peaches and plants and post-cards, jewellery, shawls, handbags, candles, incense, cheap Levi's, fake Rolexes, bootleg cassettes, anything you want, we got it, everything you can imagine, we'll sell it, any price you can bargain down to, we'll take it. What do you want? But no one is auctioning a full head of hair – except for the wig stall of course, but that's not quite the same thing. Joyce tightens her grip on her handbag and the crowd carries her on, weaving her inch by inch through the punters and past the Market, down towards where she thinks the Lock is.

After circling the maze of passages around the Lock several times, Joyce finds the salon that Liz suggested. It's under the train tracks, a bit hole-in-the-wallish. There's a man having his hair cut just outside the shop. He and his hairdresser are on display atop a small wooden platform; several onlookers gathered around. Joyce pauses to watch them as she catches her breath. The trek through the sun-shine euphoria has left her sweating, her fine wisps of hair plastered to her forehead. A blackboard is propped on an easel behind the two men. 'Reduced price for demonstration cut – £10' is chalked in alternating dusty colours of blue, pink and yellow. But Joyce is willing to pay more – much more, money-is-no-object more – to get away from the live crowd, to get some privacy, a chair inside, way in the back, in the dark, in the shadows, maybe with a partition set up nice and cosy around it.

She ducks into the salon and is relieved to find there are no customers inside – who, after all, would choose to be inside on a day like today? Who but Joyce who is relieved to find it cool in the shade of the shop, a rickety old fan spinning in the corner. As her eyes adjust to the reduced light, Joyce makes out the lone worker who is lounging in a swivel chair, sipping a Lilt, her slippered feet propped up on the lip of a sink. This is Shelagh – so says the badge over her left breast. Then, enveloping Joyce's right hand with both of her own and shaking heartily, the girl says it too. 'Hi, I'm Shelagh,' she beams, 'but you can call me She. All my friends do.'

'She?' puzzles Joyce, tingling at the girl's touch and the intimate use of the word friend.

'Yeah?'

'Just *She*?'

'Just She, that's me. As in an everywoman kind of way,' Shelagh says as she releases Joyce's hand.

But She – or Shelagh as Joyce continues to think of her – is not like *any* other, let alone *every* other, woman that Joyce has ever seen. Striking, that's the word for her – for She. Striking with her silver earrings pierced half-way up each lobe, her three silver nose rings, her two-inch-thick silver choker, her legion of silver rings on all fingers and both thumbs, and her tight silver bracelets which extend up to her elbows. Joyce thinks Shelagh's jewellery must weigh more than Shelagh, especially since she's rather petite, downright tiny. Shelagh's dressed all in black – black T-shirt, black jeans, black belt, black socks, probably even a black bra and knickers if she felt like wearing any that day. Her eyes are also encrusted with very heavy, very black eyeliner and mascara and she has very short, very black hair – so black it looks like it might smear if you touch it. She – Shelagh is all silver and black, except for a few spots of exposed skin, which is a pickled pink. To be truthful, Joyce finds her kind of frightening – until she notices Shelagh's slippers which are bright green with blue lace flowers stitched on. And then Joyce notices her smile which is crooked but warm as a freshly baked bun. Still, postergirl smile or no, Joyce is certain that Shelagh doesn't shop at Marks & Sparks.

Joyce tells Shelagh what she wants – the shaving, the stacking, the nape of the neck, the over the ear.

'I know exactly what you mean,' says Shelagh as she ushers Joyce into her chair and sweeps a cape over her, tying it tightly at the back. She eases Joyce back into the sink, twists on the faucet and begins to wash her hair.

Ohhh . . . Joyce can feel individual hairs as they cling to Shelagh's fingers and catch on her silver rings, can feel them ripping so readily free, but she doesn't protest because it feels wonderful, Shelagh's strong hands working away, kneading her skull, massaging her scalp, even the bulky weight of the rings is nice – soft, supple, soothing – tender.

'You have very, um, fine hair,' Shelagh comments as she turbans a towel around Joyce's head and tries to discreetly dislodge the clump of hair now clogging the sink.

Shelagh swivels Joyce's chair around so her back is to the mirror, so she can't witness what's about to happen, so she doesn't panic as clients so often do. Then gently, gently, gently, she begins combing out the wet hair, trying not to jerk too hard on the tangles, coaxing the teeth of the plastic comb not to be too greedy.

They both gaze into the mirror, stunned. Joyce stares at herself and Shelagh stares at Joyce staring at herself. Joyce is quiet and Shelagh is quietly concerned. And then not so quietly.

'Oh, shit,' pants Shelagh. 'You don't like it, do you? You don't like it one bit – but you did tell me to keep going, you did say that. Well, don't worry. That's the thing about hair – it grows back. Always does, never fails. Might take a while, but it'll definitely crop up.' She fiddles with the combs soaking in a container of blue disinfectant, rearranges some brushes on the counter. 'Hey, look, I've got an idea. There's a fab hat shop just around the corner and it's nearly my tea break now. Why don't we pop in there and pick out something? Velvet maybe, maybe some plumes. How does that sound?'

Joyce doesn't say anything, just keeps staring.

'They're not very expensive, the hats. I saw this lovely green one in the window this morning. It would really suit you.'

'No, no.' Joyce speaks at last, shaking her head slowly. 'No thanks, Shel– . . . She. I hate hats. Anyway, I think I have some errands to run this afternoon.'

Joyce asks Shelagh for the cuttings, says she wants to keep them as a memento. So Shelagh shakes out the cape Joyce has been wearing. Hairs fly everywhere and several puffs catch the stream of the fan, dispersed to dance until the fan tracks out of range and leaves them to settle. Shelagh sweeps it all up into a little pile, very little, then into a Sainsbury's carrier bag, and gives it to her. It is light, weightless almost, this bit of hair she has been carrying around with her for ever. And her head feels so light now without it.

Joyce is tempted to hug Shelagh – or maybe kiss her – before she leaves but decides against it. Instead, she smiles weakly and leaves her a ten pound tip.

It's not until Joyce is out of the shop, back on the street, that she realises how weightless she is. With each step she feels more and more light-headed, giddy almost, her head feels buoyant like it is bobbing merrily on a bed of jelly rather than sitting on her neck and shoulders. There's a slight breeze now, which at first, despite the afternoon's heat wave, is startlingly cold against her bare head, but then it's fabulous, fresh, it feels like air is rushing through her exposed skin, through her skull, through her mind, lifting her up off the ground by her cerebrum. It feels like each step is a leap into the stratosphere.

Joyce knows she should have said something to Shelagh to keep her from worrying. But she couldn't find the words – they were somewhere lost, snipped off at the root and fallen on the floor with her brittle hair. Of course, Shelagh was in the right; Joyce *had* told her to keep going. She hadn't planned to, to go all the way – it was the razor that did it, the musical electric razor, and the magical goosepimple effect of Shelagh's touch. Shelagh and her razor started in-back, just a shave in-back, but the pressure of her dainty, ring-clad fingers and the hum and tingle of the razor, the way it seemed to shake and tickle every nerve and fibre in her upper body, the way it made the fillings in her molars vibrate and her tongue go numb, the way it made her close her eyes tight and hum along with it – it mesmerised her so that she couldn't call a halt. So Joyce hummed the monotone tune of the razor, bowed to the pressure of Shelagh's tapered hands, and told her more, more, more, keep going and Shelagh listened obediently to both of them and kept going until there was nowhere else to go except over the other side, off with the arched eyebrows and down the steep slope of Joyce's nose. She came to a standstill there at the top of the forehead and switched off the razor. Joyce stopped humming and opened her eyes and that's when Shelagh swung the chair around towards the mirror so Joyce could face the consequences and her own image.

It wasn't the shock that had kept Joyce so quiet, or maybe it was, but it wasn't that she didn't like it. The thing was she *loved* it. Yes, it was different, mighty different, but there, especially there – with Shelagh's petite black frame as a backdrop and her silver reflections bouncing off the mirror and bouncing around Joyce, glowing and glinting around her head like a halo – it was right, it was perfect. Ultra hip and modern.

Still, not until she was out on the street could Joyce start smiling, now she can't stop, she is beaming. Bald is beautiful, she decides. Sinead O'Connor is the *In* thing, after all – less is more, and nothing is everything. And, at least in Camden, it's relatively normal. She and Sinead fit right in. No one stops and stares – well, hardly anyone except for a couple of American teenaged tourists in matching 'I love London' T-shirts – no one even blinks an eye. She runs her hand across her smooth skull. Lovely, superb.

Joyce confidently navigates the crowd. Straight past the hat shop she goes, into the nearest newsagent to buy one first-class stamp and a brown envelope into which she stuffs all of her measly cuttings. Then she darts into the second-hand clothes shop across the street where she picks out a skimpy black bikini – 'hardly worn' sniffs the muscular and equally skin-headed proprietor – and a pair of racing black Ray-Bans. A quick dash into the chemist for some sunscreen, a toothbrush, a new electric razor and batteries – she is tempted to shave off every hair on her body now, from the top of her head to her bikini line to the tips of her

Hobbit-like toes – and she's on her way. Next stop, Heathrow. And after that? Maybe Tenerife, maybe somewhere else. The first permanently sun-soaked destination will do. She'll post the package to Nick from the airport and make a few phone calls before boarding. She doesn't want Shelagh to feel guilty about anything – God bless her – or for Liz or Emmy or Rebecca (certainly not!) to worry when she doesn't show up for the next girls' night, and she wants Bonny to feed that damn cat. Maybe one of them will even want to come with her? Rebecca might have holiday due her. Could it be? Or Shelagh – She will, She will. Definitely. Joyce has a feeling about it.

CHAPTER EIGHT

DO-IT-YOURSELF

Bernard is hunting for shells for his eldest daughter's school project on 'Oceans of the World'. The November water of the Mediterranean is chilly but he rolls up his jeans and wades in ankle deep. He paddles amongst some black craggy rocks just beyond the low-tide mark then heads down the long stretch of open shore. Maxine remains on the beach. She keeps her socks pulled high and shoes tightly laced, gathers her shawl around her and crosses her arms against the wind. As Bernard continues his quest, Maxine follows at a safe distance behind, crushing the shells she encounters beneath her shoes, grinding them with pleasure into the wet, packed sand. She enjoys the crunching sounds they make, and finds it especially satisfying when the crunch emanates from a well-preserved bivalve that Bernard and his daughter might have coveted for their collection.

Bernard stops for a rest at a clutch of boulders at the edge of the entrance to an inland pool. He deposits his now bulging carrier bag of shells at the base of one of the rocks and clambers up the highest one. Maxine catches up with him there and joins him on his perch, staring out to sea.

'It's beautiful, don't you think?' he says.

'Yes, I suppose it is. I doubt I'll be getting any use from my bikini though.'

He chuckles. 'Unfortunately, winter is unavoidable, even here. All the same, I prefer it now to the hordes you have to fight in August.'

They both look back at the deserted beach, imagining it swarming with people. Maxine isn't sure she agrees. In the summer, she would stroll along here topless and tan, dodging fishing lines and squealing kids and jellyfish parts, winking at young French gigolos and stealing older men away from wives, leaving chaos in her wake. There is little indication of the crowds now, except of course for the resort buildings that hover at the edge of the sand. Villas and high-rises stretch empty for miles around the cape, biding their time until late spring when the waves of occupants will return. It's only a matter of months – but the time seems to stretch out as endless and barren as the ocean itself. Maxine kicks at the boulder beneath her.

'You don't have to stay if you don't want to, Max.'

'Max*ine*!' she hisses. Why is that such a difficult name for people to get right? Why are they so hell-bent on nick-names – abbreviated names, abbreviated brains, abbreviated lives. Bernard wanted her to call him Bernie, because 'everybody else does', but Maxine refused. It sounded too ridiculous. Working class. Common. Bernard sounded silly enough already, but at least in a more respectable, upper-class-twit kind of way. Like a Tory MP. Which would make her like a pol's mistress. Which had a nice, exciting, tabloid-selling sparkle to it. Even if it belied the reality. No one would pay for a tell-all of what she had with the anally non-political Bernard. Shame. Still, here they are. And here she is, pretending like she cares.

'You don't have to leave,' she tells him.

'That's not fair.'

'Maybe I shouldn't have come. What the hell am I going to do here?'

'Don't worry. You'll pick up the language. And as soon as you feel ready to come back to London, just come. There'll always be a job for you at the agency.' A new gust of wind cyclones around them, dashing salt spray and fine granules of sand into their cheeks. A wave crashes at the base of the boulder a few feet below them. 'No one's forcing you to stay here, Maxine. You're the one who said you wanted some time away, some time to be alone.'

'I know what I said.'

On their way back to the car, they meander through the jigsaw of piers around the harbour. The sailboats there, like the villas, are anchored and empty, sails rolled up and packed away. Seagulls swoop and dive amongst the spikes of the naked masts. Along the boardwalk, most of the shops and restaurants are boarded up, some with handwritten signs hanging in the dust-caked front windows, announcing reopenings in May. There is one small café open on the corner. An artificial Christmas tree blinks its fairy lights through the window sprayed with fake frost. Outdoors on the pavement, the café's tables are dotted with a few lone retirees who sit with rat-sized, sweatered dogs in their laps as they sip coffee and gaze out at the lifeless harbour.

Driving away from the beach and the resort area sprouted up around it, Maxine feels a sense of relief. At least the village centre, a few miles away, is inhabited – with real people, living real, year-round existences. And the town. The blackened cathedral, the half-hourly bells in the belltower, the bustling high street, the Thursday morning market, the *boulangeries* on every corner, the shabby cafés, the fountains dried up in winter. The seemingly indestructible stones of lava from the long defunct volcano that have been piled up to build this town, this town which has withstood the centuries on the bank of a dwindling river at the mouth of the Mediterranean. All of these elements conspire to give the place an air of permanence that Maxine craves for herself but can't feel. It's no Miami but at least it's not London. It would do.

Over the past two weeks, since Maxine arrived early and unannounced, they've developed a routine. They rise early each morning and pull on second-hand clothes and tattered overalls. After bowls of tea and fresh croissants, plus some paracetamol for Maxine, Bernard reviews the list of household objectives he brought down from London. From this he gleans a shorter list of daily objectives and then doles out the tasks between them. Maxine has never been a dab hand with DIY before but Bernard tells her what to do, shows her how and then leaves her to get on with it. Under his guidance, she has sanded and varnished the banister, assembled the futon and the Ikea bunk-beds where the kids will sleep, washed and painted a whole floorful of windowpanes and sills, and scraped the two flights of lava stone steps – back-breaking work that destroyed two wire brushes, all of the bristles having shedded, and left her hunched and exhausted, with blisters on her fingers and the palms of her hands.

A few minutes before noon, Bernard darts out to the *boulangerie* around the corner before it closes. If they lose track of the time, they can go without lunch until after 3 p.m. Sometimes, Maxine accompanies him to the boulangerie. Bernard encourages her to order for herself; she points to the shelf of baguettes and then holds up a single finger to the cheerful woman behind the counter. If the woman tries to say something to her in French, Maxine gets flustered and jerks Bernard forward to answer.

They eat brief and quiet lunches of fresh bread and sharp French cheeses that smell like wet labradors, washed down by half-litres of local red wine that they purchase by the jug. Then they return to their chores for the afternoon – Maxine stopping regularly to sneak refills from the wine jug. At dusk, they take turns in the shower, failing to wash away the green paint and the plaster that speckles their hands and hides under their fingernails.

By dinner time, the end of the baguette is often stale and rock-solid, so Bernard ventures out to buy another before starting to cook. He's a good cook, enjoying the chopping of vegetables, the stirring and slowly melting mélange of sauces, the heat of the stove-top as he labours over it, and the topping up of wine. They eat another quiet meal, more slowly now, savouring the spices and the fresh ingredients. Maxine only nibbles at her food, leaving great helpings for Bernard to finish. If he can't, she swears she'll have the leftovers for lunch the next day but, more often than not, they're thrown away just before they become more foul-smelling than the cheese. As they eat their evening meal, they chat about the agenda for the following day. They don't like to discuss London or Bernard's family or the office. Or the past. Conversation is kept simple, manageable, immediate. It brackets their shared experience. The house. They congratulate themselves on their progress.

Bedtime is early as there will always be more – and more taxing – work ahead tomorrow. Sometimes they leave the windows open in order to air the rooms from the paint, varnish or other fumes. They pile duvets on top of them and wear socks, itchy long-johns and long-sleeved T-shirts to bed, as much to keep warm as to keep safe from random brushes of naked skin.

*

Tomorrow the routine they have so carefully marked out will end. Even today it's disintegrating – as evidenced by the break for the beach walk. Tomorrow Maxine will have to find a new routine of her own design.

For tonight, though, their short-lived existence together still lumbers on. They linger over dinner, the last supper, which Bernard has put special effort into. There are dripless candles flickering on the table, highlighting the wrinkles etched into his face, and the scraped clean, post-crêpe dessert plates in front of them both. Outside on the street – more of a pedestrianised alley that stretches all of five feet across to the facing row – the footsteps of people passing are amplified, their gabbling words and accents ricocheting back and forth between the ancient façades that rise up around them. Maxine is always afraid that if she, inside, can hear the voices and clattering noises on the street so clearly, then anyone outside must be able to hear everything she's doing or saying behind these closed doors. Bernard assures her it isn't so, but she doubts him. She's taken to whispering most things just in case someone might overhear and understand.

She waits for the outsiders to pass, their voices tapering off as the night's weather chases them around a corner. A wind is riding through town tonight. Bernard is not sure whether it's the westerly mistral or one of the other aptly named northerly gales that blow up off the Mediterranean. Whichever, it's gathering force, slamming shutters, rustling stray rubbish, sending plastic bags soaring past in sounds of whip-cracking frenzy. Tomorrow the wind will pluck Bernard up and pilot him away from her too.

'Have you booked your ferry crossing already?' she asks.

'Oh yes. I'll need to get an early start and make good time on the AutoRoute if I'm going to catch it.'

'You'd better set the alarm for early then.'

'Yes, good idea. Mustn't forget to do that.'

'Oh no, mustn't do that.' Maxine bites her lip to stop herself from cursing. Bernard thinks swear words are coarse.

The wind doesn't drown out the cries of the neighbourhood's pets, droves of semi-domesticated cats and dogs that roam the streets, whimpering for food, brawling with each other and rigging the pavement with minefields of excrement. A cat screeches shrilly outside, as if it's clawing at the wind. Maxine stands, walks over to the as yet unshuttered window and peers out into the darkness for the animal. But she can't see it through her own reflection. She returns to the table and begins to clear the dishes.

'Don't worry about that now,' Bernard tells her. 'I've got something for you, a few early Christmas presents.' He guides her back into her chair and then pulls some parcels out of the corner cupboard. 'I didn't have a chance to wrap them properly, I'm afraid,' he says as he places them in front of her, one cardboard box and a Waterstone's carrier bag.

In the bag, she finds two books – a French/English dictionary and a vocabulary primer which promises to teach anyone the language in 'three short months!' 'Oh great, thanks,' she tells him, smiling wanly. The box with its thick duct tape is not so easy to open. Bernard grabs a carving knife from the sideboard and slices through the seals, tearing back the flaps of the box until she is presented with a Linguaphone language tape set. She attempts another smile which she hopes will pass for gratitude.

'These'll help you get by,' Bernard announces. 'With just a few hours a day of studying, you'll be chatting like a native in no time.'

'Mmm-hmm. Great.'

'What's the matter? Don't you like the presents?'

'Yeah, I do. Of course I do. It was really thoughtful of

you. Thanks, Bernard.' She begins to stuff the remains of the box and packing paper into the carrier bag. 'It's just I've never been a very good student. I'm hopeless in fact. I doubt I'll ever be able to learn French.'

Maxine sets the bag on the floor. She's feeling woozy and thick with wine, like a sponge sunk to the bottom of a basin of sudsy water. The thought of Christmas makes her feel worse. A Christmas alone with nothing but tapes to keep her company – how pathetic is that? She focuses on the candle to try and clear her head, passes her finger slowly through the blue centre of the flame. With a sideways look, she follows Bernard's eyes, watching them watch her play with the fire. 'That's all there is to it,' she tells him.

'Maxine, dear, I'm just trying to help. That's all I've ever wanted to do, you must know that.' He props his elbows on the table and tepees his hands in front of him, a negotiating gesture she has seen him employ successfully in many business meetings. But Bernard isn't nearly so good at reading bedtime partners as he is at reading business ones. He hasn't had enough experience, not like Maxine. 'Anyone can learn, so can you. You *will* learn. If you want to.'

'Maybe I don't want to.'

'Maybe not. So what is it that you do want?'

She withdraws her hand from the flame and inspects the black resin it has left on her finger. 'I don't know.'

He sighs. 'You could have kept it, you know. If that's what you wanted.'

'No. I couldn't have a baby who wouldn't know its father.'

'What do you mean? It would have known me! You know that. I wouldn't have deserted you. I mean, I would have provided as much financial and emotional support as I could. Even Georgina would have understood that. Eventually. In any case, I would never have shirked my responsibilities to you or our child.'

Maxine cannot afford to correct him, she cannot afford to tell him what she really means.

The house, like the town, is permanent. Maxine loves it and takes comfort in claiming it as her home, no matter how *im*permanent her stay might turn out to be. It is by far the nicest home she's ever lived in. Certainly much nicer than the dilapidated structure she left behind in North London. She was glad to get away from there and not just for the fear of the walls crashing in around her. The look on Liz's face when Maxine informed her she was leaving! No notice, no warning. She left an indignant Liz and Rebecca behind to explain to the landlord and squabble over the bills still owing. No doubt Liz would've been straight on the phone to their ex-housemate Emmy in America, bitching about Maxine as soon as the front door had slammed shut behind her. Then she would have called those addle-brained neighbours in to mull over with her and Rebecca the shreds of gossip they could gather. Bonny and that cue-ball Joyce.

Maxine laughed mirthlessly when she pictured them, huddled together, gorging themselves with ice-cream, moaning about their men problems. Except for Joyce – not any more anyway. What a loose screw that one was. Crying over a man one day and then just disappeared. Pitched up two weeks later with a tanned skull – plenty of freckles but not a hair remaining – and a *girlfriend*. Some Goth hairdresser from Camden with the most ridiculous nickname yet – just a pronoun. *She?* Get real. But Joyce whisked her away gratis on a last-minute package holiday. Dormouse one day, lesbo the next. Very strange. Wonder how long that would last. Still, gay or straight, little Joyce was no better or worse than the rest of that bunch. Oh, those stupid women, with their idealistic philosophies on life and relationships and friends. She knew they'd never liked her and she didn't care either.

Maxine had no time for any of that. Friendship was a minor luxury that she could afford but didn't value. Friends never gave her orgasms. And she wasn't asking them to, thank you very much, Joyce.

Not that there were many orgasms with Bernard either. But he *was* male at least and rich and guilt-ridden and he gave her other things. Much better to get out of London, catch the train and follow Bernard down here as soon as possible. Winter in London was so depressing anyway. What was there to look forward to? January? All the crap weather of December without any of the parties. Not that Maxine had had many party invitations this unfestive season. Life had just become one big hangover. Bernard wasn't expecting her so early, but Maxine knew he wouldn't dare be anything but welcoming and hospitable. His conscience – such a convenience for her – would allow for nothing less.

She'd been impressed from the moment she first turned into the tiny rue Jules Ferry and laid her eyes on Bernard's house at number 26. Sure it was no Floridian beachside villa but it was still like some kind of mansion to Maxine. Three storeys, all carved out of huge chunks of the region's ancient volcanic rock, leaning precariously out over the narrow walkway, crowded in shoulder to shoulder by equally long-lived neighbours. Inside – despite the coating of dust, the sheets thrown over the furniture and the trail of Bernard's tools and paintbrushes – was also pleasing. Spacious, single-room floors with high ceilings and thick walls, and crammed with sturdy wooden furniture – most of which Bernard had designed and built himself in his spare time, as he proudly informed her – bright electric lighting and a fully mod-conned kitchen.

As they worked on the house together day by day, Maxine developed a greater love and appreciation for it. She didn't let on to Bernard of course, but she felt increasingly justified in staking her personal claim on the place. She and Bernard bought the paint for the walls, the new shower nozzle and tap for the bathroom, the wood to build a desk; they picked out the carpet for the lounge, measuring and laying it out together in a single afternoon. And though the shade and brand, as well as the arrangement of furniture in the room, right down to the choice of throw rugs and desk lamps, was dictated telephonically by Georgina, Maxine considered it her rug, her furniture, her room, her house. To do with as she pleased. During the many hours of painting and scrub-bing, she occupied herself imagining the minor, and sometimes major, adjustments she'd make as soon as Bernard left.

After all, why shouldn't she claim the home as her own as much as possible? She was certainly entitled. It wasn't a real home to Bernard, or Georgina or their two bratty daughters. It was only a holiday place, somewhere they came for a few weeks a year if they weren't vacationing in more exotic locales. And Georgina had surely never dedicated the same amount of time or back-breaking work that Maxine had to improve the place. No, Georgina obviously didn't care, nor did Bernard. Not really, not as much as Maxine did. Twenty-six rue Jules Ferry would be her home, her entire existence for as long as she could manage it. In her mind – and maybe in reality, once Bernard was gone – the door plaque would be etched not with the two digits of the address but with her name, in inch-high block letters, just like one of the labels she'd left behind in London with the rest of her life and unpaid bills.

In the bedroom – *their* bedroom – that last night, Bernard closes the windows and the inner shutters and tries to draw a bolt across the mistral. Though the fumes from the after-noon's final treatment of the stone steps still tickle the hairs

of their nostrils, the night has become too chilly and bois-
terous to be allowed in. The bolt, of course, does not block
out the worst of the night's gale-force screams or its nimble
fingers of cold which can pick through any lock, find any
chink of access into this old house.

There are plenty too. Gaps abound from the sloped floors,
splintered rafters and misaligned doors and window frames
as the house settles into the final moments of the twentieth
century. It's a beautiful house but easily penetrated by a cold
and unforgiving winter. This is a house and a town designed
to endure hot and passionate Mediterranean summers. The
building's thick, stone walls offer a gratifying shade from
the summer sun. But its medieval architects evidently forgot
the other eight months of the year; the same walls that keep
the heat out in summer, keep the cold in in winter. Most
days now it's colder inside than out and out is pretty damn
cold. Maxine finds it tolerable during the day when she's
engaged in one of her more energetic DIY chores. But once
she completes the task and the cold grips her body's film of
sweat, it can become unbearable. No such thing as central
heating in a sixteenth-century holiday home, as Bernard had
warned her. So she's taken to carrying a portable heater
around with her which she plugs in to one of a slew of
extension cords and alternately directs at the worst affected
body parts – her hands and feet.

Heaters flank the bedroom as well. Each night, half an
hour or so before they come to bed, Bernard switches the
heaters on to warm the room. But he switches them off again
with the lights, saying it's too dangerous to leave them running all night. (That's one of the first rules she intends to
overlook once he's gone. Better to end life a shish kebab
than a popsicle, so Maxine thinks.) Their motorised fans
chug to a standstill now as Bernard climbs into bed beside
her.

'Good night, love,' he says, rolling into a ball away from her.

'Good night, Bernard,' says Maxine but she doesn't really mean it. Not in the sense of 'good night, sleep tight' anyway. Not yet. A sour slime of toothpaste sticks to her teeth but she can still taste the fermented grape on her lips. She licks them greedily.

'Bernard?'

'Hmmh?'

'I think it's colder today.'

'The wind always makes it worse,' he yawns.

Maxine snuggles into his backside. 'You're warm though, Bernard. You must have good circulation. You're lucky. I've always had terrible circulation. Just terrible. My feet, God, they're like ice cubes. Honest, sometimes I can't even feel my big toe, not to mention my little ones. And my hands, my fingers, well, they're just like icicles. Sometimes I think they may break right off they're so cold.'

She tucks her left hand under his shirt and starts to caress his warm chest, combing through his springy, greying hair. He winces as though she's attacked him with a chilled pair of tweezers but she doesn't stop. It's just the metal of her Claddagh ring – much colder even than her skin – which stings him. So she tells herself. 'Feel how cold they are?'

'Maxine . . .'

'I'm sure I'm going to suffer horribly when I'm older because of my poor circulation. What's that disease old people get? Arthritis? I'll probably get that, probably any day now.'

'I don't think you'll have to worry about arthritis for a few more years yet. Besides it's in the joints, not the blood.'

'What?'

'Arthritis.'

'Oh. Well, I *do* get cold right down to my bones.'

'I don't think it's the same thing.'

'Awfully cold, Bernard. My hands especially. It sure does help to have you here to warm them.'

'Maxine, look . . .'

Her hand strays further and further south until she feels the tip of his hardened penis nudging against the flesh of her palm. 'My hand is all toasty warm now, Bernard, thanks to you. Maybe it can help warm you up, too,' she whispers as her hand slips beneath the waistband of his cotton long-johns and begins to fondle his erection.

'Maxine, no . . .'

'Sshhh, you don't need to say a word.'

'No, no, honey, please . . .'

She strokes him up and down with the lightest touch of her fingers and tickles the top of the penis where she knows it's most sensitive. This bit drives him wild. As if in agreement, he groans, deep and guttural, from the back of his throat. She knows she's got him now.

'No!' Or maybe not. Wrenching her hand out of his pants, Bernard swings round towards her, a look of fury on his face. But he checks himself before allowing his anger to form words. Her own, startled, young eyes stare back at him. Young eyes, young face, young, young body. And mind, that too. She doesn't know any better, he thinks. This is all his fault. His features grow slack again as they revert to their normal facial expression. 'Maxine, honey, I said no.'

She retracts her hand from his grip and cradles it in her other. Damn. 'You're not going to tell me you have a headache, are you?'

'Well, the fumes are rather fearsome.' He chuckles nervously; she doesn't smile. 'That was a joke.'

'Right, I get it.' A stray shaft of moonlight has wormed its way through the shutters. She holds her arm up into it for a squinty inspection and fingers the friction burn he's left on her wrist. 'You didn't have to be so rough, you know.'

'God, Maxine, I'm sorry. Did I hurt you?' She sniffs in reply. 'I didn't mean to hurt you, love. It just doesn't seem right. This is *our* bed, you know. Georgie's and mine. I can't sleep with another woman in our bed.'

'Let's go do it on the kitchen table then. Or maybe the bathtub. Or, better yet, how about the stone steps? I'm on top though.' Bernard frowns. 'That was a joke, too,' she says.

'Very funny. But, look Maxine, you know it's not just the bed or the table or wherever. We agreed, it had to stop. It was all a mistake.'

'Cheers, mate, so now I'm just a mistake to you.'

'Of course not, you're great, wonderful. You're a wonderful, vibrant young girl. Any man my age would be a fool not to see that. And I do see it. God, I can't stop seeing you sometimes, in my mind. And I'm not saying I haven't enjoyed our time together. Have I ever!' Bernard shakes his head woefully. 'But I'm married, Maxine, I'm a happily married man. I'm no good to you. No good. You deserve someone much better, younger, handsome, single. Everything I'm not.'

No kidding, thinks Maxine. But what she deserves and what she's stuck with are two different things. And what she's stuck with now is a man who won't shag her when she's gagging for it.

'I wish I could be those things for you, Maxine,' Bernard continues. 'I really do but I'm not getting any younger, I can't afford a facelift and I am never going to leave my wife.' He says that last bit with special emphasis like it's italicised or colour-coded, writ large in red, indelible ink: *I – am – never – going – to – leave – my – wife.*

And Maxine thinks, Who asked you to, you moron!

Maxine doesn't want to be a marriage-breaking home-wrecker, just a hedonistic bitch. All she really wants is a god-damn shag. She sighs.

'I thought you understood all that. You said you did and you said you didn't want . . .'

'I know what I said,' Maxine interrupts.

The room is silent for a few minutes as they both lie on their backs, stare into the murky recesses of the darkened rafters and wonder how they ever got themselves into this mess. Bernard is also worrying for his ex-lover's emotional stability and Maxine is assessing the possibilities of some-how forcing him to relent for just this one last night. The odds are not in her favour, she realises. But if not tonight, when and how is she ever going to get laid again? It's been weeks already.

'Maybe I'll take a French lover.' She tries to glimpse his reaction from the corner of her eye but his profile is bathed in shadow. 'Did you hear me, Bernard? I said I might take a French lover.'

'I heard you.'

'That would be perfect, wouldn't it? Kill two birds at once. They say that's the best way to learn a language, don't they?'

'Yes, people do say that.'

'So that's a bonus really. Learn the language and get a shag. Probably a damn good shag, too. French men are meant to be fantastic lovers. My new lover could probably make me orgasm just by blowing on me. Can you imagine? Orgasming, just like that.' Maxine snaps her fingers. 'I could cum every single night, every single minute if I wanted to with a lover like that. Wouldn't that be nice? I wonder, though, if I can even remember *how* to orgasm properly.' Maxine turns to look more fully at Bernard but he still shows no sign of reacting.

'Yup, nightly orgasms and language lessons. He could

teach me all sorts of things. How do you suppose you say 'Go down on me now, darling' in French?'

'I don't have the faintest idea.'

'Come on, Bernard. You're so good at languages. You must know. What would it be? "*Voulez-vous lickez-moi, s'il vous plait, mon amour?*"' Maxine suggests in a sitcom, French accent.

'That's enough, Maxine,' he warns. 'I really don't know. You'll have to ask your new lover.'

'Oh, I will, Bernard. Don't worry, I will.'

They fall silent again except for Maxine's exaggerated exhalations. Bernard stifles another yawn. He's tired, he wants to go to sleep. He's got a long drive ahead of him tomorrow. Georgie and the kids will be waiting for him, he's looking forward to seeing them. But he knows this isn't over yet. 'I want you to know, Maxine,' he ventures, 'I want you to know how sorry I am I got you into this. I accept full responsibility. You are a very, very beautiful and special person and I know that someday you'll meet someone who'll make you happy. It's just not me, sweetheart. And I am so sorry.'

Oh, for fuck's sake!

Once Bernard has turned his back to her for the last time, lying there as still and dead as a three-day-old corpse, Maxine at last abandons hope of achieving any hormonal satisfaction tonight. Bernard is a fool. A well-meaning fool but a fool nonetheless. A nubile young woman – okay, well, young in any case – in his bed, gagging for it. No strings attached, no promises required. And he goes to sleep, snuggling up to his precious guilt, curling protectively around visions of tomorrow: his family, his driving schedule, his escape. Leaving Maxine here on her own in a home and a bed that, in summer months, he shares with his wife and her innocence. No strings attached, no hope in hell.

Bernard is a fool; Bernard trusts her.

Maxine has never lied to him, of course. She just hasn't told him everything – about the others or the baby. On that bleary Monday morning when she delivered the news to him along with his morning post. Some invoices to sign, some calls to return, the quotation on the Hynes' rush job and, oh yes, Bernard, I'm pregnant. That was all she said, 'I'm pregnant'. And, as his startled coffee short-circuited his keyboard, he assumed things. Like paternity. And responsibility. Which, along with the blank cheque, leave with full pay and a holiday home, were both welcome and convenient for Maxine. Sugar daddy dipped in chocolate sauce, Maxine had thought at the time, with relief. None of the others even offered her an apology. Not even Frank who she thought might show a little compassion. But he'd gone cold turkey with her months earlier, he avoided her like the black death when her condition became a common secret. Rumour around the water-cooler – when it didn't concern Maxine – was that Frank had a new girlfriend, a *real* girlfriend or at least a serious plaything, although no one at the office had met her yet or seemed to know how he had. Frank was a write-off, as were the rest.

Bernard was the only one who'd smile at her afterwards without it seeming indecent. A sad smile, a kind word, a warm touch that, though hardly charged with passion, was human and unprompted. Bernard, her wise fool, her saviour, her boss, her room-mate. These few weeks in France with Bernard were the longest Maxine had ever spent with one man, the longest she'd ever shared a room or kitchen utensils with anyone. She didn't hate it, this cohabitation thing. Not every minute anyway. She didn't like it either.

Still, at least it guaranteed a male body, however foolish, in her bed every night. Even if he is no good for a shag, he's good to have around. What *is* she going to do in the morning when he wakes, packs away his final bundle of dirty under-wear, fresh socks and a spare toothbrush and leaves her? Here alone and linguistically challenged.

Bernard brays in his sleep and slumps further into his pillow. His back flickers at her like a neon billboard losing its juice. He's wearing a black T-shirt announcing the type of industry convention which would normally repel Maxine for its subject matter if it didn't attract her for its predominance of men *with* expense accounts and *without* wives. The T-shirt's white lettering is cracked and crumbling round the edges after too many washes and too much bleach but she can just make out the year – a year when she was still fan-tasising about Spandau Ballet, waiting for her period to spout and her boobs to sprout. Just think. Every year since the year which spawned this T-shirt, as Maxine had been stockpiling hormones and a sexual history, Bernard had been dutifully attending the same annual convention, collecting business cards, making contacts, keeping appointments, and wheeler-dealering throughout the day until turning in early after an overcooked hotel meal to telephone his wife, air-kiss his kids to bed and doze off while his peers got blind drunk in seedy lounge bars and offered barmaids tenners for blow jobs and gloriously meaningless sex.

Bernard was never the type to carry on like that. He would never forget to ring home when he was – legiti-mately – working late, never lie to his wife about anything, let alone cheat on her. Never. Unless. Unless he couldn't help it. Unless one night when the computer system had crashed and the rest of the office had gone home except for his trusty, and really quite pretty, assistant who was still beavering away into the night at his inept filing system. Unless it was pitch black and freezing out, even if it was meant to be spring. Unless his trusty assistant had acciden-tally left her coat, with her Tube pass in the pocket, at home and so he felt obliged to offer her a ride home and in the car, as he pulled up to her house which he couldn't see through an overgrown hedge, she had unexpectedly burst into tears, buckets of the things. Unless when he reached a hand out to comfort her, she had clung to him, so helpless and young and unprotected, she had clung to him and next thing he knew his nose was in her ear, his eyes staring out at the world through a veil of non-grey hair, his cheek soft and wet-hot with her tears. Unless as he tried to pull away his lips unexpectedly brushed hers and then lingered and then locked, his lips on her lips, his tongue on her tongue, his hand on her . . .

But Bernard was *not* that type. And later, after he'd sneaked out and phoned home from the extension in the hall and told his Georgie that he was just working late, problems with this damn new operating system again, this blasted Windows thing, and after he'd hung up, he shuddered and he vowed never again, never again. Never. And he had meant it too. Unless . . .

It's late now, Maxine knows that. Bernard is already gone, for all intents and purposes. The sheets between them have grown cold. She prods him in his sleep for momentary reassurance, to warm herself with even the smallest fingerprint of fellow body heat. And he flinches, violently, as if even in his sleep he knows it's her. Whimpering, he curls up tighter, closing his body against Maxine and her unwelcome advances. A foolish, guilty old man.

Would it ease his guilt at all to know the truth? That he was the innocent here, the real victim, the seductee not the seducer? What would he think if he knew that the computer system had gone down that day because she'd pulled the plug on the server after intercepting a nasty e-mail the boys in production had been circulating about her? What would he think if he knew that she'd had her coat, and her Tube pass, all along but had hidden them under her desk? Or that tears for her were things that could be turned on and off as easily as a sprinkler system? Perhaps he'd feel better, but Maxine will never know because she'll never tell him any of those things.

Bernard's guilt and self-forgiveness is another luxury, like friendship, that holds no allure for her. And besides, the truth was she hasn't ever lied, not about the big things. She didn't need to. Though she'd never planned on telling Bernard that he was the father, she knew how he'd react at the mere possibility. She suspected anyway and was glad to be proved right. But even she didn't expect him to offer her a home, a much craved-for get-away. She was still more sur-prised when she saw the place, this place, with all its hints of Georgina and Bernard's family life. And so many nooks and crannies, so many places for Maxine to make her mark, so many ways to accidentally leave a clue for an unsuspecting wife. So easy for Maxine, so difficult for trusting Bernard to even comprehend.

Once, back in London, over dinner in a swank restaurant, she'd asked him why he trusted her. It was soon after the abortion, and Bernard had taken her out to console her. In an attempt at false frivolity, he'd ordered champagne and a sticky toffee dessert. The champagne gave him hiccups and she didn't touch the pudding, but he pretended not to notice. He showed her photos of 26 rue Jules Ferry and told her about its history, told her she'd be safe there, told her she'd be happy. Maxine looked at the photos with curiosity. He'd wisely removed any from the stack that included family members but he couldn't expunge their debris, the *feel* of family that infused every scene. A stray Barbie doll here, a half-eaten apple there, an open colouring book strewn with broken crayons, a plastic shovel and pail still crusted with sand, a decidedly feminine, middle-aged, middle-class sun hat flopped possessively over a chair. Maxine saw these things in this place and tried to see herself there as well. A place for everything and everything in its place? What would she be doing? Fingerprinting the shot of the straight-backed chair and floppy sun hat, she looked Bernard straight in the eye and asked, 'Why do you trust me, Bernard?'

It was more a statement than a question. A warning. But Bernard didn't hear it, not for what it really was. Or if he did, he pretended not to notice that either, like he didn't notice her aversion to food and friends, her love of wine, her unusual office camaraderie. This foolish man simply replied, 'Why' hiccup, 'shouldn't I?' Hiccup, hiccup.

Maxine lays her hand on her belly where a baby might have grown. The skin there is soft, much too fleshy and not quite as warm as Bernard's chest. But there is no kicking, no heartbeat, only a grumbling. It's been hours since dinner, hours since all the heaters were turned off, hours since Bernard rolled over, hours that she's been lying here thinking unkind thoughts, hours that seem like days. Her stomach emits one, sudden, belching sound. She's hungry, hungry, hungry. For? Food will have to do.

Dragging Bernard's bathrobe behind her, yet another layer against the winter, she plods down the newly treated, still eye-stinging stone steps. Usually the ground-level kitchen is the warmest room in the house. But now, though the scent of Bernard's sausage goulash remains, the heat that he and the oven generated in cooking it does not. Maxine picks up one of the portable heaters from under the table, switches it on to full blast and points it at her stiff and reddened fingers. After a moment of balling and releasing fists in the stream of hot air, her hands are returning to a normal colour and func-tioning. She carries the heater with her, now directing it down towards her feet, as she rummages through the cabinets for something to quiet her stomach.

Bernard went to the *supermarché* just yesterday. He knew that Maxine was terrified of not being able to do the shopping without him. So he'd stocked up – lots of tins and other foods with long shelf lives. Even a Christmas ham for one. All hers. It's a sight that makes her desperate to run out and find a magic marker and some Sellotape. But there's no need. After tomorrow she's the only one who'll ever see it. She'd still have to get her baguettes, Bernard told her, which she could just manage – plus any fruit or cheese or other perishables that ran out. Those would be more of a challenge. And, of course, sooner or later, the cupboards would run bare and she'd have to brave a trip to the *supermarché* on her own. Either that or catch the next train home at that point. Why worry about it now? It wouldn't happen for a while, she didn't eat much anyway and she'd rather starve herself than have to make a decision like that.

Even now, thinking about it and scanning the rows of neatly stacked tins and boxes, Maxine's hunger pangs are abating. She closes the cupboard doors and reaches instead for a glass and the jug of wine which she carries with her to the table. Within seconds, she fills and empties the glass, the wine watering the smallest kernel of warmth in her belly. Warm! But not warm enough. She props the heater up in front of her and points it straight into her face. Closing her eyes, she lets the heat blast her like the fiery breath of an angry god. Her cheeks begin to prick, the skin tightening across her cheekbones. She opens her mouth to swallow the heat. Every drop of saliva and wine evaporates; her tongue goes dry, dry as a desert storm, and the back of her throat starts to burn. For as long as she can stand it, she holds herself there. Hold it, hold it, take it, take all the heat. And when she can't take it any longer, not one second more, she falls back into the chair, gagging. Her mouth and nose, every sinus passage feels scalded, every hint of moisture gone. She can't breathe, she can't swallow. And her skin, her skin feels as tight and drawn as an over-inflated balloon. Maxine is about to pop.

She kneels on the cold stone floor, pulls the wine jug flush with the edge of the table and twists the valve open. Wine pours from the plastic spigot into her open mouth. It pours and pours and pours, passing like waves straight down her open throat; it rises up into her nose and pours out through her flared nostrils. When the wine touches her baked-balloon skin, it sizzles. She can hear it, *sssssiizzzzzzle*. She spins her head around under the open spigot, the wine splashing, sizzling, all over her face; her parched pores drinking it up as greedily as her mouth. More wine, more wine. Until her hair and night-shirt are drenched and she is kneeling in a puddle of wine that stretches half-way across the room. Good God, the jug is almost empty. Whoops. She laughs – then hurriedly cups her mouth. Can anybody hear her? She pricks her ears streetward but there are no human sounds to be heard. Even the cat is quiet now. She and the wind must be the only ones still up at this hour. And even the wind is tiring itself out, its howls growing weak and whining as a child. It's much too tired to listen to her. Licking her grape-stained fingers, Maxine laughs again, louder this time. She's always hated wasting good wine.

Thankfully there are many more jugs of the stuff, Bernard has made sure of that. She'll never run out of wine – well, not as long as she keeps stunts like this to a minimum. She's got Marks & Spencers mulled wine sachets tucked upstairs in her suitcase, to keep the drinking festive. And food? Well, food she can do without. She doesn't need to eat. She can cut back, conserve, abstain. Abstinence. Abstinence? This is not a word Maxine uses lightly.

Rubbing wine from her eyes, she scans the room for the dictionary and finds it, still in the Waterstone's bag, just outdistancing the flood. She flips to the back of the English section. S. Maxine will manage, she will get by, she always does. S–H. She will prove that she belongs in this place as much as anything and anyone. S–H–A. She will become as permanent as this town and this house or at least share a part of it. S–H–AAAA.

Damn, this dictionary's as useless as Bernard – not a single decent shag in it. Never mind, not to worry, Maxine tells herself as she flips forward to the Fs.

CHAPTER NINE

GETTING BACK

For a moment, you think the light in the window might be Liz. In fact, you're convinced of it. You've done it before – come barrelling around the corner from Kilburn High Road, shouldering into the wind that always seems to lurk there, squinting against a fine February drizzle that matches the fog settled on your brain from too many hours in the pub – and counted the windows wrong. Fourth floor, fifth from the left, that's where your flat starts and ends. But sometimes your eyes want to latch on to any peripheral light around that black hole – fourth from the left or maybe fifth from the bottom – and decide that it's Liz. This time, though, you stop and count the windows carefully – one, two, three, four, five – yes – one, two, three, four, five. Yes! It is your window, it is your light, it must be her. Finally she's come back to you, come to see the 'place of our own' that she refused to live in.

You break into a gallop for the ex-council tower block. The lift never works so you head straight for the stairs and take them two at a time. In the stairwell, the air is pungent with stale piss and cat sick and day-old aerosol fumes from the spray-paint that's now scrawled itself across the walls in another layer of graffiti too obscene to stop and read. You trip on some stray rubbish – a broken Tonka truck, some smashed milk bottles – and make a mental note to clean them up, Ajax the whole bloody stairwell before Liz will have to set a single toe on a single step ever again. She's overcome all of this to see you in the first place, God bless her, but she's too good for it.

By the time you reach your own door, you're out of breath, out of breath because you're so out of shape. That's another thing you'll have to sort out, first thing tomorrow – sandblast the stairwell, bleach the whole building, spit-shine the entire square block radius (including the permanent population of pissed Paddies), join a gym, get fit, buy some cookable food, lace the bathroom with pine-shaped air fresheners, stop wallowing in self-pity at the pub every night, restart this life of yours, collectively yours, you and Liz. Now that she's back. You try to catch your breath, wish you had a mirror so you could check your hair and make sure your eyes aren't too bloodshot and that you don't have any peanut husks or other bits wedged in your teeth like a moron. No mirrors in the hallway though, only the con-crete cinder-blocks to absorb your wild-eyed expression. You rake a hand through your hair, wipe the sweat from your brow and sniff your armpits. The smell's not too bad but sweat rings are visible on your cotton shirt – you'd better leave your jacket on until after you've hugged her. Hugged her so hard and long that the impression of her body will be stamped for ever on yours. So you'll never lose her again.

Just as you're starting to get your panting under control – deep breath, calm thoughts – your inside coat pocket leaps into life and your mobile phone lets rip with a shrill, heart-stopping *bbbrrrriiiiinnnggg*. Frantically, you fleece your chest trying to locate the phone and shut the damn thing up.

'Hello!' you hiss into the receiver. In the background you can hear music and many voices and then just the one voice, Edward's, screaming into your ear. 'Alex, Alex, are you there? Can you hear me?'

'Yes.'

'What? Are you there?'

'Yes, yes, yes,' you assure him, your voice now bouncing along the corridor like an errant marble.

'Alex, listen to this one, it'll just slay you.'

'I can't talk right now, Edward.'

'No need to talk, mate. Just listen. You'll thank me, I swear.'

'Ed . . .'

'Okay, so why do women have tits?' Edward is chortling hysterically before he can even get the question out. 'Are you there, Alex? Do you know, do you know why women have tits?'

'Shit, Edward, I don't know. Just tell me and let's get this over with.'

'Okay, I'll tell you, are you sitting down?'

'Yes,' you white-lie impatiently.

'So men'll talk to them!' Edward screams before erupting into another bout of laughter.

'Great, hilarious, thanks, man. Gotta go now. Catch you tomorrow. Oh, and Ed, don't call back.' As you punch the call to an end, you can hear Edward asking if you've scored. You turn the phone off to ensure he won't call again to check. What a prat to delay your reunion like this.

You turn back to the door and fumble with your keyring. Your hands are shaking badly and the keys are all wrong, wrong shape, wrong order. They won't fit into the lock. Is this the wrong door? Why is it taking so long? Ahh, but then, the right key slips into place, smooth and perfect it glides into the lock like a knife slicing through butter softened in a microwave. The door opens and . . . it is dark. It is pitch black inside your flat now. How can this be? You stopped, you counted, you saw the light. You take half a step back into the corridor and check the number on your door. It is right.

She must have turned the lights off again when she heard you coming, you think. Who could have missed that little exchange with Edward the comedian? She must want to surprise you, she must be hiding. You will play along, you will act surprised. Nonchalant. This is just you, the happy, carefree bachelor coming home to your bachelor pad after a night on the razz with your mates. No big deal, remember that. Whistling, you edge into the flat. It won't take you long to find each other after all. It's only a tiny flat, the kitchen/living area and, off to one side, a box bedroom – barely big enough to fit a double futon and a wardrobe.

You don't switch the lights on immediately; in fact, you can't. The overhead bulb has blown and you haven't bothered to go to Sainsbury's to get a new one yet. (Mental note: you'll pick one up with the hamper of cookable food in the morning.) For now, you grope your way across the black hole, tossing your phone and keys on the coffee table which nearly fails in its mission to batter your shins. But not quite. Ouch! To your disappointment, that's your only major collision, no warm flesh leaps out to impede your progress to the window. You draw back the curtains. Light from the anaemic moon and the streetlamps trickles into the room. You turn, expecting to discover her – to your great surprise, of course – and discover . . . nothing – to your great surprise, in fact. The room is grey and empty and a right pigsty as well. Worse than usual even. But then, just there in the corner, framed by the entrance to the bedroom, you see her shadowy figure. She's been waiting for you in the bedroom. This *is* a surprise! Already, blood is racing to your groin at the thought of Liz, naked, in your arms. Oh, dear God. Thank you. As you step forward to embrace her, abandoning all semblance of nonchalance, all shred of devil-may-care dignity, you switch on the table lamp. Suddenly, the room is over-exposed, caught in a light that seems too bright to be possible.

And there, just there, in the corner, where your Liz is supposed to be – looking like Liz, smelling like Liz, sounding like Liz, waiting expectantly for you – just there, just now, it is not Liz at all. It's a man. A grizzled, greasy-haired man wearing a black coat, dirty jeans ripped above the left knee and a scowl. He's carrying a duffel bag from which several leads dangle, their plugs bobbing merrily, and through the bag's open zipper you can see a stack of your CDs – Shakespear's Sister right on top. Holy shit, you think, this man is a burglar, this man is robbing you. What fucking cheek! You're angry – until you hear the man speak.

'Stay right there,' the man growls and there is menace in that voice. Then you notice that his other hand, the one not holding the bag, is in his bulging coat pocket – and there is menace in that pocket. 'Don't move.' And you don't move.

'I'm going now,' says the man. 'Don't say a word and you won't get hurt.' And you don't say a word. Roughly, he brushes past you, not smelling or feeling like Liz at all. At the door, something catches his eye. He spins on his heel and you brace yourself, preparing for the worst. He approaches again and shoulders you as he leans down to snatch your mobile phone from the coffee table which doesn't even attempt an assault. As he exits at last, you lose your balance and crumple on to the floor. And you don't move.

You are no hero. Not for one second do you consider stopping the man or chasing after him or even glancing out the window to see if he leaps into a car whose license plate you can scribble down on the pad next to the only phone you have left in your possession. Instead, you remain on the floor like a bag of dirty socks, abandoned in this flat with all the other things not worth stealing. When you finally rouse yourself from your slump, your only motivation is the six-pack of Guinness in the fridge which you're hoping the thief has spared. It's your lucky day (ha!); he has. As you lean, shaking and weak, against the kitchen counter, you suck down two cans so quick and hard that you almost inhale the tabs. The stout settles like sediment in the pond of your stomach. You belch with remorse.

You should call the police. You should call them right now, you know that. It's the sensible thing to do. You shuffle towards the phone, lay your hand on its inert back and leave it there. It's an ugly, decrepit old phone, old enough to still have a rotary dial which has been spun so many times all the numbers and letters have spun right off. It came with the flat and has no doubt been around longer than you have, a veteran to successive generations of council cast-outs. This phone is probably more familiar with this situation than you are. How many frantic calls to the police has it listened in on, calls reporting burglaries, rapes, perhaps even murder in this decrepit, old building? You hate this building and this flat, you hate this bloody neighbourhood, but most of all you hate this phone, despise it with all your being. How dare you be left with this damned phone? Your hand is tired, it needs to rest. But it's finding no comfort; the plastic against your fingers feels hostile. The receiver has turned grey and bitter from so many years of so many hands making so many calls.

Gather strength, you must gather strength. Just do it. You pick up the receiver and raise it tentatively to your ear. The dial tone is loud, piercing your ear drum, screeching out its high-pitched monotone like a haunted house warning.

'Don't say a word and you won't get hurt. Don't say a word and you won't get hurt. *Don't say a word and you won't get hurt.*' Slam the phone down, slam it again and again. Then slam it some more until the receiver is splintered and your hands bruised and bloody from where your knuckles have grazed the dial. So much for calling the police.

After a quick recce of the flat, you sprawl out on your bed exhausted. It's worse than you thought. You never knew how much you had until it's gone. And now it is, all gone. The Guinness was just about the only thing the thief had spared you. That and your Spurs strip, flung desolately to the bottom of your wardrobe. Who else but you would want it with the season they're having, the worst in the club's history? You and your beloved Spurs are bottom of the league and facing relegation and you feel it for all it's worth. You feel like being stretchered off the field for good.

That thief. He must have come back half a dozen times or had the help of a small team to have cleaned you out so completely. It isn't just the obvious value things he's taken either. Sure, the telly and VCR are gone – you were a fucking idiot not to have taken out that Radio Rentals insurance policy, now you'd be double fucked for that loss – as well as your small but prized collection of videos – all the porn flicks, the Wicked Willy series, *The Name of the Rose* (Sean Connery was the man), *Blade Runner: The Director's Cut*, and even your home recording of the 1991 FA Cup Final (he'd probably just record over it, the bastard). And as you suspected, your hi-fi and all your CDs, amongst them several birthday, anniversary and Christmas presents from Liz and even the Sade's Greatest Hits album which was your favourite for making love to. Plus your Nikon camera, three rolls of film, the second-hand microwave your mum gave you as a housewarming present, your collection of beer festival pint glasses and the silver serving platter you inherited from your gran which mum assured you would come in handy one day. And the mobile phone of course. At least that's not technically yours – it belongs to the company. No doubt your manager will dock it from next month's pay cheque. Also gone are your guitar (you'd been meaning to take proper lessons for years now), your life-sized poster of Catherine Zeta-Jones (who looked a little bit like Liz if you wrinkled up your nose and closed one eye), your safety stash (two pre-rolled joints and another half an ounce), your favourite footie trainers, your steel-capped DMs (how you wish you had them now just so you could kick the shit out of someone, anyone), two pairs of Levi 501s, some wool jumpers, your pillows and even your bed linen. All gone.

And more, lot's more you are certain. Everywhere you look, emptiness stares back at you – from the hollowed-out drawers to the deserted cupboards, vacant wardrobe and shelves wiped bare of anything but lifeless dust particles. Empty, empty, empty.

As you calculate your losses, they mount and mount even higher, even greater, even further back than tonight and this one isolated robbery. It isn't the first time you've been robbed, not by a long shot. You cast your mind back, right back. There you were just a little boy, playing Thunderbirds with a bunch of other boys your age in the nursery. You went to the pottie and when you came back there was a bigger boy spread-eagle on the floor toying with your Captain Scarlet car. Wayne Westbrook was his name – he was big and stupid and wore his hair like a pudding basin and ate his own bogeys. He was throwing around your precious red car, roughly flapping its wings, firing your Captain Scarlet rockets with his filthy, phlegmy fingers. You decided not to say anything just yet, he was so much bigger than you after all. You kept your eye on him as you went to play with Lady Penelope's Rolls-Royce in the corner. But then, when playtime was over and everybody got up to leave, Wayne Westbrook wouldn't let go of your Captain Scarlet car.

You summoned all the nerve you could find, strode up to the big thug and said, 'Wayne, can I have my Captain Scarlet car back?'

And Wayne Westbrook said, 'What Captain Scarlet car?'

'The one you got there, Wayne, in your hand,' you said, pointing at the evidence.

'This?' Wayne asked and he held the car high above your head. 'This ain't your Captain Scarlet car. It's mine.' And plain as day, Wayne Westbrook waltzed out of there and you never saw that car or a single one of its rockets again.

When you were twelve, you lost your Glenn Hoddle auto-graphed football. Or as good as. You were watching TV when your little brother Jimmy and his friends sneaked it off for a kick-round. By the time you noticed it was missing and had tracked down the little sods, the ball was muddy and scarred and half of Glenn's signature was scraped clean away.

Over the years, you'd had other things nicked: a twenty-pound note just disappeared once; your whole wallet, complete with a fresh pack of condoms, another time; a filo-fax brimming with telephone numbers of all the girlfriends you never had (pre-Liz days); your leather motorcycle jacket swiped from the back of your chair while you were right there sitting in it; the radio from a rental car you'd hired to take Liz away for a romantic weekend in Cornwall (another instance where you'd foolishly declined the appropriate insurance option); Spurs' chances of achieving footballing glory this season. All gone.

And then, the worst, the gravest loss of all and the most recent one, aside from tonight's. Liz herself. Because that's what her absence feels like to you, what it's felt like from the very beginning. Theft. It'd be a lie to say you never saw it coming. You did see it, in your worst dreams, the ones that woke you up in the middle of the night when you'd have to turn on the bedside lamp and gaze at her full on, touch her cheek and smell her hair just to make sure she was still there, still real. Sometimes she'd stir, half-wake from the glare of the light in her eyes and swat your hand away before rolling on to her other side. In the morning, you could tell yourself that it was just a dream, a silly nightmare that didn't mean anything. Worse was when you saw it in her face and her movements – the genial, enclosing gestures she would make in a group, gestures that had a way of sealing all of them together and pushing you out. Especially when she was with her girlfriends. Emmy and Joyce and even Rebecca, gorgeous though she may be. And most especially when she was with that batty Charlotte. With Charlotte, you faced a constant battle for Liz's love and attention.

That night, in front of the gaggle of girls, when you confronted Charlotte about her fake rape, when you watched her crumple into a wet, burbling mess, like tissue paper in the rain, you thought you'd won the battle. Liz's mouth dropped open as she watched her friend disintegrate. 'Is that true, Charlotte? Is it all a lie?' Liz asked in a disbelieving, sorrowful voice to which the only response Charlotte could manage was to run screaming from the room. You smiled and forced yourself to swallow a tut of self-righteousness. You had known all along. But then Liz turned on you and caught you grinning and your tut snagged in your throat, almost choked you – that's when you saw it clearest, in her eyes, clearer than ever, more frightening than your worst dreams. Hatred.

She never said it, of course, never admitted that she hated you. And she couldn't have really, not all the time, because you carried on for a while after that – you made plans and

211

willed her to play along. 'A place of our own' you told her. That would solve everything, you told yourself even though you feared, you knew, that no such place existed.

But even then, even with all the warning, even with all the unspoken doubts, when she left, it wasn't like she really left. You could almost have handled that but it wasn't that. It was so much worse. She'd been a victim just like you. And other people – like Charlotte, like those stupid girls, like all the dirty bastards who ever plied her with drinks and wanted to get down her pants – they had pulled Liz away from you. Stolen her. Almost like in those old, black-and-white Shirley Temple films your mum used to watch on Saturday mornings – the bandits broke in and kidnapped your beautiful, curly-headed girl. They left no notes, asked no ransom. She was just gone, gone as surely as your guitar and your pint glasses and your Captain Scarlet car which have joined her out there, somewhere that you aren't. And you can't call the police, can't send out a search party to find her, to get her back. She's gone. It's so unfair and so final.

You're crying now. First it is silent – quiet convulsions that shake your body – but soon you give in to it, succumb to the pain of this avalanche of losses. An avalanche of things you will never see or touch again. It overwhelms you. Oh, God Liz, why? Now you're blubbering worse than a baby whose bottle has been snatched away. Another loss, they start so early. You cry yourself to sleep in your stripped bed.

The next evening when you enter the Bird in the Bush after work, the air is already thick with smoke and alcohol-fuelled conviviality. The combination stings at your eyes and makes you rub them harshly with your knuckles which are just beginning to scab over. On nights like tonight, the atmosphere in here can be a bit cloying but it's one of the few constants you have left in your post-Liz existence, so you

stick with it, wear it like day-old underwear, feigning obliv-
iousness to how the rank and soiled cloth sticks to your
skin and rides up the crack in your buttocks.

Edward waves at you from a table in the corner. You wave
back but head for the bar first and place orders for you both.
Two pints of whatever's going. For what it's worth, Edward
is also a constant. An overblown, arrogant, comically-
challenged constant but a constant none the less. And
generally amiable. You've known Ed for ever but started
hanging out with him more when his ex-girlfriend Harriet,
another one of the bevy of heartless bitches, moved in with
Liz. He was chucked too, quite some time ago now, when
Harriet went gallivanting off to Notting Hill, literary fame and
fortune hot on her heels. Edward didn't seem much bothered
by her departure, he never really talks about it at all. But the
sheer fact that he shares this dreaded state of chuckdom
makes you feel affection for him – in almost equal measure to
the resentment you feel for his inability to be fazed by it. He
is also the only one amongst your dwindling circle of single
friends who seems to have nothing better to do with his time
and money than spend it with you every night in this loud,
substandard, off-the-beaten-City-track pub.

With minimum spillage except for the inevitable slop
down your left-hand cuff, you carry the pints and deposit
them on the sticky-topped table which Edward has been
lording over in wait for you. He's camped out with his briefcase and huge presence on the bench against the wall so you
scurry around for a spare seat. The only ones still going are
the foreshortened stools. You pull one up to the table and sit
down, feeling like a midget compared to King Edward. He
might have at least saved you a seat.

'So why did God create lesbians?' Edward shouts by way
of a greeting. It's another ritual, a constant that you could do
without. But Edward does love his bad jokes, the cruder the

better. In his flat, the only books are a *Best of Tasteless Jokes* collection, volumes one to God knows how many – and these are certainly bad enough. But the worst jokes have come since his company got hooked up to the Internet. Fashioning himself the Joke Czar, he's signed himself on to some bizarre mailing lists; people send him all sorts of shit which he then recycles and sends back out to a growing number of, often unwilling, 'subscribers'. Your only experience of this greater 'wired world' of the Internet is via Edward's comic commentary which, since you're not hooked up yourself, he feels necessary to deliver in person. 'So?' Edward repeats.

You shrug which is obviously not good enough. 'Come on, Al,' he says, 'make an effort.'

'Don't call me Al,' you reply to which Edward starts humming bars from the Paul Simon song that you detest.

'Okay, Al, I won't – as long as you can tell me why God created lesbians.'

An image of Liz's friend Joyce flickers before your eyes. She's the only lesbian person you've ever known, but she hardly seems typical. And the only possible reason you can think of for her existence is as a co-conspirator in the efforts to steal Liz away from you. Which hardly seems a very good reason at all – certainly not funny and certainly not the answer Edward's looking for. You decide it's best to co-operate – just. 'So you could tell stupid jokes about them?'

'No, not quite, but good try. Wanna try again?'

'No.'

He leans forward as if to whisper it to you in close quarters and then roars in your face, 'So feminists couldn't breed!'

You can't even muster a polite giggle for that one.

'Get it?!' Edward gasps, both hands holding his shaking belly lest it tries to make a run for it.

'No,' you say, 'it's shit.'

'So *feminists couldn't breed*,' Edward repeats as if you might have missed something.

'It's still shit.'

He sighs and changes tack. 'Well, speaking of excrement, Al, you look like day-old shit baked over.' A smug smile plays at his lips.

'Ta, mate.'

'Late night then?'

'You could say that.'

'What else could you say?'

'Not what you're thinking, Edward.'

'Really?' He studies your face before confirming that you're telling the truth. 'Damn, I thought for a minute you were making some progress.'

From his breast pocket, Edward produces a pack of Camels, pulls out a cigarette and tosses it into his mouth like popcorn with one hand as he simultaneously tosses the rest of the pack on to the table-top. He doesn't bother offering you any. Just as deftly, he magics a match, strikes it and lights up. 'So what did happen then? I tried calling you back on your mobile a few times but first it was dead and then some strange guy answered and then you just kept hanging up on me.' As he talks he puffs away, his lips multi-tasking with ease – sucking, blowing, talking. His spoken words mix seamlessly with the smoke and pub titter around you.

'It wasn't me,' you tell him.

'Who was it then?'

So you tell him that, too. You tell him just about every-thing that happened, glossing over the finer, more embarrassing details. When you look up from your now-emptied pint glass, you're startled by the sincere look of sympathy that bunches around Edward's eyes. 'God, Al – Alex,' he says, 'that really is the shits. All further drinks are on me tonight – and let's make sure there are plenty. You could do with a raging hangover tomorrow to take your mind off things.'

He nips quickly up to the bar and comes back twice, loaded down with pints which he lines up on the table in front of you next to a wad of bills and pile of loose change more than sufficient to ensure these will be the first of many rounds. 'I will get you pissed and happy if it's the last thing I do,' he promises as he slides back into his bench seat. 'So here's to the pissed.' He raises one of the glasses and waits until you do the same before imbibing heavily.

The happy is less forthcoming. You're warmed by Edward's concern, however, and his generosity in the beer department. You even manage to chuckle at a few of his jokes. But your mood can't be shifted and you don't really want it to. The scale of your burglary and the overall diabolical course of your life of late seems ample justification to indulge in some serious self-pity. Edward also appears willing to indulge your indulgence – up to a point. You just can't pass up the opportunity.

Concern lining his voice, he asks you for more particulars of the night and you recount the order of events more fully this time. Before you know it, round about the fifth pint, the embarrassing details are shooting out thick, fast and as unfiltered as a pack of Woodbines.

You're telling him how convinced you were that it was Liz, how you could almost smell her, almost feel her in your arms again. And that the most terrible thing about the entire night was not realising that a burglar was in your flat but realising that Liz wasn't. Wasn't and never would be. That revelation – after the few precious moments of hope that had gone before – had been like losing her all over again, you tell him. And you can't, *cannot* handle that. The loss is too great – intolerable the first time, unbearable the second.

Simply unbearable. This loss is beyond your realm of understanding, beyond your threshold of pain. Liz was the best thing that ever happened to you and you ruined it. You don't know how exactly but you did. It was all your fault. You'd been careless, hadn't been watching over her closely enough, hadn't protected her from the rest of the world. And now she's gone. Stolen away, you shriek. And you can't live without her.

You are slumped over your glass, your tears, snot, saliva and invective pouring into your beer. You are finished, utterly finished. Across the table, Edward is silent. He hasn't said much for a while and he must have smoked his last ciggie some time ago. He's twiddling with the empty packet on the table.

You look up at him hoping to find some solace in the face of a fellow chuckee. But the sympathy that you'd seized on earlier – was it moments or hours earlier? – has drained from his face. Bunched around his narrowed eyes now are impatience, frustration, end-of-tether annoyance even.

'Don't you think this has been going on long enough, Alex?'

'What?'

'What?!' he echoes in mock disbelief. '*This!* Whingeing, moaning, all of it.'

'Didn't you go through this with Harriet?'

'You know I didn't.'

'Don't you want to get her back?'

'Hell no. If I could, I might get back *at* her, but not *with* her. Never.'

'Don't you miss her, Edward, even a little bit?'

'No, Alex. Harriet was a fucking bitch. She just used people, all people, me included. Soon as something better came along – like a whopping big cheque for her fucking "liter-a-churr" – that was it. Goodbye Eddie baby.'

217

'She wasn't all that bad, was she?'

'You didn't know her like I did. Sure, she wasn't bad between the sheets and okay to look at. But hey, she's not even that good-looking any more. Did you see that column of hers in the newspaper? Did she look shit in that pic or what? I don't know what she's playing at.'

'Have you read the book yet?'

'Nahh. And I'm not going to. I don't have time for that chick shit. I always told her, if she wanted to stick at that writing thing, she needed to do a good action book or a bonking bonanza. Something like that, something people would bother reading. That's what really sells.'

You don't bother to point out the position of Harriet's book on the best-seller list. You stare into your beer. 'I guess you can't really compare Harriet to Liz,' you say. 'Liz is different, she's worth missing.'

Edward explodes. 'Even if I'd had Liz, even if I did miss her or want her back, I wouldn't carry on like this. It's ridiculous. You've been like this for months. I mean, come on. Enough! You've got to stop acting like such a wimp. Men just do not *do* this.'

'What?'

'*What* again! Are you thick? *This!* All this misery shit – men just don't do it.'

'But, but . . .' you stammer, desperate for him to understand.

'But nothing.' He crumples the empty Camel into a ball and flings it at you. It bounces harmlessly off your shoulder and on to the floor. 'Stop being such a, such a . . .' Edward throws his hands up in despair, his fingers working, grappling for the right word. 'Stop being such a fucking *victim*!'

You're startled. You stare at him, your mouth hanging open, drool gathering at the corner. With effort, you make your jaws come together, clench them together, try to stop

218

your lips from quivering. Look fierce, unfazed, manly. You can do it.

'Damn it,' Edward continues. 'I need a smoke and a shit. Be back in a minute.' Absentmindedly, he grabs at the reduced pile of coins on the table and charges off for the loo.

Once he's out of sight, you clutch at your shoulder as if you've been shot. Edward is right, of course. This has been going on too long. You've let yourself sink further and further until you doubt you can sink any more. It's worse now than when Liz first left in the autumn. Then you were just in shock, utter disbelief. You were sure you'd be back together by Christmas. You even bought her presents – a jewellery box and a mother-of-pearl hair clip – stolen too by that wretched thief because you never had the heart to return them. Things had slid further since the new year, accelerated by the simultaneous decline of Spurs who had lost every single game in seven. Even Valentine's Day had slithered past painfully, and you, who always said it was overly commercial hype, crying for the lack of a Valentine, your Valentine. Your Liz.

And now this. Edward's Camel projectile might just as well have been a bullet for the size of the wound it's ripped open. A victim?! Victim. What a horrible word. But that's how your best friend, if that's what Edward can be called, sees you. If you're honest, that's how you see yourself too. Victim. Certainly you feel like one. Victim of a cruel, fucked-up world. Just as certainly, you are sick of it. Sick of the victimisation, sick of the world. Sick of the losses and the pain, sick of the suffering at the hands of others, sick of the control these others seem to have over you. Sick of the *others*.

You're either a vic*tim* or a vic*tor*. (Not just *you*, that is, but anyone.) Didn't someone famous say that? Or did you read it on a bumper sticker? Either way, it has a ring of truth, a fact-of-life feel about it. So, most of your life you've been the former, but who says it's got to stay that way? If you can't beat 'em, join 'em and all that malarkey.

Edward's right, you think. Time to stop being such a nice-guy wimp. Time to get back some of your own. Time to dole out the losses rather than be on the receiving end for a change. Your lips are steady now, your jaw firm, determined. You square your shoulders and sit up straight and tall as the stool will allow. You *can* do it. Yes, you can, dammit. You drain the dregs of your final beer and replace the glass on the table with a thump so forthright that it makes the lonely coins Edward's left behind jump.

The money. Hmmmm . . . You examine it. While there's little loose change remaining, there are still a fair few notes. Swivelling your head, you make sure that no one's watching you, that Edward hasn't yet popped his head out of the gents. You count the money. Forty quid in total, one twenty, a ten and two fives. Without thinking twice, you trouser the twenty.

By the time Edward returns, last call has come and gone. Just as well, he says to your agreement. He's been pondering on the pot. 'Look, Alex, I'm sorry . . .'

'No need to apologise, Edward. You're in the right.'

His relief is obvious. 'Shit, I'm glad you finally see it that way. I was beginning to worry about you, mate.' Edward smiles now as he stuffs what's left of his money into his wallet. He doesn't bother to count it and probably won't even notice tomorrow that there's any missing. If he does, he'll most likely expect he was short-changed at the bar. So easy.

He laughs now and pats you on the shoulder as you both prepare to leave. 'Okay, Al, I've got another one for you. It's perfect. You ready?'

'Shoot.'

'Why can't you trust a woman?'

'I don't know, Edward. Why can't you trust a woman?'

You're out the door now, him heading off in one direction, you in the other. 'How can you trust something that bleeds for five days and doesn't die!' he screams over his shoulder. You can still hear his laughter as you round the corner.

The idea grows. At night, you gather strength from it. You gather strength as you lie in your stripped bed in your silent, empty flat and stare at the blank space on the wall where Catherine once lived. And you have dreams, weird dreams. Dreams where you're chasing after Wayne Westbrook who's speeding away in your Captain Scarlet car, Catherine in the passenger seat at his side. Dreams where you're chasing the greasy-haired burglar who's got the duffle bag across his back except rather than dangling leads its dangling Liz, her limbs jutting out every which way, her head bobbing around and she's calling to you and she's dropping a trail of CDs for you to follow. Dreams where they're all mixed together – Catherine, Liz, Wayne, Captain Scarlet, the burglar and sometimes even Glenn Hoddle. But in every dream, every single one, you're the one doing the chasing, always two steps behind. Then you wake up, shaking, and you think about the plan and it calms you, it gives you strength. That dream you, that is not you any more.

And as the idea and its attractiveness grows, so does the feasibility. You begin to watch people – your colleagues, your friends, acquaintances, people you pass on the street, bump into on the Tube during your daily commute, sit across from in pubs and restaurants. Everywhere. You watch them like a thief might – case them and their homes, their habits and their belongings. They are so careless, careless the way the old you, the old victim, might have been.

In the office, the secretaries leave their Diet Cokes and

salads in the communal fridge, unmarked, unhidden, a temptation for anyone with a growling stomach. During meetings and fag breaks, their handbags and briefcases and Walkmans are abandoned at their desks in plain view, along with all the little personal knick-knacks that cluster around their PCs and in-trays. Fair game. Even the boss never shuts his door when he's away. Anybody could walk into his office. Anybody.

In the pubs and clubs after work, groups of good-time girls and guys stream in, desperate to shake off the office doldrums. They peel off their coats and jackets, bags and umbrellas, consign them to a corner by the bench next to the table where they're sitting. As their numbers swamp the place, no one bothers sitting down any more. They head off in twos and threes to the bar for refills, bounce on to the dance floor once the DJs come on duty, slink into corners for drunken snogs, waddle to the loos to make room for more refills. And all night, no one casts so much as an eye in the direction of their belongings. The pile grows and grows, the tan raincoats and black overcoats and leather bags get mixed up. It will be a task picking through them at the end of the night but the good-time gang don't worry about that now. And they don't worry in the least about something going missing. Everyone's stuff is in the corner and everyone is close by so it must be safe, they think. Besides, they just can't be bothered being weighted down by so many *things* when the place is jam-packed and the music is pumping.

On the street and in other public places, bags hang loosely off shoulders or are set down, if only momentarily; pockets gape open; wallets and cheque books peek out; little kids and babies are left unattended for a pop-in to the corner store for a quart of milk; mobile phones are set on tables; shopping bags gather like lemmings and can't be told apart;

car doors are left unlocked, windows rolled down, stereos and glove compartments fully visible; and sometimes, a pair of sunglasses, a gold-plated pen, a diary, a leather glove, a scarf – anything – is dropped or accidentally left behind, remembered only later when it's too late and too difficult to retrace steps correctly.

In their homes, behind closed doors, people feel safe. But as you and your own burglar know, doors are thin; locks are flimsy; windows are left open all day; neighbours are oblivious and uninterested; and alarms, if existent, are just a screeching nuisance, barely tolerated.

And everywhere, everywhere that people gather, settle or pass through with their things, their precious and semi-precious belongings, there is always that point, if only for a split second, when a hand eases its grip, a head is turned or the eyelids blink. Attention is diverted.

Careless. So easy really. And their carelessness stokes your confidence.

Today you are not a victim. Today you are a Manchester United striker. Today you are a thief. It's a good day to be a thief too, you decide, when you tumble out of slumber and into the morning. Textbook winter grey with the omnipresent promise of rain, and a chill in the air that matches the temperature of your mood. You start off proceedings by stealing some time. Plugging your nose and gargling up excess mucus into the back of your throat, you call in to the office and cough sickness down the line to Lucy the receptionist. You despair for your lost productivity time, but Lucy clucks sympathetically and tells you to go back to bed, don't give it another thought.

It is the bed you don't give another thought to. Emboldened by the office ruse, you embark on your mission. Things do not go to plan, however. Of their own accord, they choose instead to go quickly downhill from here.

When you try to steal an apple from a high street fruit stall, you're chased across the pavement and into the traffic by a mad, Indian mullah. You only manage one vengeful bite before dropping the apple to bruise and burst beneath the wheels of the southbound bus you escape on. When you try to steal a ride on the Tube, you're caught by an inspector at your final Jubilee Line stop. He doesn't believe your confused patting-pocket-search-must-have-lost-ticket-I'm-innocent-honest-guv act for a second and slaps you with a ten pound fine on the spot. When you try to steal a *Private Eye* from W.H. Smith, your path and minuscule frame is blocked by a beefy security guard. He convinces you that you need much more than one magazine. You leave via the check-out, with half a dozen periodicals and a King James Bible (to assuage your guilt and learn the error of your ways, you assure him). When you try to steal 50p from the busking mime decked out like Elvis Presley, you're rewarded with several swift kicks in the shins courtesy of his Blue Suede shoes. He extracts a 'donation' of five pounds before he allows you to crawl away. (You don't dare ask what the point is of an Elvis-that-doesn't-sing busker.)

No, your life as a thief is definitely not progressing well. But then you spy your perfect prey. Or so you think. A granny with her shopping. About two feet shorter than you, hunched and slight of build, she'll be no threat to your prowess or, if need be, brute force. (At the thought of which, you flex your biceps just to make sure you still have some. You do, barely.) Being old, she'll also be senile and suffering from even more severe attention deficit than your normal victim. Ideal prey, ideal opportunity. There she is waiting forlornly at a wet bus stop (the rain has halted temporarily but puddles abound), her Tesco bags sitting unnoticed on the pavement at her feet as she fumbles in her bag for her OAP travel pass, a paisley-print umbrella dangling from her wrist and obstructing her rummage.

You sidle up to her and, pretending absorption in the bus schedule tacked to the post, inspect her bags. One appears to be filled with fruit, loo roll and rubber kitchen gloves; the other with an assortment of McVities' biscuits, Polygrip denture cream and other dental-care products. Hmmm, tough choice but you decide to go with the biscuits and Polygrip (might come in handy for caulking the bathtub after all?). Then, waiting for the right moment, waiting, waiting – can't wait too long, you can see the bus chugging into view down the road, just a few stops away – waiting, waiting . . . And then. Ah-ah-ah-chooooo! She sneezes, eyes blinking, body thrown even further forward than normal hunched position; you swoop, feel the plastic handle in your grasp and prepare – a mere millisecond of preparation, a pin-prick in time, trainers gripping macadam – to take flight when . . . Holy shit, who knew an old lady could move that fast? She spins on you, her liver-spotted claw shoots out, hooks the other side of the bag's plastic handle and yanks with a tenacity and strength that, like speed, you would have never credited her with. The paisley brolly baton-twirls round the wrist of her other hand until she grips the handle and thrusts it into your chest rapier-like. The blow is enough to wind you but you maintain your side of the carrier bag tug-of-war, more determined still that the McVities will be yours (and the Polygrip too, goddammit), that your first bite of this old biddy's Hobnobs will be the sweetest oat and chocolate concoction to ever grace your tastebuds. And then, she aims the umbrella lower and with her gnarled talon of a thumb, ejects it into your groin with deadly accuracy. Ballseye!

Gasping, you reel back. Your knees buckle, bringing you to the ground, as your hands relinquish the carrier bag and fly, too late, to protect your throbbing groin. The old witch delivers another brolly blow to the base of your spine which lays you out flat, your tongue licking the cigarette-butt-strewn pavement. 'Get a real job,' she screeches as her bus pulls up. She grabs her other bag of shopping and leaps balletically on to the back of the double-decker chariot. As the bus noses back out into the stream of traffic, you raise your head to see your perfect prey escaping, hanging from the rail, her brolly-clad arm held aloft in victory. 'Amateur!' she yells back, then lifts her chin and spits into the air. The gob arcs like a beauty and then goes long, zinging through the air gathering velocity, exhaust fumes and airborne bacteria until it lands, once again with astonishing accuracy, splat in your eye. The batty old bitch cheers and pumps her fist in the air at the scene of your humiliation.

At midday as you sit, dejected, in a West End café sipping Orangina and gnawing a crusty, tuna salad sarnie – *both* of which you actually had to pay full, tourist prices for – you are forced to re-evaluate your options. Aside from your initial blush of success – which, to be honest, fell more into the category of skiving than stealing – the morning has been an unmitigated, and expensive, disaster. You shudder now thinking about the parting look on the old woman's face, citrus-carbonated tuna regurgitating slightly into the back of your mouth. You gulp it down and cover your face with your hands. All you have to show for your morning of hard work and persistence is one mouthful of Granny Smith apple – and even that was too sour for your liking. A pathetic haul for a would-be crook if ever there was one. Yes, upon reflection, you must conclude that you have not been a grand success. You have decidedly non-stick fingers. Perhaps you just aren't cut out for thievery. Perhaps you aren't cut out to be a victor. Perhaps the victim/victor selection takes place before birth and, sorry folks, but the judges' decision is final. You were born a victim and there's just no messing with birthrights.

You're starting to feel sick for real now. Nausea rises again in your throat on a wave of Orangina. Fuck knows what kind of contagion landed with the harpy's spittle to infect your tear ducts. Whatever it was, it has made an impact. Ball bearings seem to have attached themselves to your eyes which have also developed a maddening itch that can't be scratched away and a permanent wetness around the rims. When you, none the less, raise your fingers in a futile attempt to wipe away the irritation, your lids feel as tender and swollen as engorged earthworms. Lucy's bed suggestion is definitely sounding more attractive to you now than when she uttered it this morning. That bed beckons; you must get back to its warm embrace with all possible haste.

You decamp the café and the remains of your lunch and walk blindly through the current spate of downpour – one promise the day has not reneged on – to Green Park Underground where you hop on to the first northbound Jubilee. The carriage is surprisingly full for an early, mid-week afternoon. The perennial smattering of tourists – predominantly American and loud – are dripping into their guidebooks and heartily declaring that they're not put off by a little rain. Aside from their excited chatter, the rest of the passengers are silent and glum; in all likelihood, a collection of dole-collectors, OAPs, skivers and other sorry sad fucks like yourself. Thankfully, the Americans disembark at Baker Street, shouting 'Elementary, my dear Watson' and 'Mind the Gap' in the most jovial, holiday voices imaginable, and leaving you and your fellow hometown losers to your fune-real gloom.

Only a few of your crowd get off with you at Kilburn. You've miscalculated as usual and are at the farthest end of the platform from the exit. The others haven't been so fool-ish and have legged it half-way down the stairs by the time the train has swished shut its doors and hurtled its remain-ing passengers to destinations even further north and scabbier than this one. You're left staggering along the deserted and blustery platform. Your eyesight has worsened, both eyes are heavy as grapefruit now and gushing citrus juices from all corners. Your face is wet and salty with tears. Posters and billboards swim past you in a peripheral blur as you muddle along, fearful of stumbling over the precipice and on to the rails. But then you see it, there on the red plas-tic smear of a bench, your very last chance of redemption.

You rub at your eyes again and, like a windshield after a flick of the wipers, revel in one brief moment of clarity. Without a doubt, there is a black bag sitting ownerless on the seat. You cast a glance up and down the platform, but there's no one in your dim sight. You take another specula-tive step towards the bag, stop and look up and down again. Definitely no one. No owner, no witness, no old biddies, no vigilante staff. Could this be as easy as it seems? It crosses your mind that the 'unattended bag' could contain an IRA bomb. Blown away to smithereens – a perfect end to a per-fect day? But you dismiss the idea. For you, unattended bags have only ever meant additional London Underground excuses for train delays rather than blood and body parts. Besides this is Kilburn.

Before allowing yourself to think of any more unsavoury possibilities, you snatch the bag and race down the stairs. Somehow, despite your half-blindness, you manage to make it all the way to the bottom, past the empty guard desk, past the *Big Issue* vendor and out of the station without once tripping or bumping into any walls or other living souls. At last your luck must be changing. You dart around the corner, away from the high street and the rain, and into the littered doorway of a long-gone-out-of-business dry cleaners. The territorial trappings of one of the area's street residents is in evidence – a blanket yellowed and damp with piss, a pair of gnawed trainers without laces, an empty bottle of El Dorado, several crushed cans of Tennant's Super and a stench that will soon bring your nausea back with a force – but you ignore the insalubrious surroundings in your anticipation.

You crouch, wiper-blade your eyes again and examine your prize. It's a woman's bag certainly, imitation black leather, of a C&A-type quality, splitting at the seams. And it's very full. You unzip its belly, and dump the contents out on to the ground between your knees. What a jumbled mess. Five kinds of lipsticks, some mascara, some blusher, and several other tubes and compacts of make-up you can't identify, a brush, a pen without a cap, an address book. You flip through the address book. It's overcrowded with names and numbers and birthdays scribbled in the margins, out of any semblance of alphabetical order. This is a girl with friends. Must be nice. A set of keys, a dangly earring without a back, a tampon, a condom, a one-day Travelcard, two letters. The letters are un-postmarked, new stamps in their right-hand corners. One is addressed to Nan in Hull, the other to a Billy in Chicago. Billy a boyfriend, a jilted lover, a cousin, a long-lost mate, a prison penpal? You'll find out soon enough. The flaps of the letters are sealed but there's ample room to slip your thumbnail in at the side. You drop them both on top of the address book and return to the spoils. A pack of Wrigley's gum, half a bag of Maltesers, two individual lint-covered Polos, lots of wadded-up wrappers and tissues, and finally, a wallet. Like the bag, the wallet is imitation leather, this time in a scaly, red snakeskin design. You unclip its change-purse at the side and shake out the loose coins, a few pounds bouncing with a heavy thud on to the pavement. Then you pull out the notes and fan them in your hand. A five, a ten, another five, and then with the final flick of the fan, a strip of photos.

They're the kind of 4-for-£2 photos found at photobooths in post offices and train stations and Blackpool Pleasure Beach. The kind where people feel compelled to strike the silliest poses possible in front of a synthetic baby-blue curtain for a backdrop. The kind that are popular with best friends and young-in-love couples. The kind that are cheap but cherished, for years to come. You and Liz had them done once. (She took them with her, probably threw them away. You would've kept them for ever.) The couple in these photos are mugging to the camera the same way you once did. She – who you assume is the owner of the bag – ruffles his hair in one, pokes horns behind his head in another, sticks her tongue out in the third. He – who you assume is her enamoured boyfriend (maybe Billy?) – tickles her chin, covers her eyes, licks her ear. And in the fourth and final shot, they are both in profile to the camera as they kiss. A kiss to end all kisses. A kiss that'll last for ever. Captured for ever on film, this single strip of film in your hand. He is fair-haired, she is dark. Like you, like Liz. And, like your long-lost Catherine Zeta-Jones, if you wrinkle up your nose and close one eye, you can just imagine . . . You try it now and are pleased to discover that it works even better with swollen eyes, through a veil of tears.

With your thumb, you caress the face of the girl in each of the four photos. So beautiful, so easy. Your innocent little bag girl who will pine for her photos and her phone numbers, maybe weep, who doesn't know who the hell you are, some joker, some loser, some thief who's stolen her bag and her memories. You worry for her, feel for her, sympathise and empathise, but not too much. You are anonymous to her, you are a victor and a victim too. You've got your own losses to worry about.

You place the photos in the pile with the address book and the letters. Then, with extreme care, you refill the wallet with the money, then refill the bag with the wallet and the make-up and the condom and the keys and the full menagerie of goods. You zip up the bag and dust it off, hug it to your chest for a second. Again, you glance up and down, but the rainswept street is as deserted as the Tube platform. It's only mid-afternoon but going on midnight. Darkness has fallen like a stone to knock the city out for good. Or at least for the night.

You arrange the bag next to the blanket and trainers and stuff the photos, address book and letters into your jacket pocket. There will be one happy bum in the Bird tonight. You smile at the thought but won't be there to witness it. Your bed is calling, your Lemsip is calling. You head for home, urging yourself along, praying that, for just this once, you won't be tempted to stop and count the windows.

CHAPTER TEN

THE HEADLINE READS . . .

DAILY MAIL, 19 MARCH 1994 – COPYCAT COLETTE CAUGHT!!
Harriet Tillings, author of the best-selling novel *Beware
the Dwarfs: A Single Girl's Diary*, has been accused of
plagiarism. An anonymous statement sent to this and
every other national newspaper alleges that her now
famous character Colette is intimately modelled on an
ex-flatmate of Miss Tillings, so intimately that the mystery woman may well have had a hand in scripting the
record-breaking book.

Sources confirm that Miss Tillings did in fact share a
flat at one time with a young woman named Charlotte
Mereville whose past bears an uncanny resemblance
to that of fictitious Colette. Miss Mereville was unavail-
able for comment at the time of going to press.

In the six months since *Beware the Dwarfs* was
released, it has become something of a publishing phenomenon. The single Colette struck a chord with
millions of single and lonely young women who iden-
tified with her hard knocks experience of men and
relationships. Her name has even entered the modern

lexicon – with the phrase 'quite Colette' signalling one's ill fortune with the opposite sex.

Bookshops across the country cannot keep the novel, now in its third edition, on their shelves and sales have now topped 100,000. The book has also spawned a regular newspaper column for Miss Tillings and a film is reported to be in the works. A bidding war for foreign rights is currently in the offing.

Beware the Dwarfs is credited with creating a new genre for women's fiction – dubbed 'single white and anxious female' (SWAF) – which many other female authors have now capitalised on. Recent additions to the SWAF category have included *Is That Your Bum or Do You Have a Balloon in Your Pants?*, *My Place or Yours*, *Mum Says I'm a Statistic Now*, *Shut Up and Kiss Me* and *Love: An Abuser's Guide*.

Psychotherapist Reginald Morrison, who famously analysed Colette for a BBC 'On the Couch' documentary and found her in need of therapy, thinks the genre captures the modern woman's malaise. 'Single young women are becoming more and more dissatisfied because their lives have not met up to their teenage expectations,' he says. 'Many women of a certain post-student age fall into this "Colette" category where they aren't married, they don't have children, their "careers" are faltering and they have never achieved the physical perfection that the fashion industry has been thrusting on them for time immemorial. Is it any wonder that major depression amongst twenty-something women has increased ten-fold in recent years?'

Miss Tillings declined comment.

Editor's note:
Get to the bottom of this one.

The reporter sees Harriet before she sees him. She has been waiting in the tea-room at the Ritz – her choice, his bill – for half an hour by the time he saunters in. Though the *maître d'* points Harriet out, the reporter does not go to her immediately. He watches her, waits, makes some notes.

She is short, much shorter than he expected, much smaller in stature than the size of her publicity might imply. Petite, but not quite because the term doesn't seem to fit her; it's too delicate, too frail-sounding for anything to do with Harriet Tillings. *Dwarflike*, the reporter writes in his ring-bound notebook.

She is wearing an expensive silk suit, designer label, understated in a shade of mauve. Tasteful but, like the term petite, it doesn't seem to fit her any more, it's too big, baggy, it hangs off her too thin body. *Recent weight loss – sudden*, the reporter notes. He gnaws the end of his pen for a beat and then adds, *Shrivelled? Emaciated? Look up synonym*.

She is positioned with a glass of champagne within reach of one hand and a china teapot, cup and saucer within reach of the other. She sips at the champagne and then the tea and then the champagne again. She crosses, uncrosses and recrosses her legs. The top leg bounces, her foot tapping the air in triple-time. She glances at her watch and creases of irritation deepen across her face – even though it is still five minutes before their scheduled appointment. *Impatient, nervous.*

Taking another sip of champagne, Harriet peers towards the entrance. Her vision is wide and then it narrows, zeroes in on him; he is in her sight now. She puts her glass down and stares at him, her lips set in a line ironed straight with suspicion. *Suspicious*, the reporter writes as he nods in greeting and begins to walk towards her.

She has red hair, cut in a short, blunt fashion that frames her face. Probably an attractive style once but now it draws

unflattering attention to her hollowed-out cheeks. *Gaunt.*
The make-up doesn't help either. Coming closer, he notices
her plum eyeliner smudged at the corners of her eyes, the red
lipstick that is bleeding ever so slightly round the rim of her
mouth, the powdered concealer smeared into the still apparent dark circles beneath her eyes. The concealer has left
streaks of chalky residue. *Make-up*, the reporter scribbles, not
missing a step as he closes in on the table, *inexpertly applied.*

He introduces himself, shakes Harriet's hand (*cold,
clammy grip but strong*) and slides into the seat across from
her. Before he can say another word, Harriet is off. 'I want
you to know that I am here under duress. My agent has
forced me to do this. Him and that brain-dead PR.'

The reporter swivels his head – the ubiquitous PR is
nowhere to be seen. 'What about the PR?' he asks.

'Absolutely useless!' Harriet declares though all he
wanted to know was where the girl was. He rephrases the
question.

'She's got the day off.' Harriet waves her hand as if this was
completely unreasonable, even though it is a Sunday. The
reporter wishes he was still in bed, in church, in traction,
anywhere but here with such an unwilling subject.

She is off again. 'I can see the headline now in screaming
block letters: "Plagiarist Confesses All!" Well, I'm afraid it's
not like that, I didn't plagiarise anything.' *Denial*, the
reporter scribbles.

'And, just for the record,' Harriet continues, 'the only
reason I've agreed to do this is with the understanding that
this is an unbiased, non-tabloid-titillation opportunity to
"set the record straight", as it were.'

The reporter nods and scribbles something (*deluded*) in
his pad. Harriet cranes her neck to try to see, but he has the
notebook expertly angled so that not even a contortionist
could eavesread. It's an uncomfortable position for writing,

gives him a cramp. One of these days he's going to learn shorthand so he won't have to be covering up all the time. 'Have you got that?' Harriet asks and the reporter nods again and makes a broad underlining sweep across the open page.

'So,' says Harriet, 'I do *not* want to talk about my childhood, my family or my private life. We are here to talk about *Beware the Dwarfs*. So let's try to stick to those parameters, all right?'

Sighing, the reporter pulls a micro-cassette recorder out of his pocket. Harriet cringes as if it were a gun. He places it on the table between them and she draws back in her chair.

'Are you happy for me to record this interview?' he asks. 'I certainly wouldn't want to misquote you.'

She sets her shoulders. 'No, that's right, of course not. Of course.'

She takes another swig of champagne, then tea, then champagne. He pushes the record button.

Q: Fine, well thank you for agreeing to the interview, Miss Tillings. May I call you, Harriet?

A: No, you may not. And it's *mizz*.

Q: Right, okay. Umm, why don't we start at the beginning. *Beware the Dwarfs* was somewhat of a surprise hit . . .

A: Not to me. What was so surprising about it anyway? What a ridiculous thing to say.

Q: Well, I mean, you were quite young. Were you prepared for such an early success?

A: It didn't seem too early to me, not early at all. I've been writing my whole life, you know – it was due me.

Q: Did you expect for it to become such a cult classic?

236

A: I'd hardly call it cult, for heaven's sake. Haven't you done your homework properly? It's been on the best-seller list for fifteen weeks now. I think that qualifies it for mainstream.

Q: And there have been several spin-offs: a regular column –

A: It's not a column, *per se*. It's a serialisation.

Q: Pardon me – a weekly serialisation in *The Times*, an audio-book version, a film script underway, bidding wars for American and European rights . . .

A: Yes, yes, all that. It's been very busy.

Q: Have you had any time to think about your next book?

A: Like I said, it's been a horrendously busy time in my life. I've got a lot on my mind at the moment, but of course I've thought about that. I've started working on something which is . . . You have actually raised a good point here. It's not easy after a first novel. You're creatively sapped, but you've got to come back and quickly. Particularly when you've signed a two-book deal, as I have. You're contractually bound to come back – bigger and better than the first time. Publish or perish and all that.

Q: So what will the follow-up book tackle?

A: What will it tackle?

Q: What themes, what subjects?

A: Oh well, it's going to be about . . . I mean, it is about. Well, it's very difficult to encapsulate just like that.

Q: Can't you give a hint?

A: No, no I can't really. That would be telling. And the whole thing is very hush-hush. I mean to say, the moment I even hint at what the next thing will be, a hundred other authors will be copying me. Just look at what's happened with *Beware the Dwarfs*. Suffice it to say that I am working on something. It will be wonderful, I can assure you. It will have the same kind of impact as *Dwarfs* has had. But I can't possibly talk about it. Not possibly.

Q: Did you expect *Beware the Dwarfs* to hit a chord with a whole generation of women as it has done?

A: It would be vain of me to suggest that I expected such a thing – and I am anything but vain. No, truthfully, I could not have anticipated that *Beware the Dwarfs* would have become such the phenomenon that it has. Having said that, I did have a very good feeling about it, especially once I'd shown it to my agent. He was extremely excited. He recognised the commercial and literary appeal of the thing. He knew we were on to something. No, we didn't realise that it would take off to quite the scale that it has, but yes, we knew we had a hit.

Q: And why do you think it appeals?

A: Why does any fiction appeal? It's got a great central character, it's well-written and it contains universal themes: disappointment, heartache, the differences between men and women. Oh, look, can we just get past these insipid questions and get to what you've really come here for?

Q: What do you suppose that is?

A: Don't patronise me. You're not dealing with that hapless PR, you know.

Q: Fine, you're right. We do need to address the plagiarism issue.

A: Yes, and . . .

Q: And, you have been accused of plagiarism –

A: By who, whom? Whom, I ask you? Anybody could have sent that rubbish to the newspapers. Anybody with a fax machine and some time to waste. Just because someone writes a letter doesn't make it true. Especially when they're not man enough to sign their name to it.

Q: So you think it was a man? Which man might that be?

A: Are you saying it's a man? Has Edward been in touch with you?

Q: Who's Edward?

A: What? Oh, never mind. Look, no, I didn't say it was a man. That's just an expression, as you very well know. I haven't a clue whether it's man, woman or child. There are plenty of people who could be jealous of the kind of success that *Beware the Dwarfs* has achieved. Plenty of people who would like to destroy it. Why don't you try asking some of those real Colette clones? All those other novelists trying to ride on my coat-tails. Not a man among them, I might add.

Q: But there are certain elements of truth to the statement. You did at one time live with a woman named Charlotte Mereville?

A: Yes, so?

Q: So, she does bear an uncanny resemblance to Colette?

A: How do you know that?

Q: So I'm told.

A: By whom? Have you spoken to Charlotte?

Q: No. Not yet.

A: Who – whom have you spoken to?

Q: I can't reveal my sources.

A: 'So I'm told, so I'm told.' What utter twaddle. Your sources. Hmpf! Nobody told you anything. You just gleaned that from that ridiculous statement. I don't know what's the matter with journalists these days. They can't seem to undertake any primary research to save their lives. It's all secondary bullshit. It wasn't like that in my journalist days –

Q: Now that was as, let me see if I can find it . . . oh yes, editorial assistant on *Fishing Digest*?

A: Oh, you know it, do you? Well, yes, that's correct. It's Britain's most respected fisherman's journal, as I'm sure you're aware. But that's hardly important to the article, now is it? And I don't like your tone.

Q: Let me put the question another way, Ms Tillings. Does Charlotte resemble Colette in any way?

A: Of course, she does. Charlotte was lonely, she wanted to be loved. Sometimes desperately so. She had that in common with Colette. It's like that quote – what is it? Oh yes, from Priestley's *An*

Inspector Calls. Did you see that at the National, by the way? Marvellous production. Well, Priestley says: 'The desire of women to live is a weakness. In another world it might be a strength, but not in the world we've made.' Anyway, what's so telling about that – two lonely women? It's hardly a remarkable coincidence to be lonely. I'm sure such a label could apply to a large percentage of women, and men as well. I know it does – why else do you suppose *Beware the Dwarfs* has been such a success? People identify with it.

Q: But you did begin working on the novel when you were living with Ms Mereville?

A: Yes, I did. Look, it wasn't just Charlotte who lived there. We had another friend, Liz – have you spoken to her? No, of course not – or so you say. Anyway, we had a friend Liz who was living with us, too. We were three young women. We sat around a lot, we talked about our problems, shared our griefs, lived our lives. There were plenty of stories. Some incredible stories.

And yes, I admit it. Charlotte in particular did have some horrendous luck with men. She wasn't a particularly pretty woman and she was a bit too forward – though I'd appreciate it if that was off the record. And she was incredibly insecure, she had no self-confidence whatsoever. So, yes, she wanted a boyfriend and she never got one – just like millions of other women. The difference with Charlotte was . . . the difference was that she talked about it incessantly, told the story, every story of every single fresh defeat in detail. She wouldn't shut up about this man or that man. I felt sorry for her, really terribly sorry. But, yes, again I admit it. Her stories did awaken in me inspirational rumblings, ideas for books to come. *Beware the Dwarfs* was the first product of this.

Q: So *Beware the Dwarfs* is in fact Ms Mereville's story, not your own creation?

A: I wouldn't say that. You're twisting my words. I would say that Charlotte's stories *inspired* me. *Beware the Dwarfs* is *based loosely* on some of Charlotte's experiences – and mine as well. What's so criminal about that? I challenge you to find me an author whose characters and stories aren't to some degree influenced by their own experiences and those of the people they're acquainted with. We have to write what we know, we have to write about the world around us. What else is there? All creativity and imagination has one foot in the real world. Unless, of course, one has the luxury of lunacy. But we're not all so lucky, and besides, even then, toes do dangle.

Q: You say you felt sorry for Ms Mereville, but you didn't have any qualms about exploiting her confidence so blatantly for your own ends?

A: I don't know what you mean. What did I exploit? We're talking about inspiration, not exploitation. A writer's greatest enemy is self-censorship, something I refuse to indulge in. I cannot prevent myself from writing what I know to be a good story. And I don't think even Charlotte would have wanted me to. She understood the nature of writers, she even supported me in my efforts. I think deep down she wanted to be a writer herself – doesn't everyone? – but she didn't have the courage or discipline to do so.

Q: Ms Mereville was an aspiring writer then?

A: That's not what I mean. Look, it's like that old saying that everyone has a book in them. That may indeed be so, but if they haven't got the wherewithal to dig it out, is it destined to go for ever unread? What a shame, I think, what a waste. No, better if someone else gives them a little help.

Q: So Ms Mereville was working on a book herself? Did she ever share any extracts with you?

A: Are you deaf or just being difficult? Asking the same question, again and again, a hundred different ways. It's ridiculous.

Q: I didn't realise I was repeating myself.

A: Let me make this clear. I do not mean that Charlotte was a writer, Charlotte never wrote anything – never, not that I saw. I just mean, I mean . . . Look, Charlotte Mereville was jealous of me. She would have liked to have been a writer. She would have liked to have been a lot of things. She was always jealous of me. She coveted my gift, my job, my boyfriend. Everything.

Q: You're saying that Ms Mereville had absolutely no hand in the writing of *Beware the Dwarfs*?

A: No . . . I mean yes. That's what I'm telling you, what I keep telling you. Of course she didn't have a hand in it. I . . . I have never plagiarised anything.

Q: Fine, of course. So why did your flat-sharing arrangement with Ms Mereville end?

A: Things end. She and Liz decided to go suburban – Hampstead Garden Suburb, that is. I don't know why they wanted to do such a thing, maybe they just wanted more shrubs in their lives. But I could appreciate it, I needed a change too. I could feel things starting to accelerate with the writing, I knew I was on the verge of something. I felt that as a serious writer I had to concentrate all my time and effort on being a writer. And that effort paid off. Soon, very soon, I signed on with my agent and then the advance came in. That allowed me to move into my own flat in Notting Hill. A much better neighbourhood for a writer really.

Q: And since then, you've been . . .?
A: I've been bloody getting on with my own life.

Q: This new book? Working on your own writing?
A: Yes, that's right, my own . . . I mean, no. What are you implying: 'my *own* writing'? I've been writing. Full stop.

Q: Have you been in touch with Ms Mereville since you went your separate ways?
A: No. No, I have not. She was a nice enough person, but neither of us tried very hard to keep in touch.

Q: And why was that?
A: For heaven's sake, stop trying to read into everything I say. We lost touch. People fall out of one's life. It happens. All the time, to everyone. It's the nature of modern society. Friends are for phases, not for life.

Q: Of course. And now you've moved on to another phase in your life?

A: Yes, absolutely. Now I am in my success phase.

Q: But don't the latest allegations threaten that success? I understand that your column – pardon me, your serialisation – has been pulled from *The Times* and that the film project has also stalled.

A: No, that's not exactly true. And even if it were, those are only temporary setbacks. Once all of this blows over, it will be plain sailing once again.

Q: And your publishers – Mercat, Millrose and Friedman – are supporting you?

A: Of course, they are. One hundred per cent. They think it's wonderful free publicity. *Dwarfs* is just flying off the shelves with all this gossip and drivel.

Q: Are you suggesting that it's all just a publicity stunt?

A: Don't be ludicrous. I would never wish this upon myself. I am just saying that there is a positive out-come – and my publishers are not giving up on me.

Q: But could publication of your second book – this masterpiece in the wings – be jeopardised?

A: I'm sure certain people would like to think so, but that is not going to happen.

Q: Would, in your opinion, Ms Mereville be one of those people? Do you think she might be behind this smear campaign – another show of jealousy?

A: I don't know, I really don't know. But obviously someone is jealous of what I've got now. Charlotte could not be ruled out. She wasn't a very nice person to be honest with you – I wouldn't put it past her.

Q: What if I were to tell you that Ms Mereville tried to commit suicide after the publication of your book?

A: What! I . . . I don't believe you. That's not true . . . it, it can't be true. Who told you such a thing?

Q: No, it's not true. But if it were, Ms Tillings. If it were, would that make a difference to you?

A: How can you lie about such a horrible thing? I don't know what you're suggesting. I really don't. I . . . I have done nothing, nothing at all wrong, nothing illegal. All my life, I have wanted to be a writer all . . . all my life. I've been writing since . . . since before I could remember. I know, I know without doubt the . . . the steeliness of my own conviction. I have written many stories, many books . . . it was overdue . . . it was due me . . .

Q: Ms Tillings, does the 'steeliness of your conviction' not include taking responsibility for the consequences of –

A: Self-censorship is . . . is the worst enemy. Look, I . . . I don't want to talk about this any more. I think we've definitely gone beyond the parameters of this interview. This was not . . . not at all . . . the angle which you agreed with my agent. You agreed to set the record straight –

Q: Which is precisely what I am trying to do.

A: . . . this is not what you agreed at all. I want you to switch that damn thing off. Off! I tell you.... I refuse, most adamantly refuse to answer any more questions . . .

Champagne, Earl Grey, interview finished. Author too?

CHAPTER ELEVEN

PRECISE MOMENTS

I'm just going to write it all down, just as it comes to me. I'll write so much to make Harriet proud, as if I cared for her pride – green with envy maybe, maybe even enough for a sequel. I've got a brand new notebook, a clutch of pens and all afternoon.

You see, I've always thought of life as a series of precise moments, definitive moments that punctuate your existence, that shape your future – this is one of them. In the past, my friends would dismiss my dogged attempts to prove this to them, to analyse their lives and mine and the overlap in between. 'Charlotte,' they might say, 'life is for living, not analysing.' They would say this in different ways, different words, different tones of voice, with different expressions on their faces, but the meaning was basically the same. And, depending on who was doing the saying, they would do other things as well – laugh (Rebecca), sniffle (Joyce), sermonise (Emmy), cheer (Bonny), worry (Liz) or imitate (Harriet – in her writing, that is). Still, I knew the truth and they did too if they stopped to really think about it and be honest with themselves. I'm not the only one who's had hardships after all.

This momentary precision take on life was comforting to me once, when I was a kid, when there were a finite number of the things and they were mostly good, when I kept them in a bag in my mind and only took them out every once in a while to blow on and polish and reminisce. I never realised then there could be so many precise moments or that such a high proportion of them could be so painful, and so potent that the longer you store them in your memory bag, the more painful they become every time you take them out for a buff and shine. I didn't realise that when I was eighteen anyway – about an Ice Age ago – but things have changed in these past few years. It seems that your twenties are chocker with just this type of painfully precise moment.

It's a strange decade, your twenties. To be fair, I think it should qualify as two decades. Your early twenties and your late twenties – but with more exact identifiers than that. In your first two decades of life you move through many distinct phases: infant, toddler, primary schooler, adolescent, teen, student. But then you hit twenty, and you're supposed to be an adult? Just like that? Suddenly life phases are measured on scales of time that you still have difficulty grasping, twenty and thirty years, *several* decades at a single pop – youth, middle age, retirement, death. But your twenties are the real pivot point, so many changes, so many significant moments jammed into a single ten-year stretch. And overall, the change in *you*, the result of all these little changes, is almost as dramatic as the metamorphosis of a child from 0 to 10 years. Certainly, you're nothing like the person you started out your twenties as.

At the moment, I'm only in my mid-twenties – I hit the half-way mark, twenty-five, in six weeks' time – and I can already see this. Today has made that clearer. Today has been one long, drawn-out moment that'll be stamped for ever, till death do us part, on my memory. It started this morning with the letter from Liz. That was jarring all by itself. It threw me into this haze that's just lifted, just a few minutes ago when . . . Well, what I've just witnessed . . . God, it was terrible, really truly awful. I'll have nightmares about it, maybe for ever. I will see that woman and . . . It was awful. But also – I hate to say it, I feel criminally guilty for saying it – but also, for me, there is an upside, it was a good thing. It has brought me here, to Trafalgar Square on this sunny, spring afternoon and it has brought me head to head with my past.

I've done my best to get away from it, my past. I've tried time and again. It's a flaw, I know, but if something bad happens, I just want to run away. The crises are often self-created, I know that too, but it doesn't make them any easier. And somehow, when I become most disgusted and disappointed with myself, I take it out on my friends. I tell myself they aren't real friends, they don't really care about me, they're too superficial, too pretentious, or not loyal enough, not nice enough, not fun enough – too much of all the wrong qualities, too little of all the right ones. I instantly tire of their company. If they were there, witnesses to my indiscretions, there's something wrong with *them* and I must get away from them. I must hide. It's like I blame them for allowing me to be who I am? I never saw it that way at the time, of course. But now, maybe I can admit, or at least consider, that that may be the reason. Whatever the reason, though, the reaction was the same – flee, hide.

London is a good place to hide. I've been in hiding for a year now. It's pretty easy to do really. I just moved east, to Mile End. I'm renting a room in a house owned by an old widow, Mrs Fairhazel. The house is okay, a bit of a time capsule, a throwback to the days of post-war rationing. Or what I imagine those days would've been like – doilies and lace, heavy oak furniture and fading black-and-white photographs, a 'wireless' in the kitchen and a permanent smell of boiled cabbage. The best thing about the place really is that it's cheap and I have my own room which is a decent size.

Mrs Fairhazel's okay too although she doesn't talk much, not to me anyway. On the odd occasion, I do hear her muttering to her late husband, who apparently was a keen gardener (his tools still sit, rusting, on the back patio), or one of the five cats which roam the entire house (with the exception of my room which I keep firmly shut against any long-haired, feline intrusions). From what I can gather, it seems she likes to keep them all, husband and pets, updated on the latest developments on the Archers.

Though she's not much for lively company where I'm concerned, I think Mrs Fairhazel means well towards me. She has these little wordless ways of showing me, like putting fresh towels out in the bathroom once a week, or saving me a slice of Sunday roast and half a Yorkshire pud which she wraps in clingfilm and puts on the second shelf in the fridge with my name on it. And some nights or late on a weekend afternoon, she'll knock shyly at my bedroom door and present me with a cup of steaming tea. I don't recall ever telling her how I like it but she seems to know instinctively – on the weak side with just a pinch of sugar. 'Okay, luv?' she'll mumble as she passes me the mug. If she hasn't woken me or interrupted something too urgent or embarrassing (I don't think we need to go into specifics, do we?), I'll nod and thank her or ask how she's faring as the tea warms my hands. 'Fine,' she'll say, nodding in return and clasping her own mugless hands in front of her nervously.

She pauses for a moment while neither of us can think of another question to ask, not a single thing to discuss. 'Fine, luv, fine,' she'll say in response again, before scuttling backwards out the door.

Like the house and the landlady, Mile End is a bit queer. It's like a filmset version of seedy London where you really do encounter bums that hurl abuse at you in cockney rhyming slang and shopkeepers straight out of *EastEnders*. Except grittier. And it's dirtier here than the rest of London, which is saying something for sure. Like when I blow my nose, the tissue turns black. Same thing when I swab my ears with a cotton bud. It's the grimiest ear wax you've ever seen. Not pleasant. Not pleasant to think what kind of pollution I might be ingesting through my other orifices either. And there are plenty more areas to avoid here – so it seems – than other parts of London. (At least the other parts I've been to.) One of the longest conversations Mrs Fairhazel and I ever had was when she mapped out for me in the A–Z the route I must walk to and from the Tube. It was rather a convoluted path but she assured me it was safest. She also advised only to use Mile End station even though Bethnal Green was slightly closer. 'You don't want to go there, luv,' she said, pointing to a grid of streets on the map. I asked her what was there and she shook her head furiously. 'Thieves,' she croaked, '*rapists!*' I blushed at the word and assured her I would most certainly not be going there.

I guess maybe I should feel scared by the roughness of my neighbourhood, sickened and weary of the crime and grime, but I don't really. I don't mind any of those risks as long as I'm safe from the other. *My past.* And I do feel safe there, my new home. Alone and totally cut off but safe in spite of it, because of it even. Just the way I wanted it.

I do panic sometimes – about my past catching up with

me. With good cause, too. Panic doesn't even begin to describe the time when Harriet's book (*Beware the Dwarfs*? Ugh!) first came out and then all that stuff more recently. But – and that's a very big but – aside from that and the phone calls from mum saying Liz's been asking after me, there haven't been many disturbances. Funny that so many of those people from my old life work in the City just a few streets away, but they've never been to Mile End. Most of them have never been further east than Liverpool Street Station. So there's little chance of meeting up in my local. At first, I worried about running into them on the Tube but there's not much chance of that either. We're always heading in opposite directions. Maybe our trains pass sometimes in the tunnel – like ships in the night, you know – Garret or Liz or Wendy, any of them, heading west for home, me heading east, or vice versa in the morning on our ways to work.

I quit my Square Mile job about the same time as I moved out of the house in Hampstead Garden Suburb. I left without working my notice, left so quickly that my workmate Wendy didn't have a chance to organise a leaving do or even a card. Now I'm working for a temping agency in the West End, just off the Strand – '*Tempo*rarities, our staff are like gold dust'. I don't temp myself, I work in the office: interviewing the girls, overseeing their keyboard and shorthand tests, placing them with clients. It's a lot like working in personnel (or should I say 'human resources', that's the proper term for it now), which was what I always wanted to do, you know, and I enjoy it for the most part. Some of the assignments are pretty good and I wish I could take them myself, sometimes they even turn into real jobs for the girls, and good-paying ones too. Other assignments are the worst though, and I know it beforehand. I wouldn't wish those kind of jobs on my worst . . . well, not even on Rebecca, not even on Harriet for that matter. Data entry work of the most mind-numbing kind in shitty, all-smoking offices in the middle of gangland nowhere (worse even than Mile End), overseen by a lary boss who wants you to work through the night, and staffed by a small team of bitter old has-beens and never-wases who just bitch about their low pay and long hours and the fact that there's no fish and chip take-away within walking distance. I feel kind of guilty sending the girls off to work in offices for people and in places I know they're going to hate. But if a client pays, we've got to find someone to do their shit. That's our business.

And I can't really complain because *my* job's okay – there's even been talk of becoming a branch manager. Some day. Wouldn't that be something?

Where I've been most at risk of running into my past is around the office. Not so much actually *at* work. Some of the girls did ask, when all those news stories came out, if I was the same Charlotte Mereville, but I just denied it and they let it go. And I can't see Liz or Rebecca showing up for a temping job although, if Harriet's been hit by this plagiarism thing as hard as the papers say, there's no telling with her. Still, really I'm most at risk *after* work. Sometimes, once we lock up the shop, if I go out for a quick drink with one of my co-workers or maybe to a play or to run an errand up on Oxford Street, sometimes then I do think, well, there's always the possibility, isn't there? Sure, squillions of people traipse through the West End every day, even more in the evenings, but within those squillions will be a few I know.

A few months ago, one Friday night after work, my fears were realised. I ran into Louis – the Trader with the fiancée back home. At lunch-time, I'd picked up a half-price ticket for *The Mousetrap* (okay, yes, it's cheesy and it's been running for like forty years – but I haven't got round to seeing it yet. And there must be *some* reason why it's still going, right?) and was getting a quick bite to eat at McDonald's before heading to the theatre. It was crowded in the restaurant and tables were in short supply, but I'd got there early enough to secure a four-seater. I would have gladly taken a two-seater – I mean, what did I need with three extra chairs – but there weren't any available when I pulled up with my tray of McNuggets, large fries, two apple pies and a large Diet Coke. As the place filled up, some people started giving me dirty looks but I buried my nose in *Time Out* and pretended not to notice. So engrossed was I that I didn't in fact notice the trio of suits when they shuffled in and joined the queue. They didn't make the smallest dent on my consciousness until, that is, they drunkenly crashed into it – and my table at the same time.

'Anybody sitting here?' a male voice slurred above me.

I looked up to reply, half a McNugget jutting from my lips, when I realised who was doing the asking. In his perma-pinstripes and squiffy swagger, Louis looked the same as the last time I'd seen him, nearly a year before. As did his gorgeous mate Derek, Wendy's old (and maybe still current?) boyfriend, who lagged a few steps behind at the condiments carousel where he was arm-wrestling the over-full napkin dispenser.

I pushed the rest of the deep-fried poultry wodge into my mouth and swallowed it whole as I fumbled for something to say. 'Hello, how ya doin'?' perhaps. 'Long time no see?' 'How was the honeymoon?' Or maybe just, 'Fuck no, get your sorry, lying tray off my nice, innocent table, you cheap, rotten wanker?'

'Well?' Louis asked again, impatient now. Which was when I twigged – he didn't know who the hell I was. He didn't *recognise* me. And though, all these months, recognition was the very thing I'd been hiding from, the fact that I should come face to face with my past, who I recognised all too well, and not be recognised myself! It was no relief whatsoever.

Why? Because I knew very well the truth. At this point, it would have been a comfort to think that it was all Louis' fault, his shortcoming – to believe that he was just a typical man, and as a typical man, I to him was one of so many passing flirtations, so many that he simply couldn't remember me from the masses of other female flesh. Sad comfort really, but better than the truth. For the truth was that I *was* barely recognisable from the girl he knew last year, and not just because I'd got older and wiser. The truth was I was now my own self-contained mass of female flesh. The truth was, the truth was, you see, that I'd got *fat*. Really fat, much fatter than I was before. There, I said it – wrote it, whatever.

I tried and tried, really and truly I did, I tried to diet and exercise, tried to lose weight or at least keep it off. But when I ran away that last time, from Liz and the girls, well, it was just too much. I wish I could be one of those women who lose their appetite when they get upset or depressed, who absent-mindedly 'forgets' to eat. At least, after the bastard leaves them, they may still cry themselves to sleep every night, but they'll look damn good when they see the prick again. With women like me – whose appetite, along with lots of junk to fill it, is about the only thing we *don't* lose during a depression – the best to hope for is that your fat will offer you a disguise in such situations.

Which was what I was praying for then, at that moment with Louis. And it seemed to be working. I coughed, shook my now bowed head and forced a husky 'no' from my mouth. Louis slid into the seat beside me, the sleeve of his jacket brushing mine, and his mystery friend slouched into the seat across from him. I didn't know this fellow, or at least didn't recognise him from my initial fleeting glance and didn't dare look at him more fully now. Neither of them bothered with anything like dinner conversation, just started ripping open their styrofoam burger boxes and tearing at the paper wrappers on their french fries. I looked at my own tray – two McNuggets, half my fries and both apple pies sat untouched and my stomach still grumbled for them to join their forebears. Should I wolf them down and then go? Should I just bin them and make an immediate break for it? Or maybe, given the speed with which the boys were wolfing down their food, the safest thing would be to shield myself with my magazine until they left to continue their boozing and then finish my meal at a leisurely pace?

A few seconds later, I realised I should've gone with option two while I still had the chance. It could've been such a smooth escape. But then Derek – who, judging by the substantial stack of napkins on his tray, had at last triumphed over the dispenser – arrived. No sooner had he sat down, dead opposite me, than his gaze settled and a spark of startled recognition lit his eyes. 'Charlotte?' he asked. 'Is that you?'

Resolutely, I stared down at my dinner, pretending not to hear, but I did hear – I heard the rustling of papers and processed food fall silent around me, I heard Louis' squeaky turning, turning, turning at my side, I heard his sharp intake of breath. And I felt my cheeks and all my chins – a Churchillian profile that Louis had a perfect view of – go red. I was acutely aware of this, as I was aware of the fact that I hadn't washed my hair that morning or applied any lipstick or powder since lunch-time. So there I was. Blotchy, greasy, unmade-up, *fat* and thoroughly by myself – dateless and friendless – scoffing junk food in McDonald's on a

Friday night. Caught. Could I pretend to be deaf or someone else – a Lithuanian maybe, someone who didn't speak or understand any English?

'Charlotte?' Louis parroted. 'Shit, it is you, isn't it?'

I tried to muster some dignity as I met his shocked stare. He looked at me like most people look at a bum on the street – or worse, a bum who they've just discovered used to be a famous multimillionaire. Like in that sequel to *Trading Places* where Don Ameche and that other old geezer brother of his wind up as winos. And not a hint of empathy, or sympathy or whatever the right word is, from Louis. Not a hint of feeling 'There but for the grace of God goeth me'. A woman might think that in such a situation. But a man, a man like Louis? Not a bit of it. Just 'Fuck, look what kind of ugly loser you turned out to be'. 'Yes,' I said. 'That's right. And you are?'

'Louis.'

'And Derek,' Derek piped in helpfully. 'Wendy's boyfriend.'

Well, that was one question answered anyway. 'Oh, right, yeah, I thought I recognised you.'

'Wendy was wondering what had happened to you, Charlotte.'

'Oh, well, not much,' I said, 'just felt it was time to switch jobs.'

I stared down at Louis' hands. They were covered with grease and Big Mac special sauces but didn't sport a single piece of jewellery – not an engagement ring or wedding band or even the shadow of one. So that was another question answered, I guess. I reached for my bag which was on the floor at my feet. 'Well, it was nice seeing you guys. I've got to run, though. I'm meeting some friends.'

'Don't you want the rest of your food?' the mystery bloke asked.

'Huh? This?' I gasped, waving away my dinner. 'Oh, no,

it's not mine, some mistake. They gave me too much, you see. Must've been somebody else's order. Anyway, I'm not that hungry really, couldn't eat another bite.' I would've patted my belly as confirmation except that would've just drawn more attention to it – not that it needed any help doing that. As I squeezed myself out of the plastic prison of immovable table and attached seat, I could actually see the thought bubbles popping up from their heads. 'Yeah, right,' Derek was thinking. 'That must be a first,' Louis was saying to himself. And his friend, who didn't know me from Cain, was already laying mental claim to my apple pies.

'I'll tell Wendy I saw you,' Derek called after me as Louis still goggled my bum in disbelief – mixed with relief that we never got involved, fiancée or not. And my own thought bubbles were screaming, 'Please don't, don't tell her what you saw, just forget you ever knew me. Please!'

Yes, that was an unquestionable nightmare. At least, at least, the one saving grace is that it happened pre-*Dwarf* days. Can you imagine what the thought bubbles would have looked like then, if they had read that stupid book? There wouldn't have even been any bubbles to decipher, just howls of laughter. Oh the shame – and Louis never even meant anything to me. I know that didn't come across very clearly in Harriet's depiction of the events in the book, but believe me, he didn't. Honest, I never even really fancied him. We only went on one official date – which cost me plenty. Now if, on the other hand, it had been Peter or, God forbid, Garret . . . well, that would've been something else. I cringe at the very thought – every single part of me cringes, from my hair to my knees to my very toe nails, we all cringe.

I mean, it's bad enough as it is. Because, though I haven't run into either of them yet, I see them all the time. Just like in that 80s pop song. You know the one – *Always Something*

There to Remind Me? Well, it's true, there is something, always, everywhere. The worst of course, the biggest reminder, was that infernal book. I didn't want to buy a copy of the wretched thing, but I couldn't help it. So I bought it, and I read it. And there they were, Peter and Garret, leaping off the pages at me, in my own words no less. Only their names had changed and none too cleverly either. Peter became Perry, Garret became Gerard. I mean, really. Couldn't she have at least picked another letter – there are twenty-six in the alphabet.

Anyway, if it's not the book, it's always something else. Usually just another bloke, a face in a crowd that's a similar shape, the same colour hair, the same cut, the same shoulders, the same height, the same jacket, the same shoes, or a gait that looks familiar. I can see a man walking towards me, he's still half-way down the street, but he struts like Peter and I'm sure it's Peter, so sure that I want to duck into a shop or run the other way or lace up a boxing glove. Or sometimes I hear a real plummy accent, or a sarky comment or someone who utters the word 'ebullient' and I turn and I do see Garret, for just a second. Or a man sucking a cigarette like a nipple, a bilingual dictionary, a song on the radio or a National Gallery print. They all holler Peter, Garret, Peter! Or places, places do it every time. Places we met, places we used to go to regularly, places we planned to go to, places I'd hoped we'd go to. Places I didn't even remember us going to.

Places are everywhere, of course, because everywhere is a place, *some*place. Does that make sense? I'm not even totally safe from those eerie kind of places in east London. The other day, for instance, I was walking my normal route to the Tube on my way to work in the morning. And suddenly, I looked up from the ground, and I noticed a small blue and white sign – a sign, a sight I passed twice a day, every day but had never really taken in until that second when the words leapt out at me – 'the best curry in all of London' it read. Could it be? Could it really be the same place? I glimpsed the inside of the restaurant and sure enough, there were the pink and white tablecloths and the full collection of Taj Mahal watercolours. I couldn't see the waiter with the cleft lip but, no doubt, he'd come on duty later. It *was* the same place, the exact same place Peter had taken me that last time we saw each other, that night when I hit him and almost caused a road accident.

I recognised it all in an instant even though it was day-time and had been night-time when we were there before. The one-pump petrol station on the corner, the kerb he parked his car next to, the spot where we'd crossed the street. And I could just about visualise the route he'd taken to get us there, where he lived and I lived in relation to right there. Everything fell into place – like clues, bits of evidence in a murder mystery. And I, the sleuthful detective, was returning to the crime. Except that I didn't feel sleuthful. I felt scared. I started to tremble, just like that night when he told me. I could see his lips moving, see him sipping at his beer, hear him telling me that he wanted to get it out in the open, that he *didn't mean to hurt my feelings*. A wave of nausea crashed over me and I wanted to excuse myself and run into that restaurant, run past the pre-laid, table-clothed tables, past the waiter whose face was slipping off, straight to the back and hide in the dinky loo, and just cry. Or vomit.

The next day I changed my route. Just slightly of course, not enough to take me into Mrs Fairhazel's no-go zone – let's not even say the r-a-p-e word – but enough to avoid that encounter again.

Which is what I try to do with any sight that will conjure up their faces. It's not a very successful strategy but I do do my best to avoid them – Peter and Garret. In the real world. Sometimes, though, in my dream world – where I am slim and svelte and detest jammy dodgers, McDonald's and Häagen-Dazs – I seek them out. I zero in on them in their homes and offices; waltz right up to their doors and rap loudly, confidently; bask in their startled, lustful gazes; shun their pathetic attempts to win me back; hush their begging; and confront them. The scripts change slightly depending on my mood, but a few lines are always there, often in my opening or closing. With Peter, I usually greet him with a swish of my perfectly formed hips and a dimpled smile (in reality, the only dimples I have are nowhere near my face) and smoulder, 'So, Petie, any luck finding perfection yet?' Then I take pleasure in throwing all of his worst chat-up lines back at him – which he laps up like a dog in heat – before I knee him. With Garret, the convo is kept to a min-imum. 'This is all your fault, you selfish, fucking tosser!' I scream before punching him over and over and over again. (There's a lot of needless – though quite enjoyable – violence in my dreams.)

Sometimes, I wake up with a smile on my face which I try to cling to even if my pillow is sodden with tears. And then I head for the kitchen for a late-night snack. Comfort food can be so very . . . well, comforting, you know.

Women are different. The women I've known, my friends and ex-friends, ex-flatmates, ex-colleagues. I don't really see their faces in the crowd. Maybe I'm not looking for them. And I don't have dreams about castrating them (for obvious reasons really). But I do think of them sometimes. Miss them even. Like when I want to go to the pub and share a few rounds with someone, I miss Wendy. When I want someone to lie to me and say I don't look fat, I think of Rebecca. When I want to be reassured that fat is not such a cross to bear anyway, I guiltily imagine Joyce (I mean, you can *lose* pounds right, but you can't *gain* hair very easily). When I'm watching an American sitcom and don't get the jokes, I wish Emmy was around to explain them to me (as long as she'd leave again in the commercial breaks). When I want someone to share my bag of crisps so I don't feel like such a glutton, I pine for Bonny (I definitely wouldn't be so knee-deep in Fatsville if she were around). I even think of Harriet sometimes – though I try not to. Sometimes I can't help it though. Like when I'm racking my brain trying to remember some stupid quote or other and who said it or when I have a question about fish (okay, it does happen occasionally).

And then lots of times, lots and *lots* of times, when I want someone to comfort me or laugh with me, gossip and confide, remember my birthday and even the anniversary of when I lost my virginity, hold my hand, give me a hug, pose for a photo, make me a cup of cocoa or one of a hundred other things that I just can't do on my own, I think of my best friend. I think of Liz. And I miss her terribly, honest I do.

I feel really guilty sometimes, just having dumped them all, Liz in particular. And especially when she keeps trying to call and write to me. When I got that letter of hers this morning . . . that just choked me up. But. Well, more on that later.

Harriet hasn't tried tracking me down. In fact, I'm sure she wishes I'd stay hidden. I knew, you know. At the end, anyway, I knew how she intended to use our journal. I just didn't think she'd have so much success with it. I was very glad I was hidden when that book came out. So glad no one I knew now knew me before. They would've recognised me for sure. Later, after the plagiarism story broke, several journalists managed to track me down. They kept calling and calling. One in particular, he even showed up on my doorstep. He asked me all sorts of things about Harriet. Oh, the trash I could've told him – well, you know. But I didn't. I didn't see the point. I mean, I don't blame her for what she did. She was obsessed with writing, hell-bent on being famous. I don't *blame* her for grabbing what she saw as an opportunity for making her dreams come true. I just hate her for it. No, I wasn't going to be a part of it, but I certainly didn't shed any tears when she got such a roasting. Yippee, I thought, this is an upside that was long in coming. But come it had, the shit finally hit the fan.

Serves her right.

Let's be honest, though. In spite of all this hiding, all this honorary EastEnder rubbish, I haven't really escaped them. Not my friends, not these men. I've *become* them. No, not in an *Invasion of the Body Snatchers* kind of way, but in much smaller, much subtler ways. Little parts of me becoming little parts of them. Like this, right now, this urge to write everything down – this is Harriet. And the other day, I looked in the mirror and realised I'd somehow grown Rebecca's hairstyle (though not blond and it doesn't look nearly as good on me). I've even developed her way of telling a story – that tilt of her head, that lilt in her voice. Now my tilt, my lilt. The other day at work, I noticed myself doing it, saw myself in the reflection of the agency window. I shuddered. And Liz's terry-cloth robe, in the exact shade of forest green – I picked that up from Selfridges (I mean, it did always look so comfy). Peter's taste in music, I've got that too. All those stupid tapes he made for me, the ones I took such care in destroying. I went out and bought them all up again. It took me for ever to figure out the song titles and the groups from the snatched lyrics I could recall (why don't people ever write these details down on home-made compilation tapes?) but I did it. Every time I listen to Richard Thompson I ache, but I do that too, I do it anyway.

It's scary really when I stop to think about it. It's like I'm a cookie-cutter cut out, a copy-cat by nature. Is anything really me or mine? Do other people do this, I wonder. They must do, mustn't they? Unintentionally, we all become one another. Phrases, turns of speech, laughs, mannerisms, ways of working and flirting, tastes in clothes and music and literature. Anything. We all must have got those little quirks from somewhere. I'm not sure whether this is comforting – that people never really leave us, that relationships never really end – or depressing. Probably the latter. What am I saying? Yesterday, anyway, it would have been the latter, *definitely* the latter.

Because I wanted these things, these relationships, these people to be over, for good, you know. I didn't want to become them or remember them or miss them, I wanted to forget them. Because all of them together, collectively, they *are* my past. And that's what I've been trying to get away from. That's what this is all about, right? What it's always been all about!

But I guess that's just the point. I'm so frigging stupid sometimes because of course it is. That's just *exactly* the point. I can never hide from my past, I can't escape from it because I'm fucking lugging it around with me everywhere I go. And it is really fucking heavy. How can I have such a heavy past at not-quite twenty-five? It's like the two stone I've gained over the past year, but even heavier than that. I'm weighed down by them both. At this rate, if I ever reach thirty, it'll crush me. At least that's what I thought yesterday.

But enough of all that, enough of it. I've written it down, got it out. It needed to be said and I feel better. But now I want to think about today. Because today, some terrible things happened. Today changed all of that, everything that's gone before.

It started with the letter from Liz. It arrived even before I left for work which in and of itself was unusual – the post never arrives before 9 a.m. ordinarily – but I didn't think much of it at the time. Mrs Fairhazel brought me the letter as I sat in the kitchen buttering my third piece of toast. She even smiled as she handed it to me, muttered 'Good morning' and then shuffled off to the pantry in search of cat food. Of course, I recognised the handwriting immediately. It's a penmanship I'd grown intimate with over many years – notes sneaked to each other in school, postcards sent from holidays, phone messages and shopping lists scattered around shared flats. The address written in Liz's hand was my parents' address but that had been crossed out and my own address scribbled next to it in my mother's handwriting. My mother had passed on other messages from Liz since we'd been out of touch, but mainly phone messages and none of those for a few months now. I'd begun to think Liz had given up. This was the first proper letter she'd written, the only written correspondence I'd received from her since last year's birthday card.

I hesitated in opening it. Maybe she was angry with me, maybe she was writing to tell me off, tell me what a stupid, selfish bitch I was. Even if she wasn't, did I really want to be reminded – again – about that whole period of my life? I buttered another piece of toast, slathered it with jam and devoured it before I felt ready. Then I read the letter. It wasn't very long and it started off innocently enough, real chatty in fact, kind of like a Christmas newsletter that you send to second cousins and distant school chums to bring them up to date with your life.

Emmy had finally gone back to the States, just in time for

classes, and was now about to graduate but wasn't sure yet whether she'd be able to come back here. She was hoping against hope that she could, and not just for her Brit friends and the London nightlife – there was a man involved (of course) but Emmy had never dished many details. Joyce and Bonny and Liz still met up sometimes for girls' nights – out more often than in these days, Emmy had introduced them to a very cool club for it – but the tone had changed somewhat after Joyce's big revelation. Revelation? Joyce, Liz wrote, had dumped Nick (good riddance), shaved her head (well, why delay the inevitable?), found a girlfriend who was also a hairdresser (does that mean what I think it does?) become a rally-organising, armband-wearing lesbian (guess so), quit her old job and got a new one with the RSPCA as an animal rights activist (say what?). She seemed all the better for it (well, good on her then); she and She (huh???) were very happy together.

Liz meanwhile had moved out of the dump in Hampstead Garden Suburb – losing her deposit in the process (typical Lurid). After Emmy went home and someone named Maxine – who Liz referred to interchangeably as 'the bitch' and 'the tart' – got knocked up and left, she and Rebecca couldn't stomach fighting with Slumlord Lurid any more. Rebecca? Yes, wrote Liz, Rebecca was back and she was 'ever so sorry'. 'Can't you find it in your heart to forgive her?' (hmmm . . . no! well, maybe . . . well, not yet anyway). After that, Liz decided to rent her own studio flat – she'd been promoted so could just about afford it. 'A Place Of My Own' she called it, in capital letters, just like that. She liked living on her own, she could get used to it.

Then, slipped in right at the end of a very long paragraph, the real shocker – she'd broken up with Alex. She said she didn't see him at all any more but heard through the grapevine that he wasn't doing so well. 'I know you always thought he was no good for me, Charlotte,' Liz wrote. 'I think now you were right.' I reread that bit. Now you may have expected me to feel happy about that, or relieved, but I didn't – even to my own surprise. In fact, I felt more than a tad guilty. Honest, I may have harboured some resentment towards Alex, but I never told Liz that and I for certain never told her he was no good. No matter how much I wished he wasn't around so I could have more of Liz to myself, it was always obvious how much he cared about her. I hoped she'd let him down easy.

Liz had met another bloke named Frank, or 'the body', in some apparently peculiar circumstances. 'Now there is a story!' Liz promised, followed by a few parenthetical ho-ho's. But she refused to call Frank her boyfriend. She hadn't lost one just to find another. She was 'playing the field and loving it'.

After that, the tone of the letter changed. It got much more personal, much harder to read. Liz said she missed me, she wished she'd been a better friend, she understood why I did everything I did. 'I read Harriet's novel,' Liz penned, 'and I was mortified. Oh, Charlotte, why didn't you tell me? I would have listened. I should have suspected, I should have known you were upset for good reason. I am so, so sorry and so very angry for you (see enclosed).' She pleaded with me to get back in touch with her. And she signed it, 'your best friend' followed by a string of XXXs for kisses next to which she'd jotted 'remember?' Which was a silly thing to ask, because of course I remembered. Liz owed her snogging prowess to me and for years, I was the first person she'd always run to squeal to whenever she'd had an opportunity to practise it. How was I going to forget that?

Oh, shit, now I was late for work. I stuffed the letter into my bag, polished off a final crust of toast and ran out the door. On the Tube into town, as I clung precariously to a ceiling strap and tried not to topple over into anyone's lap or tread on their toes, I looked at the single sheet of A4 attached to the last page of the letter. It was the original of the plagiarism statement reproduced in all of the newspapers. Well, who knew Liz had it in her? I held it curled around the edges so that no commuting snoops could spy it over my shoulder, and I reread every line, every word five times. Then I stuffed it, with the letter, back into my bag.

Several times this morning, in fact, I took the pages out to skim again. I read them so much that I memorised certain phrases. So even when I wasn't reading them, Liz's words were rattling round my consciousness. I couldn't get them out of my mind and, consequently, couldn't keep my mind on anything else. I forgot to time one girl who was taking a shorthand test and left her sitting in her cubicle with the tape machine replaying itself for 45 minutes. I put another girl who was supposed to be demonstrating her PC skills in the cubicle with a five-year-old Mac which was on the blink (she became very distressed). A complete daze was what I was in. A really ditzy daze. And several times, when I took Liz's missive out again, I thought about tearing it up, throwing it away or resealing the envelope and typing *return to sender* across the front of it. But I didn't do any of those things. Each time, I carefully refolded the sheets of paper and put them back in my bag where they seemed to be burrowing into a permanent home.

At lunch-time, I thought I'd better go outside to try to clear my head. Maybe some yummy comfort food would assist my efforts. I headed up to Covent Garden in search of the perfect antidote and found it in a bakery, around the corner from the Opera House, which sold enormous chocolate-chip-studded muffins and tubs of strawberry Häagen-Dazs.

I bought a portion of each and roosted in the piazza to wolf them down as I watched acrobatic buskers throw their skinny little bodies about for loose change.

To my disappointment, though, the sun and the crowds and the food and the acrobats didn't do much to disperse the fog settling on my brain. At the end of my lunch hour, feeling fatter and foggier, I steered a course back for the office. Which was when the *really* terrible thing happened.

At the Strand, I was feeling too lethargic to amble the few yards in the wrong direction to the crossing so I joined a huddle of other pedestrians waiting at the kerb for a break in the traffic. A young businessman, swinging a briefcase and gassing into his mobile phone, held the lead. He'd nudged two steps off the kerb already and kept rocking forward on to his front foot like a sprinter readying for the start gun. Behind him stood a middle-aged woman loaded down with several bags of shopping from the Tesco Metro round the corner. She was bundled up like it was still winter – long woollen coat and a stripy scarf – despite the day's onset of proper spring weather. I lined up behind the woman and behind me a couple of truant, tattooed teens were already jostling for position.

I raised up on my tiptoes and craned my neck right towards Trafalgar Square. The traffic was pretty steady but not gridlocked enough to be able to weave your way across the macadam without harm. A constant stream of midday drivers were going about their business, thankful to not be held up on this short stretch of their journey and making up now for time they would surely lose later at more congested junctures. Lorries, delivery vans, courier bikes, taxis, mini-cabs, buses, tour coaches and other garden-variety vehicles whizzed past. We'd have to wait for one of the traffic lights further up to redden and create a break for us. That obviously wasn't going to happen soon enough for the double-breasted sprinter, however. He must have spotted a sooner break, however slender, because by the time I'd swung my head back in his direction, he was off. It really was like a race then. The woman, seeing the runner ahead of her, her opponent, gaining a lead, also sprang into action. She didn't even look left or right, just at the heels of the businessman which she followed like a reflex. My foot flinched too and the kids behind me pushed forward impatiently. It was like a chain reaction. We were all in so much of a fucking rush.

But then we – the truants and me – heard the horn and less than a split second later this really god-awful screeching. I don't remember hearing anything for a second or two after that. Like I lost that sense – my hearing – altogether as my eyes went into sensory overload. My entire field of vision contracted into one sphere of action. The woman. She was running, her coat and scarf trailing out behind her, her too heavy bags knocking about her shins, sharp corners of supermarket packaging punching holes in the plastic as the bags took the motion strains. And she was almost across that first lane – she wasn't nearly as fast as the briefcase man who was already perched atop the mid-Strand traffic island looking for a westbound break – when into this field of vision stormed an Iceland lorry. She'd have been better off if she'd never seen that lorry full of frozen TV dinners. But she must've had the briefest glimpse of it out of the corner of her eye and it made her turn to look and that turn, that momentary delay, cost her. If she hadn't turned to look, she just might have made it an extra two paces to safety. By the time she saw the lorry full on, though, by the time she realised she was in real danger, it was too late.

I have never seen a person hit by a moving vehicle before, let alone a lorry. If I'd ever thought about it, I suppose I'd just imagine that they got hit and they fell down. Or maybe like in the movies when the cop rolls up on to the bonnet of a car, cracks the windscreen, then rolls back down on to the ground and continues chasing the bad guy. But it wasn't like either of those scenarios. As I watched, this woman was thrown. Her body, like nothing more weighty than a feather, flew through the air, seemingly suspended for several minutes, until it landed with the most horrific, squelching thud. That sound was the only thing that penetrated my eardrums. Like the sound you might expect an overripe tomato to make if you smashed it against a brick wall – but louder and squelchier. And that's what I thought of too, when I saw her splayed out on the pavement. Her legs were contorted in ways that would make a gymnast blanch and her face – which was not unkind – was turned sideways, her cheek resting on the white-painted lane demarcation. And from her head spilled the innards of a smashed tomato – thick and red and pulpy, her blood and brains radiating out of her head and into the road, into the tasselled ends of her stripy scarf, no hope of ever being whole again.

I had to stick around for a while along with the teens and a few other witnesses to answer questions when the police arrived. The businessman was long gone, his appointment must have been very urgent indeed. I felt terrible, everybody felt terrible and shocked, the lorry driver most of all. I mourned for him. He was only young, younger than me for certain and probably not much older than the truants – and he was hysterical. Moaning and sobbing. He'd leapt out of the lorry as soon as it came to a stop and raced to where the woman's body lay – screaming 'Oh my God, oh my God, oh fuck' the whole way – but it was too late of course. So he paced up and down beside her as people gathered to gape – him screaming and sobbing and wringing his hands the whole time until he was carted away in the back of the police car.

It was funny – not in a ha-ha sort of way, of course – but I used to have dreams about being run over, killed by a lorry. You know, they were those sort of childish, vengeance dreams where you wish yourself dead just so you can see how sad and guilty all your friends and family would feel after you were gone. And in my dreams, Peter and Garret and Louis and – God, what was the name of that Royal Navy guy? – oh yeah, William and Liz and whoever else would rally together and vow to get that horrible, blasted lorry driver. Today, it very well could have been me whose life this lorry driver snuffed out – if I'd been second in the kerb queue rather than third, if my reflexes had been just a little bit quicker. But even if it had been me, I wouldn't want anyone – not my family or even this woman's family – laying their blame or hatred on the shoulders of this lorry driver. Okay, yes, he was probably driving too fast but it wasn't his fault, not his alone, not even mostly his. Not she nor the businessman nor me nor the truants, none of us should've been crossing there or at that moment. Why are we all in such a fucking blind hurry all the time?

He was so badly shaken, that kid and, even though it may not be his fault, even if he's never convicted of anything, he'll have to live with that woman's death for the rest of his life. Dead. One minute she was someone's mum, someone's wife, someone's friend, someone's colleague, just running her errands during her lunch hour, getting impatient about crossing the street, worried about the work piling up on her desk back at the office. So she makes a dash for it. And the next minute, less than a minute even, she is dead and her shopping is scattered across the Strand – to be flattened under the wheels of fast-moving cars or picked over in the gutters by slow-moving bums. A very definitive moment indeed. For that woman of course, and the driver, but for me as well. For me – as sure as anything.

Like the driver, I was shaken too. Shaking badly. After the police were finished with me, I went back to the office just long enough to vomit and be told to take the rest of the afternoon off. It came as a welcome instruction. I grabbed my bag, a notebook and some pens and headed here, to Trafalgar Square.

Of all the hiding places in London, Trafalgar Square is one of the best. Assuming you're hiding from the locals, that is. I come here often but, aside from the pigeon-feed vendor, I must be just about the only Londoner who does. Tourists and exchange students, on the other hand, can't stay away. Which is why I like it so much – it's a great place to find a seat and people-watch without any fear of being recognised.

When I first got here – goodness, it must have been a couple of hours ago now – I was trembling and I could still taste the chocolate-tinged vomit on my tongue. Seemed like I was always vomiting, an emotional reaction that came almost as automatically as blushing. How then, I wondered, could I be such an easy vomiter but such a failed bulimic? One of life's great mysteries. I washed the bile down with a handful of crisps and some bottled water I'd picked up at a newsagent's on the way as I found a seat on a bench with my back to the National Gallery. Looking around me, I tried to erase the image of that woman and her crown of blood from my mind but I couldn't do it. And so as I gazed at the scene around me, everything was overlaid with her. It was like a spliced film. Frame one – water spraying rainbow effect in fountain. Frame two – woman sprinting. Frame three – toddlers feeding pigeons. Frame four – woman being thrown. Tourists posing for photos in front of Nelson's Column – woman dead. Kids romping on stone lions enacting scene from Urban Jungle Book – woman dead. Young man stretched out on bench, lazing peacefully in sunshine – tyres screeching, woman dead.

I could feel the sun myself, tickling the hairs of my exposed forearms, warming the backs of my ears. A couple of pigeons landed near my feet and raised their beaks quizzically in my direction before acknowledging that I had no food and gobbling off to greener pastures. And I could hear the pattering feet of children chasing pigeons, the rain of seeds being thrown, the squawk of peckish, squabbling birds, the splash of water that shimmered and churned and sprayed on unsuspecting friends who sat too close to the edge of the fountain, and everywhere squeals of laughter and people talking and moving and interacting around me.

Then suddenly. Suddenly, I was no longer trembling, suddenly I was no longer scared or sad or shocked. I was smiling. I was smiling because I was so happy, no ecstatic, because I was so damn lucky because *I was alive!* It could so easily, so nearly have been me. But it wasn't. It wasn't me. It was that woman, not me. She's dead but I'm not. I am here, I am alive. I am no longer in a daze. *I am alive.*

And this feeling, it just washed over me like, like . . . Oh, God, would I upchuck the crisps and the Perrier? No, not like that. For once not. But I started doing this funny thing. Like laughing and crying and snorting all at the same time. My face is wet with tears and I must look a state, still pale and stunned and crazy or something.

Thinking about how insane I must look makes me start laughing and snorting some more. And smiling, smiling like I probably never have. Because it is this absolutely gorgeous day – warm and sunny and full of promise. I don't even mind seeing all these kissy-faced, PDA-possessed couples (and there are plenty of them here in the Square – something about being on holiday I guess, the romance of foreign climes). They don't make me feel like shit, sick with my own loneliness, they don't bother me in the least. In fact, I enjoy seeing them – today they encourage me instead of embittering me. Because today is wonderful. And my past? It's still there, it's still with me. I'll always be carrying it around – because I have to, because it's part of me. But it's not the only part of me, not even the most important part of me. It's *past* for God's sake, it's over. What matters now is today. Today and all the things I'm going to do with it. And tomorrow too.

It's days like this when you think everything really is going to be all right. It's days like this that you remember or maybe – like now, like with me – that you first realise, but in any case know, without a shadow of a doubt, *know*, what real love is, the ultimate love. The love of life. The upside in life is life itself. Okay, okay, I know that sounds just totally Walt Disney but it's true. That's how I feel and, after what I've seen, I know it's right, I know it's real. It's days like this that make up for all the rest. Does everybody have days like this? They should do.

So that's about it, I've just about written myself out. As far as this journal goes anyway. You know, maybe, if my life makes such damn interesting reading, maybe I should write my own book. This could be a good start. I'll go on from here, then package it all up and call it *Charlotte Mereville's <u>Real</u> Diary*. Or possibly not Charlotte Mereville. I've never really liked my name, you know. Maybe I'll use a pen name or, or . . . what do they call it? An *alter ego*. Yeah, I'll set up an *alter ego* with a shorter, snappier name and a more interesting job. Heroines don't really have jobs in personnel – sorry, human resources – do they? It's got to be law or the City or publishing or, you know, something glitzy. A media babe or something. So it'll be a media me and they'll make a film about it and I'll make a million squid. That'd be nice, eh?

For now, though, I think I'll just go home. Maybe make Mrs Fairhazel a cup of tea and write a letter for a change. Or maybe I'll just pick up the phone. I'll ring Liz and surprise her. I'll tell her thanks for defending me, thanks for exposing Harriet and we'll have a good old laugh at the witch's expense. And then move on. I'll invite Liz to my birthday party for two – just me and my best friend. And I'll tell her I miss her too and that I want to see her and I want to hear all about this guy Frank and her flat and all about her life, and that I want to be a part of it again, and I'll ask if she knows of any good diets. Or literary agents.

TRAPLINES
Eden Robinson

Set within the harsh and insular milieu of contemporary urban Canada, these four novellas approach timeless themes of adolescence, parenthood and belonging from a unique and challenging perspective. In beautiful prose of deceptive simplicity and searing invention, *Traplines* marks the emergence of a writer certain to assume a place alongside Carol Shields and Alice Munro in the vanguard of Canada's literary talents.

'Canada seems to have an inexhaustible supply of excellent women writers. Now there is another young and striking voice. This volume contains four novellas in which Robinson takes us into the underside of family life, from the point of view of the teenagers involved. Her writing is fresh and often harrowing'
Observer

'Combining pathos with biting humour, each of these beautifully crafted narratives has a sting'
Independent on Sunday

'A Generation X laureate'
New York Times

'This is a fine book – unflinching, moving and shockingly, bloodily funny . . . she writes from the heart'
A. L. Kennedy

'Robinson is good, frighteningly good'
Gail Anderson-Dargatz, author of *A Cure for Death by Lightning*

SEX AND THE CITY
Candace Bushnell

Wildly funny, unexpectedly poignant, wickedly observant, *Sex and the City* blazes a glorious, drunken cocktail trail through New York, as Candace Bushnell, columnist and social critic *par excellence*, trips on her Manolo Blahnik kitten heels from the Baby Doll Lounge to the Bowery Bar. An Armistead Maupin for the real world, she has the gift of assembling a huge and irresistible cast of freaks and wonders, while remaining faithful to her hard core of friends and fans: those glamorous, rebellious, crazy single women, who are trying hard not to turn from the Audrey Hepburn of *Breakfast at Tiffany's* into the Glenn Close of *Fatal Attraction* and are – still – looking for love.

'Intriguing and highly entertaining'
Helen Fielding, author of *Bridget Jones's Diary*

'Imagine Jane Austen with a martini, or perhaps Jonathan Swift on rollerblades'
Sunday Telegraph

'Hilarious . . . a compulsively readable book, served up in bite-sized chunks of irrepressible irreverence'
Marie Claire

'Irresistible, hilarious and horrific, stylishly written . . . Candace Bushnell has captured the big black truth'
Bret Easton Ellis

GENERATION X

Tales for an Accelerated Culture
Douglas Coupland

'Funny, colourful and accessible, this is a blazing debut'
The Times

Andy, Dag and Claire have been handed a society priced beyond
their means. Twentysomethings, scarred by the 80s fallout of
yuppies, recession, crack and Ronald Reagan, they represent the
new generation – Generation X. Unsure of their futures, they
immerse themselves in a regime of heavy drinking and working
at no-future McJobs in the service industry.

Underemployed, overeducated, intensely private and
unpredictable, they have nowhere to direct their anger, no one
to assuage their fears, and no culture to replace their anomie. So
they tell stories: disturbingly funny tales that reveal their
barricaded inner world. A world populated with dead TV shows,
'Elvis moments' and semi-disposable Swedish furniture . . .

'A New Age J. D. Salinger on smart drugs'
Time Out

'Dizzying sparkle and originality'
The Times

'Quirky, witty, with an affection for its characters which lifts it
above the level of such as Bret Easton Ellis's *Less than Zero*'
Mail on Sunday

'A landmark book'
Daily Telegraph

PARIS TRANCE
Geoff Dyer

'People talk about love at first sight, about the way that men and women fall for each other immediately, but there is also such a thing as friendship at first sight.'

In his latest novel Geoff Dyer fixes a dream of happiness – and its aftermath – with photographic precision. Erotic and elegiac, funny and romantic, *Paris Trance* confirms Dyer as one of Britain's most original and talented writers.

'A beautifully composed rave generation rhapsody . . . In prose dripping with eroticism and aching with melancholy, Dyer masterfully dissects the vicissitudes of twenty-something love'
Sunday Times

'Dyer reasserts his credentials as the Poet Laureate of the Slacker Generation'
William Sutcliffe, *Independent on Sunday*

'Voluptuously enjoyable'
Literary Review

'A *Tender is the Night* for the Ecstasy Age'
Tim Pears

'A skilfully crafted map of the human heart'
Independent

'The irresistible quality of the book steals up, like sun through a plain curtain'
Candia McWilliam, *New Statesman*

Now you can order superb titles directly from Abacus

☐ Traplines	Eden Robinson	£6.99
☐ Sex and the City	Candace Bushnell	£6.99
☐ Generation X	Douglas Coupland	£6.99
☐ Paris Trance	Geoff Dyer	£6.99
☐ The Colour of Memory	Geoff Dyer	£6.99

───────────────── ⟨ABACUS⟩ ─────────────────

Please allow for postage and packing: **Free UK delivery.**
Europe: add 25% of retail price; Rest of World: 45% of retail price.

To order any of the above or any other Abacus titles, please call our credit card orderline or fill in this coupon and send/fax it to:

Abacus, 250 Western Avenue, London, W3 6XZ, UK.
Fax 0181 324 5678   Telephone 0181 324 5517

☐ I enclose a UK bank cheque made payable to Abacus for £ . . . . . .
☐ Please charge £ . . . . . to my Access, Visa, Delta, Switch Card No.

▢▢▢▢▢▢▢▢▢▢▢▢▢▢▢▢▢▢▢▢▢▢

Expiry Date ▢▢▢▢   Switch Issue No. ▢▢

NAME (Block letters please) . . . .

ADDRESS . . . .

Postcode . . . . Telephone . . . .

Signature . . . .

Please allow 28 days for delivery within the UK. Offer subject to price and availability.
Please do not send any further mailings from companies carefully selected by Abacus ☐